Beyond the Grave

THE MINISTRY OF CURIOSITIES SERIES
#3

C.J. ARCHER

Series by C.J. Archer:

The Emily Chambers Spirit Medium Trilogy

The 1st Freak House Trilogy

The 2nd Freak House Trilogy

The 3rd Freak House Trilogy

The Ministry of Curiosities

Lord Hawkesbury's Players

The Assassins Guild

The Witchblade Chronicles

Stand-alone books by C.J. Archer:

Redemption

Surrender

Courting His Countess

The Mercenary's Price

DEDICATION

Thank you to each and every one of my readers. Your support keeps me going.

CHAPTER 1

London, autumn 1889

Lincoln Fitzroy was an excellent kisser. Not that I had experience kissing anyone else, but considering I was re-living it in my head three days later, it went a long way to proving his prowess. When I closed my eyes, I could still feel his warm lips on mine, the press of his hand at my lower back, the tingles rushing down my spine. I'd always thought kisses would be messy affairs, but now I knew the appeal and why first kisses usually led to seconds…and more.

Unfortunately, I was yet to experience a second. All I had was the memory of our first. Lincoln had avoided me for three days. After a full minute of enjoying one another's company in his rooms, we'd sprung apart upon hearing footsteps approaching. It was only Gus, sent by Cook to ask when Lincoln wanted dinner to be served, but it had ended the most thrilling moment of my life to that point. Lincoln had picked up my crutches from the floor, where I'd discarded them, and handed them to me. He then turned his back and strode to his desk. His brisk order of, "Serve my dinner in here, alone," seemed to be for my benefit as much as Gus's. It was a signal that our kiss was over and that there would be no more.

I'd hobbled out of his private sitting room on my crutches and shut myself in my bedroom. It turned out to be one tumultuous evening, as I seesawed between triumph at having cracked Lincoln's hard shell of a façade, girlish silliness over my first kiss, and self-pity at his rejection. It didn't help that my sleep was troubled by nightmares. As proud as I was of myself for escaping from Captain Jasper, the kidnapping had left its mark.

During the days, however, the autumn sunshine managed to banish the nightmares and doubts, but not all of my self-pity or the triumph. The kiss still occupied my thoughts while I completed mending tasks in the library, my sore foot propped up on a footstool.

"Charlie. Charlie, wake up." The clap of hands beside my ear had me jumping out of my skin.

"Bloody hell, Seth, what was that for?" I gathered up the shirt that had slipped off my lap and checked the needle was still stuck in it.

Seth grinned, giving me the full effect of his dimples. It was impossible to stay mad at him when he smiled like that, and I suspected he knew it. It was no wonder he got away with so much mischief, particularly with ladies. "You were asleep."

"I was not. And if I were, was there any need to wake me so rudely?"

"You have to vacate the library. It's time." He nodded at the clock on the mantel.

"Already!"

"Not asleep, eh? Time must fly when one's alone in the library, sewing." He picked up the shirt I'd been mending. It was his, as it happened. A thorn had rent a small hole in the sleeve the night before. Apparently his latest paramour kept rose bushes beneath her window. I'd heard from Gus that Seth had acquired the hole after leaving in a hurry when the husband returned home early from his club. "Oh, look, you've done all of seven stitches."

I snatched the shirt off him and stuffed it into my sewing basket. "Did Fitzroy send you in here to torment me?"

"No." He passed me the crutches and, with a hand on my elbow, helped me to stand.

"Has he returned from wherever he went this morning?"

"Yes."

My heart skipped a merry tune whenever I knew Lincoln was in the house. Being under the same roof meant we might bump into one another. Unfortunately, he'd managed to avoid me so completely these last three days that the only time I'd seen him, we'd been in the company of Cook, Gus and Seth. There'd been no opportunity for private discussion. I could have sought him out, but in truth, I wasn't sure what to say. It seemed somewhat childish and pathetic to bluntly ask him why he'd been avoiding me.

"I suppose he returned for the meeting." I glanced at the clock again. The committee members would be arriving soon.

Seth picked up my sewing basket. "I'm sure."

"Do you know where he went?"

"No."

"You're full of witty conversation this afternoon," I said as I hobbled out of the library.

"Forgive me, Charlie." His serious turn had me eyeing him sideways. He gave me a flat-lipped smile that was much too pitying for my liking.

"Stop feeling sorry for me," I snapped, trying my best to streak ahead. "There's no need. I'm perfectly fine."

He caught up to me. That was the problem with crutches and only having one good foot. Storming off became much less effective. "If you'll permit me to say, you don't seem fine."

"I'm just frustrated with the slow pace of my recovery. The doctor said I should stay off my foot for another week. A week! He ought to spend a week using these contraptions and see if he likes the way it rubs the skin under his arms raw. Not to mention how dull it is to do nothing but sew all day. While it's nice to be able to read without guilt, I do miss my work, not to mention my training." I sighed. I definitely missed my regular afternoon combat training sessions with Lincoln. Even though he shut down his emotions for the duration, I at least got to touch him.

"He's a turd," Seth said as he entered the kitchen behind me.

"Dr. MacDonnell?"

Gus looked up from the central table where he was arranging cups and saucers on a tray. "He ain't so bad, for a medical man. Bit unfair to call him names just because other doctors have been causing problems lately."

"I wasn't referring to Dr. MacDonnell," Seth muttered.

"Then who be a turd?" Cook's face was blotchy and his bald head shiny from the heat given off by the range. His bandaged hand held a spoon near his nose. A thick dollop of creamy liquid slipped off and plopped back into the pot on the stove top.

"Fitzroy," Seth said.

Three sets of sympathetic eyes turned my way. I pretended not to notice as I directed Seth to deposit my sewing basket beside the chair in the corner, but my face flamed nevertheless. So much for discretion. I'd tried to keep my feelings for Lincoln a secret from them, but clearly I'd failed. I suspected they even knew about the kiss.

I half expected Lincoln to walk into the kitchen at that moment. His ability to know when people were talking about him was more than uncanny, it was a supernatural talent, most likely inherited from his mother. But he did not come. Not this time. I was being thoroughly and unequivocally avoided.

"Can I do something?" I asked, surveying the arrangement of cups, saucers and small plates and cake forks. "Pass me that other tray."

Gus refused. "Go sit down, Charlie. We don't need help."

"An extra pair of hands can't hurt." I leaned the crutches against the table and reached for the tray only to snatch my hand back when Gus slapped it.

"Sit. Down."

Before I could voice my indignation, Seth scooped me up and flung me over his shoulder. "Seth!" I cried. "Put me down! I am not a sack of pumpkins."

"Oi! Put her down! She ain't one o' your hussies." Gus sounded quite horrified, bless him.

Seth merely chuckled. "If she behaves like an obstinate woman, she gets treated like one."

"It's no wonder you're unmarried with that caveman attitude," I said, wriggling to make it difficult for him to hold me.

But he was much too strong for my pathetic attempts and didn't even grunt when I kicked him. "That, dear Charlie, is not why I'm unmarried."

"Don't be so sure." I thumped him in the back where I hoped his kidneys were.

He arched his back and swore loudly. "That bloody hurt!"

"Good."

"Put her down." Lincoln! I couldn't see him from my position facing Seth's lower back, but his sharp order sliced through me nevertheless. I could feel Seth's shoulder tense too as he swung round to the door, almost knocking my head against the sideboard.

"Sir! I was just, er, assisting Charlie to a seat." He deposited me on the chair and sidled sheepishly back to the table, avoiding Lincoln's glare.

A glare that he turned on me. It was the first time he'd looked at me directly since the kiss, and there was nothing in his eyes that I'd hoped to see there. No joy or humor, no longing or desire. Just a blackness so dark that it swallowed all the light.

"It was a little bit of harmless fun," I said.

Poor Seth's gulp was audible from where I sat. He shook his head slightly, warning me not to stoke Lincoln's temper.

"Have fun on your days off." He thrust his chin toward my foot. "I came to see how you were."

I was about to give him the standard polite answer when I decided to tell the truth. "Miserable. Thank you for asking."

My honesty seemed to confound him. The silence felt as if it stretched forever before he tucked his hands behind his back. Then he simply gave a nod and turned away. "Seth, the door. They're here."

With a sigh, I picked up my sewing. Seth filed past Lincoln just as the front door knocker announced the first visitor. Lincoln cast me a brief, indecipherable look before he followed.

I spent the next hour watching Seth and Gus come and go to serve our master and his guests. Mostly Gus, as Seth remained in the library for much of the meeting's duration. Unlike Gus, Seth was considered a gentleman, albeit one whose circumstances had been considerably reduced. His presence among the esteemed members of the Ministry of Curiosities committee was tolerated. Gus's was not. Nor mine, for that matter. Not only was I a gutter snipe turned housemaid, I was also a necromancer. The latter meant I couldn't be trusted with their secrets. Little did they know that Seth would tell me everything anyway. Once, I'd thought Lincoln would keep me informed, but I was no longer certain of that.

"Well?" I asked Gus upon his return with the empty tray. "What are they saying?"

"Nothin' in partic'lar. Lady H is tellin' 'em how Buchanan can barely wipe his own arse, let alone take care of himself if he got mixed up in somethin' supernatural."

Cook snorted a laugh. "I'd like to hear her say 'arse.'"

"Perhaps, if you ask nicely, she'll use her sultry voice." My teasing sent Cook into a fit of chuckles that shook his belly. "And?" I prompted Gus.

"And that's all I heard." He shrugged and lowered himself onto a chair with a groan. I felt sorry for him. He and Seth had been working extra hard ever since I'd incurred my injury. Although they'd done all the housework before my arrival at Lichfield Towers, my standards were higher than Lincoln's, and they'd tried to maintain them.

The meeting had been called by Lady Harcourt when her stepson, Andrew Buchanan, disappeared. While it wasn't unusual for the dissolute rake to spend all night gambling and doing whatever it was dissolute rakes did, it wasn't normal for him not to return for three days *and* have books on the occult in his rooms. The rest of the committee had finally agreed to look into it after Lady Harcourt's constant petitioning had worn them down. To be fair, she did seem quite upset by his disappearance, which surprised me. Their relationship had appeared to be a rocky one, on the brief occasion I'd seen them together, and I thought she'd be glad to be rid of him.

Then again, he was family, and if he was as good at getting himself into trouble as she suggested, and as hopeless at getting himself out of it, then perhaps he was in real danger.

Thirty minutes later, Gus disappeared again when the bell for the library tinkled. I could just make out sounds of the guests leaving. It wasn't until Seth and Gus came in to fetch trays and announced that all visitors had gone that I finally relaxed. I hadn't realized how anxious I'd been about seeing them again, particularly Lord Gillingham and Lady Harcourt. Gillingham because he was a toad with a mean streak, and Lady H because the last time I'd met with her she'd blackmailed me into raising the spirit of Lincoln's tutor, Mr. Gurry, to ferret out Lincoln's secrets. He'd walked in on the event and Lady Harcourt had blamed me for the entire thing. She didn't yet know that Lincoln was aware she'd put me up to it.

"Is Fitzroy still about?" I asked them as they returned once again carrying the trays laden with dirty dishes.

"He left with Lady Harcourt," Seth said.

"Oh." I pulled hard on the thread, breaking it. "Damn."

"Only to investigate Buchanan's rooms for himself. She assured him she hasn't touched a thing."

The journey in a closed carriage back to her Mayfair house gave her an opportunity to speak ill of me to Lincoln and to use her feminine charms on him. It was one distinct advantage she had over me. My charms were insignificant compared to her curvaceous ones. She might even close the curtains and use the gentle rocking of the cabin as an excuse to rub those ample charms all over him.

I dumped the sewing in the basket and hauled myself to my feet. Being inert for so long allowed my imagination to run rampant. I grabbed my crutches and followed them into the adjoining scullery. "Does she have any clue as to what Buchanan might be up to or where he has gone?"

"None," Seth said. "Charlie, should you—"

"Yes," I snapped. "I'm going mad with boredom in that corner, with nothing to do but sew. If I don't do something else, I'll make everyone miserable. Gus, fetch me some water."

He hurried out of the scullery, and I apologized as soon as he returned with a pail full of warm water. "Just ignore me when I turn into a curmudgeon. I'm feeling somewhat frustrated at the moment."

"The sooner you're healed, the better for us all." He poured the water into the washing tub and set the pail down. "If it is your injury that's makin' you frustrated."

Seth cleared his throat pointedly as he piled up the dirty cups beside me. I rolled my eyes. As if I hadn't detected the innuendo in Gus's tone.

"Lady H wanted to speak with you, but Fitzroy said you were still recovering from your injuries and weren't up to it," Seth said.

"He did?" It seemed he'd read my mind on the matter of avoiding her. I wondered if that was simply because he'd come to know me well enough to know my thoughts, or if he'd used his nominal seer's instincts.

Lincoln was gone for the rest of the day and into the evening. He sent word back that he would be dining out after it had already grown dark.

"But he isn't wearing his dinner suit," I protested upon reading the missive delivered by one of Harcourt's footmen.

"Perhaps he doesn't need a suit where he's dining," Seth said.

That only conjured up images of Lincoln dining off Lady Harcourt's naked belly in her bed.

I lost my appetite and ate little. The men asked me to join them for cards after dinner, and we played a few rounds before we heard the front door open and close. Seth went to investigate and returned alone.

"He's home," was all he said, rejoining us.

"Did Lady H's coach bring him back?" I asked.

He shook his head. "Hackney."

"Then he didn't come directly from her house?"

He shrugged. "Why not ask him yourself?"

I eyed the door. "He's not coming down?"

"He said goodnight, so I assume not."

"Not even to report on what he found in Buchanan's rooms? But that's not fair! We need to know."

"We need to know only what he wants us to know."

Gus nudged my elbow. "Your turn, Charlie. Keep up."

I played a few more rounds then retired for the night. My rooms were along the hallway from Lincoln's, and I thought about knocking on his door.

But I didn't. It would only make me look lovelorn—which I was, but I didn't want him to know. I wanted to retain some of my dignity.

I remained awake most of the night, partly because it meant the nightmares couldn't get their claws into me, and partly because I was thinking up ways of confronting Lincoln. By the time daylight edged the curtains, I'd decided that I had to confront him over the kiss and his subsequent aloofness. If nothing else, it would be good to get it off my chest.

I must have fallen asleep, however, because a soft knock on my door startled me awake. The clock on my mantel chimed ten. I'd overslept by hours.

"Who is it?" I called out as I scrambled for my crutches beside the bed.

"Charlie?" It was Gus. "Are you all right?"

"Yes. I slept in." I reached for my cloak on the clothes stand to throw it around my shoulders and ward off the morning chill, but knocked it off instead in my haste.

"Right-o then. We was worried, that's all. Go back to bed if you're tired."

"I'm not tired." I stifled a yawn as I bent to pick up the cloak. "I slept poorly last night and…never mind. I'll be down shortly."

"There's a parcel for you. I'll leave it here."

Parcel? For me? "Who is it from?"

But Gus didn't answer. I flung the cloak around my shoulders and hobbled out of my bedroom, through my small sitting room, to the door. I opened it and peeked out. A rectangular black box, a little larger than my hand, sat on the floor. The buttercup yellow ribbon tied around it made a bold, tantalizing statement against the black.

It was too awkward to carry the box and use my crutches, so I dispensed with the latter and hopped to the nearest chair with the former in my clutches. With my heart in my throat, I carefully untied the ribbon and lifted the lid. Nestled on a bed of rich black velvet was a silver chatelaine. The large clasp was intricately engraved with the figure of a classically robed woman, a bird perched on her raised hand. She stood on a balcony overlooking the sea, the tiny etched waves rippling around a partially visible dolphin. A vine twisted around the column at her back, its leaves spreading into the rest of the space surrounding the scene. Objects hung from three of the chatelaine's chains—a pair of miniature scissors in a scabbard, a thimble holder shaped like an acorn, and a timepiece—while another two hung empty for the wearer to fill with items of their choosing. The chatelaine was similar to one my adopted mother had worn, yet so unlike it too. Hers had been plain tin. This one was beautifully worked silver, the detail clear and exquisite. According to the inside lid of the box, it had been made by a jeweler in Bond Street.

Did Lincoln expect me to wear such a fine piece around the house? He must, or it wouldn't hold scissors and thimble. Either he had no idea what housekeepers' chatelaines ought to be made of, or he was making a statement of his wealth for everyone to see. The thing was, Lichfield received few callers, so who would see it?

I placed the chatelaine back in the box and hopped to my crutches. I hurried to get dressed in my maid's uniform then attached the chatelaine to my waistband with shaking fingers. The silver flashed against the stark black, improving the entire outfit.

But a quick glance in the dressing table mirror confirmed that it was much too fine. Why had he given me a gift that I couldn't wear? I removed it and returned it to the box.

With a sigh, I headed to his rooms. At least now I had an excuse to speak with him in private.

CHAPTER 2

Lincoln wasn't in his rooms, and I found him in the library instead. He sat in one of the chairs at the central table, his back to me, his head bent over a book. Several tomes lay before him, some open. He didn't look up, so I snuck quietly behind him to see what he was working on. It appeared to be a journal, but the loose, flowing script was difficult to read.

"Good morning, Lincoln." I wasn't sure if my use of his first name would earn me a smile or admonishment, but I used it anyway. I refused to call him Mr. Fitzroy in private after that kiss.

"Good morning, Charlie. You're up late." He finally stood and faced me. He was dressed casually in trousers and shirt, and wore no waistcoat or tie. His gaze slipped to my waist, where he perhaps expected to see the chatelaine. I couldn't tell if he was disappointed that I didn't wear it.

I tried to peer past him at the books, but his impressive frame blocked my view. It would seem I wasn't welcome to peek. "What are you doing?"

"Reading a journal." He leaned back against the table in what would have been a relaxed stance, except his hands gripped the edge so hard that his knuckles turned white.

"May I sit with you? These crutches become painful after a while."

He hesitated and I imagined him warring with himself. Eventually the gentleman won out and he nodded. "You shouldn't be up and about."

"I wouldn't be, except that it seems if I wish to talk to you, I must make the effort. You've been avoiding me."

He pulled out a chair for me beside his and steered me toward it with a hand to my elbow. "If I were avoiding you, I wouldn't be speaking to you now."

"I did sneak up on you, cutting off an early escape."

"I heard you. Crutches are not made for sneaking."

"I'll keep that in mind if an opportunity for eavesdropping presents itself."

"If I wanted to escape, I could have."

"Then why do you look as if you want to be anywhere but here with me?"

He whirled around and stalked toward the door. I was much too shocked at his behavior to even squeak a protest. All I could do was stare at his broad back with my mouth open. I snapped it shut when he turned to me after closing the door. I'd mistaken the intention of his purposeful stride. He'd only wanted to insure privacy for our conversation. That boded well. At least the conversation had the potential to go beyond simply discussing Andrew Buchanan's journal.

"Is there something I can do for you?" he asked, taking his seat once more. He picked up the journal and perused the page.

"I wanted to thank you for the gift."

"You're welcome."

"Why did you give it to me?"

"Housekeepers have chatelaines for their keys and other things."

"Not silver ones made by one of London's finest jewelers."

He said nothing.

"Thank you, it was very generous. But a gentleman shouldn't buy his housemaid gifts."

"Considering you're more than a housemaid, I thought to make an exception."

"More than?" I asked, my voice breathy.

"A ministry employee. Her Majesty's necromancer. An overworked housekeeper, housemaid, scullery maid and more besides."

But not his lover. I swallowed heavily. "A plainer one would suffice. I'll have Seth collect it from my rooms and give it back to you."

"No."

"No?"

"I don't want it back. Wear it or not, I do not care. Sell it, if you prefer. It's yours to do with as you wish."

Sell it? He was joking, surely.

"Is there anything else?" he asked, still not looking at me.

"Yes. You can stop treating me like just another member of your household staff."

"You *are* a member of my household staff. I treat you all the same."

"Oh? You're kissing Seth and Gus too?"

He closed the journal and set it aside. His hand flattened over the stamped leather cover, and his finger traced the top edge back and forth, back and forth. "We should have spoken about that…incident earlier. I'm sorry, but it cannot happen again."

It was as I expected, yet hearing it put so bluntly felt like a body blow. His capacity to switch off his emotions and speak with utter blandness was boundless. It was a long time before I could trust my voice not to quaver.

"I see. Am I to receive an explanation as to why?"

"You know why." His quiet mumble hardly reached me although we were not sitting all that far apart.

"Perhaps I do, but I'd like to hear you say it." Making him feel uncomfortable was the only weapon in my arsenal.

It was pathetic, but it was my only hope for a triumph of any kind, and I was sorely in need of just a little win.

His finger stilled. He turned toward me. "I cannot wed you, Charlie, and I will not bed you. You are too…young to be ruined."

My heart pinched. "Ah. I see. The vicar's daughter, fallen on hard times, is not good enough for the son of a gentleman."

His gaze skewered me. His hand curled into a fist on the book "You think I care for society conventions?"

My own gaze faltered. "I…is that not what you meant? Not that I was expecting a proposal after just one kiss, but I do see how a gentleman—albeit one of dubious morals—would think that I did." *Stop babbling, Charlie.*

"No," he growled. "That's not what I meant. Must I spell it out to you?"

I lifted my chin. "It would seem I'm a little slow to grasp your meaning. It must be because I'm too *young* to understand it."

He grunted. "Your wit is as sharp as ever, I see."

"Your avoidance in answering is as obvious as ever."

He sprang to his feet, making my already restless nerves jump. "You think I'm enjoying this?"

"I don't know. It's sometimes difficult to tell what you think." Our gazes locked in a brutal clash that was both thrilling and disturbing. I was caught between wanting to slap his cheek and kiss him senseless. I grabbed his hand, trapping it. "Tell me, Lincoln. Tell me why you would kiss me with such tenderness and passion then abandon me." I had hoped to appear defiant, controlled, but my trembling betrayed me.

He looked down at our linked hands and expelled a measured breath that seemed to expunge some of his anger along with it. "Because it's better I abandon you now and not later."

I tightened my grip. "Why would you abandon me at all?"

He snatched his hand away and strode to the fireplace. He stood with his back to me, one forearm resting on the enormous marble mantel. "It's not in my nature to be the man you wish me to be. The man you deserve."

"Oh, Lincoln." I sighed and stood on my good foot. "Why not let me be the judge of that?"

He slapped his hand against the mantel, startling me into plopping down on the chair. He stalked back to me, all predator again; a sleek and powerful animal that was both beautiful and dangerous, and utterly compelling. It never ceased to amaze me that he could switch from perfect gentleman to beast within the blink of an eye.

He stood over me, a powerful, raging force trapped inside thick, impenetrable walls. "You romanticize me. You defend my actions and tell yourself that I've been forced to commit the sins I have. That's why. But the truth is, I am not capable of selflessness or compassion, and I am certainly not capable of love. I'm a tool, honed to do one thing—lead the Ministry of Curiosities—using whatever methods are at my disposal, no matter how immoral or illegal. Expect more of me than that and you will be disappointed."

I felt as if all the air had been sucked out of me. I sank into the chair, a deflated, empty balloon. Not even tears welled. This man was so different to the one who'd kissed me that I began to wonder if he was right, that I had romanticized him. That he wasn't the man I'd hoped he could be.

"The kiss was a moment of weakness on my part," he said, voice cooler. "You are not to blame." He turned away and headed for the door with giant strides.

"You could have bedded me, Lincoln." I was surprised to hear how steady my voice sounded, but even more surprised at the conviction behind my words. Yet I suddenly felt very strongly about what I wanted to say, and I would shout it at him if he continued to walk away. Fortunately, he stopped before opening the library door, but he did not turn around. "You had ample opportunity that night and since, and I would not have put up any resistance beyond what is expected of a well brought up young woman. Yet you chose not to. You chose to protect my honor. What's more, you haven't blamed my lowly position for your rejection, but taken all the blame upon yourself. The amoral man you describe would have done neither of those things."

For one heart-pounding moment I thought it had worked. I thought he was going to come back to me and beg my forgiveness for his cruel words. But he did not. He reached for the doorknob.

"You're a coward, Lincoln. Your feelings trouble you and you don't know how to—"

"ENOUGH!"

My scalp prickled. A cold chill crept into my bones and settled there.

He regarded me from beneath long black lashes, the muscles in his face rigid with fury. I swallowed. I'd gone too far this time. My hot temper had often caused me problems, and this time I'd let it off the leash for too long. I prayed I had not done irreparable damage.

"I'm a man of my word, Charlie, and that is perhaps the only admirable trait you can lay at my feet. I will do what I can to protect you, because I promised to do so. I will endure your presence here because you have nowhere else to go. But more than that, I cannot offer."

Endure? Is that what I was to him? A thing to be endured, like a dull lecture? Had I got him so completely wrong after all, and he did not have tender feelings for me?

How would I even know for sure? I'd thought I did from that kiss, but it seemed I'd been wrong. I couldn't trust my instincts when it came to Lincoln.

He jerked open the door and left me alone with my misery and confusion. His footsteps were so light that I couldn't tell in which direction he went, but the front door opened and closed so he must have gone outside.

I swiped at my damp eyes and gathered my frayed nerves together. It was good to have it out with him. I needed to know where I stood. Knowing was better than wondering and hoping.

Yet it was not the outcome I'd hoped for. Not even close. I'd been a fool to expect anything at all from a man such as Lincoln, but that didn't make me feel any better. Hope could turn even a sensible girl into a silly one.

"Charlie?" Seth's voice startled me, even though I'd been staring at the doorway. He inched into the library, Gus and Cook crowding behind him. Their concerned faces left me in no doubt they'd heard at least part of our exchange.

"Fitzroy shouted," Gus said with a glance over his shoulder.

"We ain't never heard him shout before," Cook added. "Usually he don't need to shout to get his point across."

"It would seem I was a little slow in grasping his point," I said wryly. "We had an argument."

"About?"

"A private matter."

"Charlie, be careful." Seth passed me the crutches. "If you push him into a corner, he will fight to get out and not care who is in his path. Even you."

Gus patted my shoulder. "Best to avoid him when he's in a temper. Just get out of his way and take cover, next time."

"I disagree," I said hotly. My own temper was still simmering near the surface, despite the heaviness in my heart. I felt as if I hadn't quite got my point across to Lincoln, and that only frustrated me more. "It's when he's in a temper that he should be confronted. It seems to be the only time he speaks the truth. I prefer it to the cool mask he presents at other times."

Seth shook his head. "I don't know whether that makes you a fool or very brave."

"A brave fool?" I looked down at the books and papers gathered from Andrew Buchanan's rooms.

"Just be careful. I wouldn't put it past him to remove you from Lichfield."

My head almost swiveled off my neck to look at him. "Because I challenge him when he's in a temper?"

"No, because he thinks getting you away from here, from him, would be for your own benefit."

"Or that of the ministry," Gus added with a shrug, as if he were apologizing for placing the ministry alongside me in Lincoln's scale of importance.

I stared at them. "I'll keep that in mind."

Cook kissed my cheek rather sweetly. "I'll bake scones to have with your tea later."

Seth rolled his eyes. "I think this is beyond the work of your scones."

Cook scowled at him and left the library. I asked the other two to stay. "Have you seen these?" I indicated the array on the table.

"No." Gus pulled a book closer to read the title. "Death ain't spoken to us about Buchanan, yet. Maybe he don't want to involve us, seeing as it's a Lady H family matter."

Seth picked up the journal Lincoln had been reading and flipped the pages. "He just left them here with you?"

"Perhaps that wasn't his intention," I said, "but after storming out, he couldn't retrieve them without swallowing a little of his pride."

"We shouldn't touch them then."

"Or perhaps we should look through them."

Seth grinned. He and Gus sat around the table, and I resumed my position on the chair and scooped a stack of slender books toward me. They seemed old, going by their worn hide covers. The spine of one was stitched and the thick pages protected with two blank boards, front and back. It was beautifully illustrated inside, the gold of the initial lettering shining against the yellowing parchment. It smelled earthy too, as if it had been secreted away underground for centuries.

It was written in an old style, but I was able to gather the general meaning. The book was about witches and spells, but I wasn't sure how much of it was real and how much simply stories, made up by non-supernaturals, to explain strange phenomena. Lincoln would probably know.

Lincoln. I hadn't thought about him, or our argument—or kiss—for almost five minutes. Keeping my mind occupied was clearly a good way to blank him out. I must continue to keep busy.

Gus interrupted me to show me some objects he'd found in a small wooden box. The box and its contents were the only things in the collection that weren't books or papers.

"Jewelry," Gus said, holding up a star-shaped pendent hanging from a worn leather strip. "And not quality, neither. Not for a fancy toff like Buchanan."

"Not jewelry; charms." Seth swiveled the journal he'd been reading to show us. Each charm's likeness had been sketched onto a page with artistic skill. The diagrams were labeled with what appeared to be explanations of each particular charm's power. The star was supposed to ward off illness.

It reminded me of the eye pendent I'd found in Lincoln's room. His charm protected the wearer against spells cast by someone with the evil eye. The pendent had come from Lincoln's mother, whom he'd never met and knew very little about. He didn't know that I'd discovered it was gypsy in origin.

"What else does that journal say?" I signaled for Seth to bring it closer so we could both study it.

He moved around to my side of the table and flipped to the beginning. "It belonged to Lord Harcourt—"

"Lord Harcourt? I thought it was Andrew Buchanan's journal."

He pointed to the lines written in an elegant looping hand on the front page. "Warren Buchanan, third Baron Harcourt, is the late Lord Harcourt, not the present one."

"Lady H's husband," Gus added, craning his neck to see. "What's it say then? Anythin' about his courtin' her ladyship?"

"If you mean does he describe climbing through her window to ravish her, then no. It's not that kind of journal." Seth leafed forward through the pages. "It's more of a random collection of information, perhaps designed to jog his memory. There are hastily scribbled verses and quotes, for example, and several sketches of the supernatural objects contained in that box. Names and dates for appointments, addresses, and what appear to be the odds of runners at Royal Ascot and the like. Our committee members feature heavily." He tapped an entry near the middle of the book.

"General Registry Office,'" I read. Below the page's heading was a list of names and years, written in different ink each time. The script grew scratchy and thin toward the end. "'Marchbank '77. Harcourt '78. Gillingham '79. I think it's a list of which committee member was to be alerted if certain public records were accessed at the General Registry Office."

Both men stared at me.

I cleared my throat. "I have some experience with the triggers set there. General Eastbrooke isn't listed, I see."

"He would have been posted overseas during those years," Seth said. "He hasn't been retired long."

He pointed out some more entries that could be attributed to ministry business. I slapped my hand down at the first sighting of Lincoln's name, halting his progress. There was no date associated with it, but it did mention Lichfield Towers. Underneath was a sketch of the house itself. The entry was very close to the final pages of the entire journal.

"That must be when the committee purchased this place," Seth said.

"And when Mr. Fitzroy moved in and came to be in charge," I added. "Lord Harcourt died shortly after, did he not?"

"Aye," Gus said. "Before Seth and me came to work here. Years of plannin', only to be pushin' up daisies when all the fun starts."

"You have a strange definition of fun. Are there more entries for Fitzroy?"

We searched through the remaining pages but found very little. They mostly consisted of dates written beside "Lich" and the abbreviated names for Fitzroy, Marchbank, Eastbrooke and Gillingham. They must have been meetings held at Lichfield with the entire committee, including the general who would have retired by then.

"Nothing about Lady H then?" Gus asked.

"Aha!" Seth spun the book around with a flourish to show Gus. "An entry describing how he bedded her for the first time, in luscious detail."

Gus grabbed the journal and poured over the page. He handed it back with a withering glare. "Turd," he muttered, returning to his own book.

Seth chuckled. "She does rate a few mentions. Here's one. 'My dearest Julia' he usually refers to her. 'For my dearest Julia, a ball gown of pink silk, Madame La Mondelle the modiste, £12.'"

I pointed to a sketch of a necklace and matching earrings on the next page. "I recognize those. She wore them the night of the ball. 'Diamonds for my dearest Julia, Ogden & Sons jewelers, £1,050.'"

Gus whistled. "He must've been made of money."

I flipped back through the journal, but there were no earlier entries for her. "I think these were written after they married, or perhaps when they were courting. There are no entries for when they met, as far as I can see. She seems to have suddenly burst onto the scene. I expect a mention of her as Miss Something-or-other, but there's nothing prior to him buying her jewelry and dresses."

Seth took back the journal and snapped it shut. "None of this has anything to do with the missing Andrew Buchanan. It's not even his journal."

"No, but he had it in his possession. Fitzroy was also looking through it when I came in. He wouldn't be interested if it had no importance."

"Then you look through it. I need some tea if I'm to be stuck in here for hours."

He left Gus and me searching through the remaining books. I kept coming back to the journal, however. When Seth returned with a tray of tea things, I picked the journal up again and studied it in more detail. What would Andrew glean from pages upon pages of his father's notes? Which name, event or date in particular would interest him?

It struck me when I saw a long list of phrases. The list began with "Department of Oddities" at the top and ended with "Ministry of Peculiar Things" underlined at the bottom. It was the original name for the newly-formed Ministry Of Curiosities, headed by Lincoln. Lord Harcourt and the other committee members acted as custodians of the archives and ministry affairs, while Lincoln did all the real work. "I wonder if Buchanan came to realize that his father was involved in something quite extraordinary. It might explain his new interest in the occult." I indicated the other books, many of which were basic primers on various supernatural subjects. "Perhaps he discovered the ministry's existence through this journal."

Seth nodded thoughtfully. "Could be."

"I wonder if it bothered him that he was never told anything about it."

"I wonder if he knew he and his brother were overlooked as heirs to the secret in favor of their step-mother?"

"The luscious Lady H," Gus said with a frown. "You sure she ain't mentioned more in there? Maybe in some code or other. Only, if I were meetin' on the sly with a girl who were beneath me, I'd have put her name in code."

"No one is beneath you," Seth rattled off rather automatically, as if his heart weren't in the jibe but he felt compelled to say it anyway.

He and I exchanged glances, then both fell on the journal. We flipped to the pages before the first mention of Lady Harcourt's name, and searched through the listing of dates and other bits and pieces. In the end, I gave up with a sigh.

"Nothing," I said, slumping back into the chair. It wasn't lost on me that I was spending far too much time searching for information about Lord Harcourt's relationship with Lady Harcourt and not on the missing Andrew Buchanan, but I dismissed it as a result of my still being upset over Lincoln's rejection. Although I no longer held much respect for Lady Harcourt, I felt we had an affinity with one another now, both having been set aside by him.

"He went to the theater a lot," Seth said, pointing out a series of entries on several pages that I'd dismissed. "But then he suddenly stopped, directly before the first appearance of "my dearest Julia.'"

I pulled the journal closer. "'The Al?'" I shrugged.

"The Alhambra Theater. It's a music hall in Leicester Square."

I smirked. "Ah, yes." I knew of The Alhambra and its allure. The theater held performances of spectacles and ballets, but was better known as a place to ogle the scantily clad dancers who would join the young bucks for a drink during the long interval. I'd even heard of whores slipping inside in the hopes of securing a customer. The gentlemen were easy pickings for us pickpockets when they left drunk as sailors and unable to walk straight, let alone catch us.

"Blimey," Gus said. "You think old Harcourt was entertainin' himself with the doxies at The Alhambra?"

Seth nodded. "I also think he met with the future Lady Harcourt there. Look at this." He tapped his finger on the initials J.T.

I shrugged. "It could mean anything."

"Templeton was her maiden name." He flipped back through the preceding pages, pointing out every entry of "The Al" with the initials J.T. beside it and a date. There were many, but the further back we went, the entries changed. J.T. was simply J, and prior to that, alongside "The Al" appeared the words "Miss D.D."

"Who is Miss D.D?" I asked.

"An actress or dancer?" Seth shrugged. "Perhaps he replaced her with Julia Templeton."

"The Alhambra is an odd place to meet the daughter of a school master. I couldn't imagine her father being too pleased to know she was there."

"P'haps she just liked the theater," Gus said.

"Then she'd more likely choose one with a better reputation."

Seth chuckled. "One doesn't go to The Alhambra to watch the stage. Except for the can can."

"Speaking from experience?"

He grinned. "Entirely."

"We ought to find out more about Miss D.D. and why Lord Harcourt listed her in his journal."

"Why?" Gus asked.

"Indeed?" Seth chimed in. "What has it to do with the investigation into Buchanan's disappearance?"

"I'm not sure," I said, "but we ought to look into it. If nothing else, it's something to do."

"*You* need to rest your foot."

"I will, but after it's healed we should investigate all loose ends from this journal. Buchanan most likely found something in here that intrigued him, something that he went on to investigate."

"This is interesting." Seth flattened out both sides of the journal. "A page is missing. It's been torn very close to the spine."

I peered closer. "So it has. And look. You can make out the impression on this page of something that was written on the torn one. It was underlined." I flipped to the next page. "The impression even appears here too. One only writes so heavily when one is angry."

"I think it's a name. Estelle Mary…Pearson."

"I wonder who she is."

He flipped a few pages, but her name did not reappear. "There are some dates and times here, perhaps for appointments, but no names or places beside them. If they are associated with this Estelle Mary Pearson, we'll never know."

"It's the most vehement writing throughout the entire journal. I wonder if Buchanan recognized the name."

"Ask her ladyship if she knows it," Gus said.

"Good idea. I'll suggest to Fitzroy to do so."

They both looked at me with sympathy. "Is that wise?" Seth asked.

"Best wait for him to calm down," Gus added.

They had a point. "I'll do it later."

Seth took the journal off me. "I'll do it."

I took the book back. "No, I will. I have to speak with him sooner or later. I promise not to argue with him this time. I'll keep the conversation to ministry business only. There? Happy now?"

Gus responded with a snort. Seth muttered, "Hardly," and continued to read.

"You can do one thing for me," I said to Seth. "There's a gift box on my dressing table. Please return it to Mr. Fitzroy. I find it difficult to carry things while using the infernal crutches."

"What's in the box?" he asked.

"Oi! Mind your own bloody business," Gus snapped. "Don't answer him, Charlie."

Seth merely shrugged. We all returned to reading through the books, until finally we heard Lincoln return, but not through the front door. His hair was a little more tangled than when he'd left, his face flushed. His gaze didn't meet mine, but slipped straight to the table and the things on it.

"What's this?" he growled.

It would seem the exercise and cool air hadn't improved his mood. At least he wasn't shouting.

Seth and Gus got to their feet and edged toward the door as Lincoln strode in. "We was just, er…" Gus looked to Seth.

"Leaving," Seth finished.

"Cowards," I muttered, earning me a glare from Gus. "I was tired of sewing so decided to do some investigating," I told Lincoln, as the other two filed out. Their departure left me feeling somewhat exposed and vulnerable. The bruises from my earlier battle with Lincoln were still raw, and I had no inclination to earn any more. I was determined to keep this conversation away from matters of the heart.

"Have you learned anything?" His manner seemed less threatening, his growl not quite so harsh. Perhaps he had resolved not to clash with me again too.

"Lord Harcourt's journal is the most interesting thing here."

"Agreed."

"You read it?"

"Only a few pages." He sat. "Did you?"

"We deciphered a few entries. If Buchanan is clever enough, he would have worked out that his father was part of the ministry, but whether he understands its function is unknown."

"The jury is out on whether he is indeed clever enough."

It may have been a joke but I didn't feel like smiling. "The only interesting thing of note is the missing page."

He leaned forward, but being on the opposite side of the table to me, he was still somewhat far away. I opened the book to where the page had been. He ran his finger over the indentation left behind by the vicious scribble of Estelle Pearson's name. "He was angry when he wrote this."

"There is no other mention of her. Linc—Mr. Fitzroy, perhaps you could ask Lady Harcourt if she knows the name."

"I will. Anything else?"

I bit the inside of my lip. There was no indication that Miss D.D. and The Alhambra theater had anything to do with Buchanan's disappearance, but I couldn't put it out of my mind. "There are some odd entries here, associated with Lady Harcourt and The Alhambra."

A small crease connected his severe black brows. He followed the entries back through the journal to where the initials J.T. were replaced with Miss D.D. His expression didn't change, not even to add an extra blink, but even so, I detected something shift in him. The entries *did* mean something.

"Do you know why Lord Harcourt would be meeting his future wife at The Alhambra?"

His slight hesitation had me sitting forward. "No."

"Do you know how they met?"

"No. He was a staid, steady gentleman. I wouldn't have thought The Alhambra was his sort of thing."

"But how did they meet? It's not as if schoolmasters' daughters socialize within the same circles as lords. Harcourt has only sons, so she wasn't a governess for him."

"She's never told me the story of their introduction."

"You never asked?"

"No."

I frowned. "Why not?"

"It never came up."

"But you were…" I swallowed the rest of my sentence. Saying it aloud might betray my jealousy. *She* had at least shared his bed, and it was becoming more and more obvious that I never would. "I would have thought you'd like to the know everything there was to know about your…paramours."

"Is that what you think?"

"Investigating her seems like something you would do before you…became involved with a woman. Checking on their situations, their families, interests and so forth." I cleared my throat and shifted my weight in the chair. Sitting for so long was becoming tiresome. I needed to get up and move about. I needed to get away from Lincoln and my growing humiliation.

"My liaison with Lady Harcourt was fleeting, and over almost as soon as it had begun. I never bothered to ask her about her private life, and she never offered up the information." It was considerably more than I expected him to give. Indeed, I'd expected avoidance altogether. His words shocked me into looking at him once again.

He met my gaze with his level one. "Does that explanation suffice?"

Was he mocking me? Teasing me over my jealousy? I doubted it, since he was trying to cut off my feelings for him before they blossomed. I lifted my chin. "It will have to do. So what's next? How will you find Buchanan?"

"I'll make inquiries at the places he frequents. I've already begun, but there are several more on my list."

"And you'll search for this Estelle Pearson?"

"I'll see what I can find in the public records, but it'll be a painstaking process unless she lives in the same house in which she was born."

"It's likely she's in the same parish."

"True. Or Lady Harcourt may know something."

"And what of The Alhambra?" I asked.

"I have no intention of going there."

"Why not?"

"Those entries appear to be a private matter between Lord and Lady Harcourt, nothing to do with the disappearance of Buchanan."

"But you can't know that for certain," I said.

"Instinct tells me otherwise."

"Instinct?"

"It rarely fails me."

I hobbled away on my crutches. "How fortunate for you."

"Charlie."

His quiet command set my nerves jangling again. I stopped. "Yes?"

He approached, but did not come too close, and stood with his hands behind his back. The distance was more of an indication of how he felt than his closed face and hooded eyes. "I need to apologize for my earlier behavior. I should never have allowed anger to rule me. If I scared you then I'm sorry. If I offended or wounded you, then I'm doubly sorry. I'm usually not in the habit of allowing my temper to get the better of me, but lately…" He shook his head, as if he couldn't quite understand how it had happened.

"It seems I bring out your temper," I mumbled.

"The fault is entirely mine, not yours. Forgive me." He offered a brief bow then moved past me and strode away.

I stared at his back, grateful that he had broken the ice and apologized, yet uncertain how we could ever be comfortable around one another again.

With a sigh, I headed into the kitchen. By the time I reached it, I'd decided to find something to do to keep my mind off Lincoln. Housework wasn't enough. It allowed far too much thinking time. What I needed was a puzzle. Aside from searching for Andrew Buchanan, the biggest puzzle I knew was finding out what Lord Harcourt had been up to at The Alhambra, and how Miss D.D. had been replaced by the future Lady Harcourt.

CHAPTER 3

It was another three days until the doctor returned and declared I could dispense with the crutches, as long as I didn't put too much weight on my cut foot. He suggested using a walking stick, and Gus went to fetch one from the attic. It had been left by the previous owner of Lichfield Towers, a gentleman of advanced years, and sported the carved wooden head of a mastiff. It was quite ugly and not at all feminine. It went against Seth's fashionable sensibilities to allow me to leave the house with it until I told him I'd leave the house anyway, with or without the stick.

"Why won't you tell us where you're going?" he asked, as I put on my warmest cloak, the one Lincoln had given me only a few weeks before. His question made me wonder if his reluctance to let me go had more to do with his concern for my safety than the stick's ugliness.

"Because you won't approve."

"Better go with her," Gus said with a grim set to his mouth.

"You can't," I said. "Neither of you can. You're about to head out yourselves." They were going with Lincoln to a gambling den in the east end that gossip suggested Andrew Buchanan liked to frequent. So far, their search had not produced anything more substantial than rumor and innuendo. Several of Buchanan's acquaintances had suggested he was being held prisoner by someone he owed money to, had offended, or ruined. Apparently they'd laughed themselves into fits at the prospect.

"At least tell us what you're up to," Seth said as he slid a dagger up his sleeve. "It'll ease my conscience if I know where you are."

I sighed. "It's like having two overbearing big brothers."

"Three," Cook chimed in with a wave of his vegetable knife.

I smiled. In truth, I quite liked the idea of having brothers. They weren't yet stifling me, but I did wonder if the novelty would wear off if I had to report on my whereabouts every day. "The Alhambra."

All three stopped what they were doing to stare at me.

"It's broad daylight, there will be no disreputable gentlemen about, and not a chance that I'll be mistaken for a doxy in my maid's uniform or this cloak." Hand on hip, I dared them to gainsay me.

"Does he know you're going out?" was all Seth asked.

There was no need to mention names. We all knew who he meant. "I was just about to inform him." Right on cue, Lincoln strolled in, looking magnificent in full-length coachman's cape and leather gloves, his hair neatly tied back, and his black boots gleaming. He would cut quite an imposing figure on the driver's seat, particularly if he drove at his usual breakneck speed through the city wearing that scowl.

"Tell me what?"

"I'm going to The Alhambra Theater. Hear me out," I said before he could order me to stay at home. "I know you don't think Lord Harcourt's meetings with Lady Harcourt are of importance to the investigation, but it seems to me you've come up empty handed so far. It can't hurt to at least cross it off as a possible reason for Buchanan's disappearance."

He considered me in silence for a moment then inclined his head in a nod. "I'll drive you. Be sure to take the walking stick and hire a hackney for the journey home." He fished some coins out of his pocket and handed them to me. "And take an umbrella. Dark clouds are approaching."

I accepted the coins in silence, too dumbfounded by how easily he'd acquiesced. Gus fetched an umbrella from the hallstand and I decided to use it instead of a walking stick. Taking both was too cumbersome.

We took the brougham. Gus kept me company in the cabin while Lincoln and Seth occupied the driver's box seat. He grumbled much of the way to Leicester Square, complaining how he was "no toff" and shouldn't be sitting inside like a lady.

"At least it's warmer in here," I reassured him.

He slouched into the seat. Honestly, there was no pleasing some people.

I waved them off from the pavement outside The Alhambra. The theater was Moorish in design, as befitted its name, with arches and columns in abundance, and domes topping the crenelated roof. The main doors were locked, and I was about to knock when someone strode up to the smaller door at the side and pushed it open.

"Excuse me." I hurried over to him as fast as my hobbling gait allowed. "Do you work here?"

"The theater is closed," he tossed back at me. "There is no matinee today."

"My name is Miss Charlotte Holloway."

"Holloway?" The gentleman finally looked at me. He took in my umbrella and cloak then removed his bowler and bowed. "Pleased to meet you. Mr. Jonathon Golightly, at your service."

"I wish to speak to someone who works at this establishment. Preferably someone who has been employed here for some years."

"I work here." The smile he gave me as he straightened was rather dashing, particularly coupled with his pencil-thin moustache and sharp beard. I pegged him to be about fifty or so, but he was unlike any man of that age that I'd met. For one thing, his waistcoat was the brightest fuchsia and he wore a cravat, not a tie. "I'm the stage manager at The Alhambra and have been so for some eight years. Prior to that, I was an actor, also here. Would you like to come inside?"

"Thank you. You're very kind."

He opened the door for me and I found myself in the promenade, an area that encircled the entire theater. It was eerily quiet. While I'd never been inside The Alhambra before, I'd often peeked through the windows as I lay in wait for a drunkard to stumble out. The handsomely dressed gentlemen, mingling alongside pretty barmaids and leggy dancers, had dazzled me as much as the richly colored carpet and the gilt-edged arches. But daylight and emptiness revealed the stains, the gaudiness, and the cobwebs hugging the corners.

"Come through to my office, Miss Holloway." He led the way along the promenade, past the bar and through a door. "Mind your step down this short flight." His voice was light, his steps short and quick. He had to stop frequently to wait for me.

Mr. Golightly led me through to a small office. A series of colorful posters were laid out on the desk, advertising a variety performance for the spring. Someone had written corrections across them in a large, looping hand.

"Please be seated, Miss Holloway." A piano struck up a tune deep inside the building and a clear female voice instructed, "Higher, higher!"

"Rehearsals for tonight's ballet," Mr. Golightly told me. "Miss Redding!"

A moment later, a tall, slender woman with a severe part through the center of her blonde curls glided into the office with a grace that reminded me of Lady Harcourt. She seemed to move without so much as a flutter of her skirt hem. Unlike Lady H, however, she wore a simple woolen dress striped in two shades of brown and a matching jacket in a style that showed off her tiny waist. She wore color on her lips and cheeks, perhaps hoping to detract from her pockmarked complexion. Unfortunately, it did not.

"Yes, Mr. Golightly?" It was difficult to tell how old she was. Her golden hair and slender figure suggested twenties, while the lines around her mouth and eyes made her seem at least mid-thirties.

"Tea, please, Miss Redding. I have a guest." He beamed at me and once again took in my rich velvet cloak with its intricate embroidery. "This is Miss Holloway."

Miss Redding wasn't quite so interested in my clothing. Her gaze remained on my face as she smiled a tentative greeting. "Right away, Mr. Golightly. The water has just boiled."

"Miss Redding is my assistant," he told me as she disappeared. "A most valuable asset to the theater."

"Has she been your assistant long?"

"Only a year or two, but she's been at The Alhambra for considerably longer. She used to dance here."

I made a mental note of the fact. "I have a rather strange series of questions to ask you, sir. At least, they may seem strange to you."

He leaned back in his chair behind the desk and rested his elbows on the chair arms. "How intriguing."

"Do you know anyone by the name of Estelle Mary Pearson?"

He shook his head. "The name is not familiar to me."

I didn't think there was a link, since the name hadn't been mentioned on the same pages as the theater, but asking couldn't hurt. "What about someone with the initials D.D?"

"That could refer to anyone."

"Only to someone with the initials D.D."

"Quite right," he said with a laugh. A nervous laugh, if I wasn't mistaken.

"This D.D. is a woman, and she would have worked here a few years ago."

He clasped his fingers together and pressed them to his lips as he thought. "No, I'm afraid I don't know any Miss D.Ds."

I had not said she was unmarried. "Not a single one?"

Another shake of his head. "I'm afraid not. Ah, here's Miss Redding with the tea."

Miss Redding backed into the room then turned gracefully and placed the tray on top of one of the posters. She poured and handed me a cup with a smile.

"I hope you'll stay a few moments more," Mr. Golightly said. "Perhaps I can give you a tour of the auditorium. We might even catch a few moments of the rehearsal." The piano player completed the tune with a flourish, but no applause followed, only a shouted direction to begin again.

"That's very kind of you," I said. "But I do have more questions, as it happens."

His face tightened, ever so slightly, but the friendly smile remained in place as if it were painted on. "Indeed. May I inquire something of you first, Miss Holloway?"

"Of course."

"What relation are you to Mr. Holloway of Belgravia? Cousin? Sister?"

"I'm afraid I don't know a Mr. Holloway from Belgravia."

His smile slipped off. He dropped his cup in the saucer with a loud clank, causing Miss Redding to pause on her way out. She narrowed her gaze first at her employer, then me.

"You are not here to discuss investing in The Alhambra at Mr. Icarus Holloway's request?"

"No, I'm here to make inquiries about Miss D.D. and a certain woman once known as Julia Templeton, before her marriage to Lord Harcourt."

Miss Redding's gasp was almost drowned out by the piano. She tried to cover it with a cough. And then she did the most extraordinary thing. She screwed up her face as if she'd tasted something sour, huffed out a miffed sound through her nose, and exited the office.

"I am sorry, Miss Holloway," said Mr. Golightly, rising. "I know no one by the name of Templeton, Harcourt or D.D. Allow me to assist you up the stairs." He extended his hand toward the door, his forced smile once more in place.

It would seem I wouldn't even be allowed a single sip of my tea. I followed him out of the office and up the stairs to the public part of the theater. This time he did not offer me a hand or friendly smile, and left me there alone, in the gaudily decorated promenade, to find my own way out. It was the most fortunate turn of events that I could have hoped for.

Once he was out of sight, I reopened the door and headed back the way we'd come, my ears alert for any sounds beyond those of the piano. Mr. Golightly's office door was closed, thank goodness, so I continued further into the bowels of the theater. The corridor was narrow and airless, its musty smell not at all pleasant. The housemaid in me saw dust and cobwebs at every turn, but not even a thorough clean could hide the peeling paint, scratched skirting and patches of mold.

I found Miss Redding in a small kitchenette near the end of the corridor. She just stood there, her fingertips pressed to the scratched surface of the small table, her head bowed as if she were praying or thinking. I cleared my throat, and she jerked in surprise.

"Miss Holloway!" She smiled and peered past me. "Is Mr. Golightly with you?"

"He was called away." I hoped he didn't suddenly appear behind me and order me off the premises. "Forgive me, but I couldn't help noticing your reaction when I mentioned Lady Harcourt. Did you know her?" There was no time for subtlety or veiled questions. I would have to be blunt if I wanted answers before Mr. Golightly discovered I had not immediately vacated the premises.

"I..." She shot a glance to the doorway and bit her lip.

"Perhaps a little privacy for such a delicate matter is required." I shut the door and gave her my sweetest smile.

"May I ask what this is about?"

"Of course you may, but I must press upon you the need for discretion. You see, there are rumors circulating that connect Lady Harcourt to The Alhambra, and her husband's family would like to have them confirmed or denied."

"His family?"

"Yes. He's dead, you see."

"I know that."

"The family hopes the rumors will prove false, which I'm sure they are. They're quite scandalous in nature." *And you, Charlie, are quite the liar.* I blamed my misspent youth and an insatiable curiosity regarding Lady Harcourt. It had become more and more obvious to me that she must be associated with The Alhambra. I also hoped that I'd read Miss Redding's reaction correctly. She did not like Lady H.

"Of course." Miss Redding tilted her chin and her eyes brightened with an unkind gleam. I wondered if she'd been waiting to impart gossip about Lady Harcourt for some time. "I'm not one to spread rumors, you understand," she began.

"I understand completely. A woman in your position must be the soul of discretion."

"Indeed. I detest gossips, and Lord knows this place is filled with loose lips. But I must make an exception in this case if, as you say, the gentleman's family wishes to know."

"They do. Most sincerely. You can be assured that your name will not be associated with any information I pass on. Anything you tell me will only be kept within the family too."

"Oh." She seemed quite put out by that. Was she hoping the gossip would reach the newspapers? If so, she could have skipped this interview and gone directly to the editors of the more low-brow weeklies. They would have fallen over themselves to print something scandalous about the late Baron of Harcourt's second wife. "You're right, Miss Holloway," she said, rallying. "That good family doesn't deserve to be duped any longer, do they?"

"Duped, Miss Redding?"

She stepped closer and dipped her head. Being quite a lot taller than me, she had to dip it further to whisper in my ear. "Lady Harcourt has a…a *past.*" She said it as if the very word tasted foul.

To London's elite, a lady harboring any scandal in her background was indeed shameful and would ordinarily be scorned, ridiculed and ultimately drummed out of the best circles. She could not hope to marry well and would never be asked to so much as drink tea alongside a respectable lady. A lady with a past had no hope of dragging her good name out of the mud—ever. A past clung to her forever, like a stain on her very soul.

It was why I could never be more than a housemaid. As a vicar's daughter, I *might* have married above my station and been admitted to polite society. But as a waif who'd lived on the street for five years, marriage to a pig farmer was more than I could aspire to. It was fortunate, then, that I had no intentions of marrying anyone, since Lincoln had declared himself unavailable.

"Did she work here?" I asked the stage manager's assistant. "Do you remember her when she was known as Julia Templeton?"

"I do. We were dancers together on that very stage."

"You were a dancer? How marvelous. I could see from your bearing and grace that you were a cut above the average." My shameless flattery earned me a smile from Miss Redding, albeit a wary one. I'd best not lay it on too thick, or she might detect my insincerity. "Thank you for confirming my suspicion about Lady Harcourt. How did she come to dance here? Her father was a schoolmaster, wasn't he? Weren't her family appalled at her decision to dance at The Alhambra?"

"How should I know? Anyway, beggars can't be choosers, so I always say. She's not the first girl from a respectable family who had to put her dainty little toes on those boards out there, and she won't be the last."

"She needed the money?"

"So we all assumed. Her father died and her mother was ill, so she said, and she squirreled away every penny, half starving herself to hoard her wages."

My sympathies for Lady Harcourt rose, and I felt awful for thinking ill of her. Of course she must have been poor to accept work as a dancer. No respectable girl would dream of doing so unless she were desperate. "Why not work as a governess?" I said, more to myself.

Miss Redding sniffed. "She made sure to tell us that her dancing career would be a temporary one, and that she would be leaving as soon as she could secure an appropriate position in a respectable household. Indeed, she reminded us of this frequently."

"Did she catch the eye of Lord Harcourt from the stage?"

"Blimey, no. She wasn't a very good dancer, but she had the sort of figure men notice."

Unlike Miss Redding and myself. She was tall and slender while I was short and still rather skinny. Neither of us could claim a bosom to rival Lady Harcourt's.

"He noticed her in the promenade at interval," she went on. "When she found out who he was, she latched onto him pretty quick." The more she spoke, the more her accent changed from the crisp tones of an efficient assistant, to the flat vowels of a working class girl. "He weren't the first gentleman to notice her, mind, but he were the richest and had a title and all. He was also in need of a wife. When Miss D.D. learned that, she wouldn't let the other girls near him."

"Was Miss D.D her stage name?"

Miss Redding nodded. "We all had stage names what we gave out to the gentlemen at interval. Mr. Golightly didn't want us using our real ones. He said it kept us safe."

"Mr. Golightly is probably correct. So Miss D.D. captured Lord Harcourt's attention and the rest, as they say, is history."

"That's right. But…" She leaned down close again. "He weren't her first…admirer. Not by a long shot."

"A woman like that would have many admirers, I'm sure. She's quite beautiful."

Miss Redding lifted her hand and seemed to be about to touch her scarred face in a self-conscious move, but at the last moment patted her bouncy curls. "She knew it, too. At first she were shy, out there on the promenade, but after one or two bucks showed some interest, she learned mighty quick how to attract 'em. After less than a week here, she was batting her lashes at the gentlemen, and lowering her costume at her chest and hitching it high up her leg. Shameless, she was. Course, the gentleman fell over themselves to buy her drinks or give her gifts."

"Gifts?"

"Fans, combs, baubles. She kept some and sold others."

"This is very interesting, Miss Redding, and thank you for the information. But what I don't understand is, how could she go from that life to her current one and not a whiff of it reach society?"

She shrugged. "Toffs only see what they want to see. Miss D.D. wore a blonde wig and painted her lips. She also put on a hat when she were out on the promenade, something with feathers or veils to cover her face. No one knew her real name, not even us, but I learned it after I saw her likeness in the papers when she married Lord Harcourt."

That did explain the anonymity. It would be inconceivable to the society matrons that a dancer could elevate herself to a baron's wife, so they'd never suspect. "It was good of you not to reveal her secret."

She humphed. "Mr. Golightly pretended the new Lady Harcourt in the papers weren't our Miss D.D. but a lookalike. Then he threatened to dismiss anyone who breathed a word, which only told us she *were* Miss D.D." She laughed a brittle cackle that made me feel even more sorry for Lady Harcourt. Her secret hung by a tenuous thread that was in very real danger of snapping one day. "I suspect he got paid handsomely, and still does, to keep mum. Now, Miss Holloway, if you will answer something for me."

I backed a little toward the door. "If I can."

"Who really wants to know about Lady Harcourt's past? The newspapers?"

"I told you, Lord Harcourt's family."

"I doubt that." Her eyes flashed as she stepped toward me. "You're too young and the wrong sex to be a private inquiry agent, and I happen to know that Lord Harcourt's family are already aware of his widow's past."

I halted my retreat. "They are?"

She nodded. "At least one member, anyway."

"Her stepson," I said on a breath. "Andrew Buchanan."

She seemed surprised that I'd guessed. "You know how he knows about her then?"

"Not quite."

"What I'm about to tell you will come as quite a shock. You must prepare yourself, Miss Holloway, as your fiancé has a past as colorful as his stepmother's."

My eyes almost popped out of my head. "My what?"

"You're hoping to marry him, aren't you?"

"Uh, yes. How did you know?"

"I see you're from good family." She fingered my velvet cloak. It almost completely hid my maid's uniform except for the bottom half of the skirt. "You're young and pretty, just the sort he likes." Her finger brushed the underside of my jaw. "And all these questions can only mean you're trying to solve a puzzle about your intended's family. Perhaps your own parents have voiced concerns about Lady Harcourt's origins, so you took it upon yourself to learn more. Did Mr. Buchanan hint about The Alhambra so you decided to start here?"

"You are very perceptive, Miss Redding. I admire your powers of deduction immensely."

She smiled a genuine smile. "I hear he's very eligible, and I know him to be handsome."

"He comes here?"

"Not anymore." She sighed. "Such a pity, but after she broke his heart, he hasn't set foot in The Al."

"She?"

"Oh, I am sorry." Her hand fluttered at her chest as she gave me a pitying look. "I see that I have shocked you, and you don't even know the worst of it yet. Yes, your fiancé used to spend many an evening in the promenade with us dancing girls. He was very well liked for his generosity and his charming manner. He could have had his pick. But I'm sure you know how he is. You can't blame a fellow for cutting his teeth here when he were but a mere lad."

"How long ago was this?"

She counted on her fingers. "Four or five years ago."

"He would have been quite young." I didn't know Andrew Buchanan's exact age, but I didn't think he was more than twenty-two or twenty-three.

"He just started university, I believe. He would come here on holidays, sneaking out of the house when his father thought he was asleep." She merely shrugged one shoulder, as if it were not unusual. "As I said, I am sorry to be the one to tell you about his past, but you cannot be surprised." She didn't look sorry. From the cruel twist of her mouth and the spark in her eyes, I'd say she was enjoying every moment. Perhaps it wasn't just Lady Harcourt's good fortune she resented, but Buchanan's rejection of her, if she was one of the dancers who had admired him.

"That would have been during the time Lady Harcourt performed here," I said. "So he must have seen her."

"Oh yes, he saw her. He also fell in love with her."

CHAPTER 4

I had to wait until the following day to impart my new knowledge. Lincoln and the others hadn't returned by midnight when I sank into bed, too tired to concentrate on my book. Seth and Gus emerged from the attic bedrooms late morning, yawning and rubbing red-rimmed eyes, but there was no sign of Lincoln.

"Did you have any success?" I asked them as they joined Cook and me in the kitchen.

"None," Seth said, inspecting the contents of a pot on the range.

"He's disappeared good and proper," Gus said. "Ain't a stick of truth in any of the rumors we been chasin' down all night. Nobody knows where he is."

"Nobody particularly cares, either, except those who claim he owes them money. They're worried they'll never see their debts paid if he's dead." Seth dipped the soup ladle into the pot and lifted it to his pursed lips.

Cook snatched it before his mouth could touch it. "Where be your manners? Get a bowl."

"It was just a little sip!"

Cook clicked his tongue and shook his head. "And you be raised a gen'leman, too."

Seth pouted and fetched himself a bowl from the cupboard.

"Get one for me too," Gus said. "Charlie?"

"I've already had some."

"Did your expedition to The Alhambra produce any results?" Seth asked, holding out the two bowls for Cook.

"Yes, as a matter of fact, but I don't want to repeat myself. I'll wait for Mr. Fitzroy to come down."

"He already been down," Cook said. "He went out while you were cleanin' in the parlor."

"Oh. Well. I'd still like to wait."

I occupied the next little while with dusting. It felt good to be able to perform my duties once again, even though I used the walking stick to get around. Lincoln returned when I'd just completed the library. I saw him ride up the driveway at speed, then a few minutes later, Gus came to collect me.

"Death wants you to wait for him in the parlor," he said in a plummy toff accent.

"You have to stop calling him that. It's neither accurate nor fair."

"I think it bloody well is. Wherever he goes, a dead body is sure to turn up sooner or later."

I sighed and followed him across the entrance hall to the parlor. Lincoln and Seth joined us a few minutes later. Lincoln had removed the leather strip tying his hair back and the locks fell in waves to just below his collar. He ran his hand through it in a self-conscious move that was rare for him.

"Seth tells me you have information about Lady Harcourt's past," he said.

"And a good afternoon to you too." I gave a little curtsy which he couldn't fail to notice mocked his lack of gentlemanly greeting. He did not move a muscle. "I have indeed learned some things from The Alhambra staff. Lady Harcourt met Lord Harcourt in the promenade when she was a dancer at that establishment."

Seth's jaw dropped, and Gus's eyes bulged. Then he tipped his head back and laughed. "Her ladyship were a dancer at The Al? I'd wager she was popular at interval with her big—"

Seth smacked his shoulder and Gus choked on the rest of his sentence. "She's a lady now," Seth said, "and one doesn't blacken a lady's character by discussing her figure, or her past."

"But what if it's true?"

"Even more reason to sweep it under the rug and nail the rug down so tightly that it can never be lifted again. This news goes no further than this room." Seth arched his brows at me. "Charlie?"

"I'm surprised at you, Seth." I was rather put-out, to be honest. Lady Harcourt was no better than me, yet he was prepared to protect her honor. Would he have done so for mine, or was it because she was a proper lady now, through her marriage? "We have to confront her about her past."

"No," Lincoln said. "We let the matter rest here."

I leaned on my walking stick, gripping the mastiff's head tightly in my fist. "You knew, didn't you?"

"Suspected. She always seemed more…worldly than a schoolmaster's daughter ought to be."

Gus snickered.

"I wondered how she met someone of Harcourt's standing, and long suspected it was under circumstances that some would frown upon," Lincoln went on. "I didn't know it was at The Alhambra until you found those references."

"If you already knew, and you weren't prepared to take the matter further, why allow me to investigate?"

His gaze slipped away. "You would have gone anyway. I thought it best to get it out of your system."

"Get what out of my system?"

Several seconds passed before he answered. "You can see now that Lady Harcourt has had a difficult past. Sometimes she acts in a particular way to preserve herself because she's afraid of losing what she's gained."

I blinked at him. "Are you saying you want me to be friends with her? After she threw me to the wolves?"

"I am not a wolf."

"Then stop growling like one."

Gus and Seth exchanged glances, clearly lost by our conversation. They didn't know Lady Harcourt had used me to betray Lincoln's trust and then scarpered so that I would take the blame. Lincoln did, however, yet he wanted me to sympathize with her and excuse her behavior.

I would not. It was unthinkable, and it hurt that he expected it. It hurt even more that he still held her in high regard.

"So the matter will be forgotten," I said. "I think that's a mistake."

He shook his head, but it was Seth who spoke. "One does not ask a lady about her past, Charlie, particularly in matters of the heart."

"She wasn't a lady then."

Gus grunted a laugh. "And I'd wager the heart had nothin' to do with it."

"All the more reason to let sleeping dogs lie," Seth said. "That's the etiquette when a gentleman discovers these things."

"I doubt other ladies would be so blind," I said.

"They would savage her," he agreed. "I can't have that on my conscience. I suggest that this goes no further than the four of us." He arched his brows at Lincoln.

Lincoln nodded. "It has nothing to do with our search for Buchanan, so I will not mention it in her company or elsewhere. Nor will any of you." He glared at Gus and Gus swallowed heavily and nodded. Then he looked to me.

"You may be wrong," I said, trying to keep the smugness out of my voice. "There *is* a connection with this piece of information and Andrew Buchanan, as it happens."

All three men gave me their full attention.

"Buchanan used to frequent The Alhambra too. He fell in love with the dancer known as Miss D.D.—Julia

Templeton—but was quickly set aside when a more eligible gentleman took an interest in her—his own father. Such rejection from a mere dancer would have angered him. Couple that with jealousy, and then to have the same woman become his stepmother! Can you imagine it?"

Gus was the first to recover his voice. "Blimey," he muttered. "That's a kick in the bollocks that he'd feel for years."

"Precisely. Perhaps Buchanan had finally had enough of seeing her every day and decided to walk away from his life, and her, forever."

Seth stroked his chin and pulled a face as he thought. "It doesn't sound like something he would do. Why now? Why not when they married?"

I shrugged. "He had no money and needed the financial support of his father, and now his stepmother perhaps."

"But nothing has changed. He still has no money. The long list of creditors proves that. Fitzroy?"

"It's an interesting fact, but irrelevant."

As much as I was in the mood for an argument with him, I couldn't do it over this point. He was right. If there was a connection linking this piece of information with Buchanan's disappearance, there was no evidence of it. Yet. Hopefully I would uncover it some other way, as questioning Lady Harcourt was out. I wouldn't go against Lincoln's wishes.

Seth shook his head over and over. "Imagine being usurped in your lover's bed by your own father. Not that I've ever fallen madly in love, but it would gall me to have found my father's fat arse in the bed of one of my conquests."

"He were married to your mother right up to the end, weren't he?" Gus asked.

"Marriage vows never stopped him from exploring outside the matrimonial bed."

"I wonder if Lord Harcourt knew about his son and wife," I said to cover the awkwardness I felt at hearing Seth reveal such information about his own father. He rarely spoke about his family, but I suspected they'd cast him aside when he did whatever he'd done to disgrace himself. One day I would ask him about it.

"Buchanan was very much sought after in those days," Seth said. "This was before he ruined his reputation by racking up debts and the maidenheads of virgins."

"That's what Miss Redding at The Alhambra told me. Minus the part about debts and maidenheads. Apparently the dancers were besotted with him."

"Girls of good family were, too. A wealthy nobleman for a father and a handsome face is a combination that appeals across the class divide."

"It ain't done you much good," Gus said. "Or Buchanan. He's been livin' off his stepmother and you been livin' off Mr. Fitzroy."

Seth batted his lashes. "You think I'm handsome?"

Gus rolled his eyes.

"Besides, my family are no longer wealthy, and the title is a noose around my neck. It tends not to be of help when one's mother has run off with the second footman."

I gaped at him.

He touched my chin and closed my mouth for me. "Yes, Charlie, the *second* footman. Not even the first."

Lincoln cleared his throat. He seemed unperturbed by Seth's revelation, so he must have known about it. Gus too. "Were there any girls in particular who were associated with Buchanan?" Lincoln asked.

Seth nodded in thought. "One rumor had legs. He supposedly put a girl in the pudding club."

Gus gave him a blank look. "Huh?"

"Got her with child, you dolt."

"One of The Alhambra's dancers?" I asked.

Seth shrugged. "I don't know for certain, but since it was a rumor circulating among my set, I'd say she was rather more than a dancer. I can't recall the details, not being particularly interested in Buchanan at the time, and I have no idea if the child was born at all."

"Thank you, that may be useful," Lincoln said. "An ear for gossip is a skill I lack, but you don't."

Seth puffed his chest out like a rooster at the rare compliment.

Gus flicked his finger at Seth's temple. "Pity you didn't mention it sooner, eh?"

Seth shot him a murderous glare and rubbed his forehead.

"Our visitors will arrive shortly," Lincoln told them. "If you could help Cook prepare, I'm sure he will be grateful."

"Visitors?" I asked as Seth and Gus left us. Clearly they already knew who was expected at Lichfield.

"Lady Harcourt is joining me for afternoon tea with her other stepson, the current Lord Harcourt, and his wife. I want to question him about his brother's habits, friends, that sort of thing."

"That'll get confusing with two Lady Harcourts in the same room."

"Lord Harcourt's stepmother—Julia—is referred to as the Dowager Lady Harcourt, but you should continue to refer to her as madam or Lady Harcourt, as you've always done. I'm sure the ladies will work out who you're speaking to. If you need to speak to them at all, that is."

"Ah, yes, maids should be seen and not heard, isn't that right?"

He flinched and I was taken by surprise. I'd not expected my silly barb to impact him at all. "You'll be expected to behave as a maid ought to, yes." He clasped his hands behind his back and added, "I don't like it either, but we must maintain our respective roles in front of the committee members or pressure will mount for me to send you away."

"You're right. Of course. Thank you, Lincoln."

He shifted his weight ever so slightly from one foot to the other. "You don't need to thank me."

"I do. I've forgotten in recent days how fortunate I am to be here. As…disappointed as I am, that you set me aside after that kiss, I'll always be grateful to you for allowing me to stay on in *any* capacity. I don't resent being a maid here. Far from it."

He was silent for so long that I forced myself to look at him, catching him staring at me. His gaze darted to my left ear. "You earned your position here, Charlie, and I'm very aware that it's beneath you, as the daughter of either Holloway *or* Frankenstein. Your gratitude is misguided."

I twisted my hand around the walking stick knob and was about to admonish him for not accepting my thanks gracefully when he added, "But it is appreciated."

He turned on his heel, and since I couldn't run after him, I had to call out. "Why are you protecting Lady Harcourt so fiercely?"

He stopped in the doorway and unclasped his hands. He turned. "I'm not protecting her."

"You are. If it were another woman, you would have questioned her about her past and her relationship with her missing stepson in particular. You wouldn't leave any stone unturned, even if that stone appeared to be small and insignificant."

"Usually small and insignificant stones prove to be just that and nothing more. Besides, she has endured enough humiliation in her lifetime."

"You think dancing to earn enough money to live off is humiliating?"

"I imagine it was for her. She's a very proud woman."

He sounded as if he admired her greatly. Or pitied her. Either way, he was clearly no longer angry with her for pressing me to question the spirit of Mr. Gurry, the tutor he'd killed. "I see." I busied myself with fluffing the cushions on the sofa to hide the tears welling in my eyes.

I was jealous. I knew it as clear as day, even though I'd never experienced the emotion before. That didn't mean I could extinguish it as easily as blowing out a flame.

I didn't hear his footsteps receding, but he had an extremely light step so I abandoned the cushion plumping and turned to leave. He was still standing in the doorway, his gaze on me. Intently.

"Charlie," he murmured.

I limped toward him. "Yes?"

"I…congratulate you on learning so much at The Alhambra. May I ask how you forced your informant to talk to you?"

That was it? That's what he wanted to say to me? "First of all, I didn't treat Miss Redding like an informant, but more of a confidant. With the application of a little sugar for sweetening, and a large dollop of lying, I simply allowed her to tell me what she wanted to tell me. It helped that she disliked Lady Harcourt when she was a dancer there, and her resentment has only deepened over the years."

A resentment born of envy and, perhaps, jealousy too. I hoped I would never be like Miss Redding, bitter and unhappy, and eager to knock another woman down from her pedestal when the opportunity presented itself. Good lord…*was* I as bad as her?

My conscience weighed heavily on my shoulders and I could no longer look Lincoln in the eyes. What must he think of me? Probably that I was an immature, jealous little viper.

"Excuse me," I mumbled, stepping around him. "I have work to do before our guests arrive."

"Well done, Charlie," he said softly from closer behind me than I expected. "I doubt I could have learned what you did from Miss Redding."

He strode off in the direction of the stairs while I headed to the kitchen, again feeling a little bruised from our encounter, but not quite in the same way. This time the bruises had been inflicted by my own fists.

"Her brain is full of wool, and she's not much to look at," Seth was saying as I limped into the kitchen, "but she's got a malleable personality. Not to mention old Edgecombe was fond of his only daughter and handed over a plump dowry."

"Who?" I asked.

"Lady Harcourt—the younger, not the dowager." Seth sat on the edge of the table and put one foot up on a chair, only to have Gus shove it off.

"Talk and work," Gus snapped. "If your own woolly brain can manage to do two things at once."

I grinned, and Gus grinned back at me. Their banter was just what I needed to get out of my glum mood. "Pass me those cups and I'll arrange them."

"No, you sit. Seth and me'll do it."

"But—"

"No buts," Seth said. "You've been dusting for hours. Your foot must be aching."

It did hurt a little. I decided to take them up on their suggestion and rest for a few minutes before the guests arrived. "The new Lady Harcourt sounds nothing like the dowager. I certainly wouldn't call *her* mind malleable."

"And she weren't rich," Cook noted from where he stood at the opposite end of the table, layering cream in a halved sponge cake.

"What's the current Lord Harcourt like?" I asked.

"Very different to Andrew, his brother," Seth said. "He doesn't gamble, and stopped attending most social engagements once he secured his bride. They rarely come to London and live quietly on the family estate. I didn't know him well, but he seems like a steady fellow, much like his father."

Gus laid out the Spode tea set on the tray. "Wonder if he topped his stepmother too."

"Gus!" both Seth and I cried. Cook chuckled into his chins.

"Go and look out for them," Seth said, shooing Gus off with a sweep of his hands.

"Why can't you do it?" Gus grumbled.

"Because Lord Harcourt will remember me."

"Aw, poor Seth, embarrassed that he has to stoop to my level, eh?" He dodged Seth's fist and shot his friend a grin from the doorway. Seth responded with a crude hand gesture that set Cook chuckling again.

"It's hard on you, isn't it?" I said gently. "Forced to serve the people you once socialized with."

"It's not so bad. I've never been all that proud anyway, and I am grateful to have a roof over my head and my debts paid. But the Buchanan brothers are of a similar age to me, and we have several acquaintances in common. Or should I say, *had* them in common. Andrew has offended most, and Donald—Lord Harcourt—has simply not remained in touch. And I've only kept up with a few."

"Aye, the wives," Cook added.

I patted Seth's arm. "Don't envy Andrew Buchanan or his brother too much. They appear to have problems of their own."

"At least *their* mother didn't run off to America with the *second* footman."

Gus entered and announced the coach was approaching, then he disappeared again to open the front door. Upon his return, he reported on the initial encounter between Lincoln and Lord Harcourt. It was their first meeting, apparently.

"Fitzroy told his lordship that he was doing everything he could to find his brother, and you know what Harcourt said?" Gus shook his head. "He said he supposed his brother was just up to his rapscallion, selfish ways again, and he'd turn up sooner or later."

"He's not worried about him at all?" I asked.

"Not that I could tell. The dowager lady looked like she wanted to clock him there in the entrance hall. She said it weren't like Buchanan to disappear for this long, partic'larly without clothes, money, nothing."

"And what did the other Lady Harcourt say?"

"Nothing, just stared daggers at her mother-in-law."

"And Fitzroy? How did he respond?"

"Said he was going to continue looking for him anyway, as a favor to his friend, the dowager. Can't go mentioning the ministry to his lordship without a bunch of questions coming up."

"Or the occult books," Seth said. "Fitzroy did the right thing in not talking about the ministry."

Seth seemed determined to remain in the kitchen, so when it came time to deliver the cake and tea, I volunteered to help Gus.

"You can't carry a tray and use the walking stick," Gus told me. "Let Lord Muck do it."

Seth pouted and heaved a sigh. I set aside my stick and picked up the tray with the cake and plates. "Come on. Follow me."

I did my best not to hobble or limp and discovered my foot didn't hurt much. Perhaps I could dispense with the walking stick altogether. Lincoln's gaze narrowed upon seeing me enter the parlor, and I suspected he would admonish Seth later for allowing me to serve.

I conducted myself as any good maid would and didn't acknowledge the guests, not even Lady Harcourt—the dowager, that is. I did, however, study them from beneath lowered lashes as I sliced the cake.

The younger Lady Harcourt was a short woman with nut-brown hair arranged in ringlets that spilled out from beneath her brown, wide-brimmed hat. The ringlets gave her soft, round face a sweet youthfulness. That very same soft roundness made it difficult to see her eyes, sunken into the puffy flesh as they were. Her high lace collar frothed beneath her multiple chins, in an attempt to hide them, I suspected, but the russet colored skirt and matching jacket brought out the apples of her cheeks. Beside her mother-in-law, she looked like a country school mistress, and I think she felt it too, if her twiddling fingers were an indication. She had moved herself to one end of the sofa, as far away from the dowager as possible, as if she were afraid of breathing the same air as her.

The dowager seemed not to notice. She was as elegant as always in her perky black hat with a lavender trim, and tight black princess-cut gown with smart jacket buttoned to the collar. It was the plainest, most demure ensemble I'd seen her wear. She tended to wear half-mourning now, so the full black seemed like a regression. I suspected she wanted to play the part of grieving widow out of respect for her stepson.

"I'm sorry I cannot give you more names," Lord Harcourt was saying to Lincoln. "Those were Andrew's closest friends growing up, but I'm afraid I know little of my brother's acquaintances nowadays."

"It doesn't matter," Lincoln said. "I have already gathered the names of several more."

Lady Harcourt pounced on the slice of cake I served her, but the dowager refused hers with a mere flick of her finger. She did not meet my gaze. Lord Harcourt accepted a piece, allowing me to study him. He was a moderately handsome man, although not striking, like his younger brother, with fair hair and a strong jawline. But whereas I'd only seen Buchanan's mouth lurch into a lazy sneer, Harcourt's remained in a flat line. He was softer in the middle too, his jacket struggling to contain the bulge. He needed to have a new one made, which told me his weight gain was new, or he was perhaps unconcerned with his appearance.

"Your father's journal was found in your brother's rooms," Lincoln said. "It's possible his disappearance is related to something he read in it."

"Or it may not be," Harcourt said.

"We must turn over every stone, even those that seem small and insignificant."

I almost tripped over my own feet upon hearing my phrase quoted. Fortunately I wasn't holding anything, and no one seemed to notice.

"If you must." Lord Harcourt accepted tea from Gus. The lines scoring his forehead drew together as he took in Gus's lack of livery. He pursed his lips ever so slightly and exchanged a glance with his wife. She didn't appear to notice.

Having finished her cake, she'd taken to staring at the rug, her face blank.

"Do you have the journal here?" the dowager asked Lincoln.

"It's in my study, but I recall most of the details." At Lord Harcourt's questioning look, he added, "I have a very good memory."

"Is anything in the journal of particular interest?" she asked casually. Too casually. Where before she seemed quite concerned about her missing stepson, she now seemed as if she were merely tossing out the question as a matter of course. Her gaze didn't meet anyone's either, yet she gripped the teacup firmly. I suspected she wasn't asking in relation to Buchanan's disappearance but her own secret.

If either Lord or Lady Harcourt noticed, they gave no indication. He was waiting for Lincoln's answer, and she continued to stare at the rug, her expression unchanged. She lifted her cup to her lips, sipped daintily, then set it down again in the saucer in her lap, all without blinking. I'd never seen an automaton before but Seth had described one to me once, and to my mind, it resembled Lady Harcourt's empty expression.

"One name in the journal caught my attention," Lincoln said. "It was written in bold lettering and underlined heavily. It was important to your father, at least, and perhaps Andrew recognized it."

"The name?" his lordship prompted.

"Estelle Pearson."

The younger Lady Harcourt dropped her cup, spilling the tea over the rug, and swooned into the corner of the sofa.

CHAPTER 5

Lincoln was the first to reach Lady Harcourt. Her husband was next. The dowager twisted on the sofa but didn't rise. She picked up a weekly newspaper from the table beside her and handed it to her stepson.

"Flap that in front of her face," she instructed. "And loosen her collar. It's much too high and tight."

Lord Harcourt did as instructed, while Lincoln stepped back. "Fetch the smelling salts," he told Gus.

Gus rushed out but Lady Harcourt was already coming around. She placed a hand to her chest and opened her eyes.

"Donald?" she said weakly.

"It's all right, my dear." He patted the back of her hand. "You fainted."

"I have been feeling a little unwell lately."

"Charlie, more tea," the dowager ordered. "Marguerite, you look quite peaky. Tea will put the color back in your cheeks."

I poured tea into the cup that had been intended for Lincoln but he'd refused, and passed it into the shaking hands of Lady Harcourt just as Gus returned carrying a green glass bottle of smelling salts. He gave the bottle to his lordship, who waved it under his wife's nose.

She drew in a deep sniff that ended in a snort. "Thank you, I feel much better. I'm so sorry to inconvenience you, Mr. Fitzroy." She sipped her tea then set it aside.

"Think nothing of it," Lincoln said.

I eyed the rug and wondered how long it would be before I could soak up the tea. It was imperative to get to spills early to stop staining. I knew that from having once deliberately spilled tea on Lincoln's floor in his sitting room. The stain was still there, a permanent reminder of my temper.

"I think my wife would like to retire to Harcourt House," Lord Harcourt said, referring to the Mayfair home of the dowager and Andrew Buchanan. She had inherited it from her husband upon his death, leaving his youngest son with nothing. Buchanan must have resented being overlooked, but as far as I was aware, Lincoln had not questioned her about it. He'd not questioned her about much at all.

"Of course," he said, taking Lady Harcourt's arm while her husband took the other. Together they helped her to stand. "Before you go, the name of Estelle Pearson…does it mean anything to you?"

"No," Lord Harcourt said. "I've never heard it."

"Nor have I," Lady Harcourt said, leaning heavily on her husband's arm. "Once again, thank you for your hospitality, Mr. Fitzroy. You've been most kind." Her eyes crinkled at the edges as she smiled.

The dowager rose and settled her hand on Lincoln's. "A word," she intoned, as Lord and Lady Harcourt exited the parlor slowly, Gus having gone ahead to assist with coats.

"Is this regarding Estelle Pearson?"

"No. I don't know who that is. It's regarding Miss Overton."

Ugh. The sweet and lovely Miss Overton who lacked spine and character; the girl the dowager Lady Harcourt was encouraging Lincoln to court.

"Not now, Julia. I must see to my guests." For someone who rarely gave away his thoughts or feelings, he sounded quite irritated.

She clung to his arm, anchoring him in the way only a lady can anchor a gentleman. He was much too polite to extricate himself. At least, I hoped it was merely politeness keeping him locked to her. "She and her mother are dining with me tomorrow night. I told them you would be there."

"Julia, that was unwise. You'll have to make my excuses."

"Can you not carve a little time out of your schedule for her? She's quite besotted with you, and you know how marvelous a wife she would make."

"Julia. Stop this." He removed himself from her grasp and headed to the door with long, purposeful strides as if he couldn't get out fast enough.

"You know she's perfect for you," she called after him. But he was already gone. "He does know it. He'll succumb sooner or later." She wasn't in the habit of talking to herself, so I knew her words were meant for me. Had the entire scene been for my benefit? She suspected I had feelings for Lincoln, so perhaps she was trying to show me that I could never have him when there were far more eligible women in London. She wanted him to marry but not to her. Although she claimed to love him, Lady Harcourt had admitted that he wasn't wealthy or titled enough for her. So she was trying to place him with a wife he could never love. One who could never supplant the place she believed that she herself held in Lincoln's heart.

I'd been quite sure there was no longer a piece of his heart reserved for her, but since his refusal to question her about her past at The Alhambra, my conviction had wavered. It was only a short step from sympathy and admiration to love.

I watched her glide out of the parlor with a dancer's confidence and grace, then collected the dishes and returned to the kitchen, while Lincoln farewelled his guests. Gus was already there, regaling Seth and Cook with details of Lady Harcourt's swoon.

"It were in reaction to hearing the name," he said with all-knowing solemnity. "She knows the Pearson woman."

"Or has heard her name before," I added. "I wish Fitzroy had questioned her about it."

"One does not question a lady over matters that have caused her to faint," Seth said. "Particularly when she pretends it was ill health."

"One doesn't, does one?" I said in my best imitation of him.

"No. One waits until he corners her alone." He winked at me. "I suspect that's what Fitzroy will do."

"I wouldn't be so sure. For one thing, how will he get her alone?"

"Climb into her room tonight," Gus offered with a shrug, as if it was something Lincoln did frequently.

"But her room must be on the third floor at least!"

"That ain't a problem. The problem will be doin' it quiet enough that she won't scream the place down first."

I put my hands up in protest. He was being ridiculous. Lincoln wouldn't climb into Lady Harcourt's room in the night. I asked him as much when he joined us.

"No," he said. "Her constitution is too delicate. She'll probably faint again. I can't get answers out of an unconscious woman."

I didn't know why I was surprised. If Lincoln wanted answers, he would get them any way he saw fit, gentlemanliness be damned. "Then what do you propose?" I asked. "It was clear to everyone that she knew the name Estelle Pearson. We have to find out how she knows her."

He glanced at the clock on the shelf. "I'll inquire at the General Registry Office tomorrow. A birth, marriage or death record will at least narrow down the parish or parishes the Pearson woman has lived in."

"I don't think Lady Harcourt likes her mother-in-law," I said, removing three cloths from the top drawer.

Lincoln tilted his head a little. "Why do you say that?"

"She couldn't sit far enough away from her, for one thing, and I never heard them exchange a single word or even a friendly glance. I thought it odd, considering they are quite close in age and have family matters in common."

"I see." He nodded slowly. "Thank you for your observation."

I limped into the scullery and dipped one of the cloths into the pail we kept filled with cold water by the back door, then fetched a canister of baking powder from the pantry and one of Cook's mixing bowls. Since my adopted mother had a housekeeper, I'd never learned how to make cleaning pastes or remove stains in my childhood like the girls who'd been thrust into service at a young age. When he'd seen my dilemma, early in my tenure as Lichfield's maid, Gus had called upon his great aunt and asked her to reveal the secrets she'd learned in forty years as a charwoman. He'd taken dictation and given me eight-pages of densely packed scrawl, rolled up and secured with a piece of string. It was still my most treasured possession, even over my cloak from Lincoln.

I returned to the kitchen only to find Lincoln gone. He was waiting for me in the parlor. Or rather, perhaps not waiting for *me*, just for me to bring the materials for cleaning the rug. He looked up from the tea stain and held out his hand.

"Pass me the powder."

"You have to soak up the excess liquid first," I told him.

"Then pass me a cloth."

"I can do it."

"Allow me, Charlie. You should be off that foot."

"I'm perfectly capable of performing my duties, thank you."

I set the cloths, bowl and canister down on a table and he picked up one of the dry cloths while I picked up another. It would seem he wouldn't be swayed from helping. So be it. I doubted I could change his mind, no matter what I said.

We worked in silence, side by side, to soak up as much of the spilled tea as possible. I wanted to ask him for his thoughts on Lady Harcourt's invitation to dine with Miss

Overton, but decided against it. It was not the sort of discussion an employee had with her employer, and he'd made it clear that was what we were to one another from now on. Nothing more.

To my surprise, *he* brought the subject up, however. "I have no intention of marrying Miss Overton," he said.

I stopped sponging and sat back on my haunches. "Lady Harcourt thinks she'll make a good wife since she's so…malleable," I said, borrowing a term from Seth.

"I don't want a malleable wife." His sponging became more aggressive, stamping the cloth into the damp rug in time to the beat of my heart. "Or any other sort of wife. I won't be marrying at all. Not Miss Overton, Lady Harcourt or…anyone. Marriage is not for me."

The cold tea from my cloth seeped into the skin on my palm. I stared at it and blinked. My eyes were dry, thankfully. I didn't want to shed any more tears for him. Not over this. Unrequited love was pathetic, and I detested being so needful. I'd managed for years without needing anyone's love, and I would do so again. It was time to move on and be thankful for what I did have. I had so much more than most. "Why are you telling me this? You don't owe me an explanation."

"I do. I didn't want you thinking that I was in the habit of kissing a woman one day then setting her aside to marry another the next. I won't marry you, Charlie, but I won't marry another either. It's imperative that you understand that."

"Is it?" I couldn't keep the disdain out of my voice. At least disdain was better than sounding confused and wistful, which was how I felt.

He stopped sponging. "You mock me."

"No, I… I don't know what to say or do or think." It helped to hear his stance on marriage in general. It was one thing to not be able to keep him to myself, but it would be worse to see him wed another woman, even if it were a marriage of convenience to a spineless twit like Miss Overton.

"Is it ready for the powder now?" he asked.

It took me a moment to realize what he was talking about. "Yes."

He popped the lid off the canister and sprinkled the baking powder over it until I told him there was enough. He watched as I rubbed in the powder with the clean, damp cloth. With the task complete, he stood then held out his hand to me. I took it and rose. A small jolt passed between us and his fingers tightened.

Then he extricated himself quickly and strode out of the parlor without another word or glance back. With a sigh, I picked up the cleaning materials and limped to the kitchen.

* * *

"She's dead," Lincoln informed us when he returned from the General Registry Office the following afternoon. "Estelle Pearson died five months ago at Queen Charlotte's Hospital For Lying-In."

"In childbirth?" I asked, picking up another pea pod.

"In an accident. The records don't mention how it happened. She worked there as a midwife."

"Damn," Gus muttered. He'd been snoozing in the armchair in the corner but had jumped to his feet when Lincoln entered the kitchen and pretended to look busy rearranging things on the sideboard. Lincoln had hardly spared him a glance, but I doubt he was fooled. "Dead end, eh?" He snorted at his lame joke.

I tossed the empty pea pod into the pail. "I could raise her spirit."

Lincoln considered it for a moment then shook his head. "It's too dangerous."

"How is it dangerous? I can control her spirit and will do so from the outset. As long as nobody alive sees, my secret will remain just that."

"We know nothing about her." Lincoln accepted a cup of tea that Seth handed him. "She could be dangerous."

"But if I control her—"

"No."

"But, sir—"

"No, Charlie, and that's the end of it." He removed himself from the kitchen with his tea.

"You're being unreasonable!" I called after him.

He didn't answer; nor had I expected him to.

"Careful, Charlie," Seth warned. "Push him too far and he's likely to snap back like a rubber band."

Gus snorted and returned to the chair. "More like the kick from a canon."

I sliced open another pea pod and spilled its innards onto the mountain of peas in the bowl. "He *is* being unreasonable. I have the means with which to help his investigation, and he's refusing it. I don't understand why. Have I not proven myself useful in the past?"

"Have you not been kidnapped and nearly killed?"

I threw an empty pod at Gus. It bounced off his forehead and landed in his lap. He lobbed it and whooped when it landed in the pail.

Seth joined me at the table and pulled the bowl of peas between us. "He allowed you to go to The Alhambra."

"Only because he thought it would be harmless, not to mention somewhat irrelevant to the investigation. He admitted he was simply trying to appease me."

"I agree wiv Charlie," Cook said with a shrug. "Ain't no reason that I can see for her not to use the gift God gave her."

I wasn't entirely sure my necromancy could be called a gift, let alone a God-given one. It seemed rather more devilish than divine and more of a curse than a skill. But it was what it was, and it was as much a part of me as my blue eyes and short stature.

Neither Seth nor Gus spoke again, which was as good as saying that they agreed with Cook but didn't want to say so out loud. They were more afraid of Lincoln, perhaps because they'd seen him kill whereas Cook had only heard about the killings second-hand. Their silent approval was all I needed to make up my mind. I would raise the spirit of Estelle Pearson tonight.

* * *

Raising spirits that had passed over to the other side was something I'd done quite a few times, but it still sent a chill down my spine. Not all spirits were happy to be wrenched from their afterlife, and not all were friendly. While I could control a spirit, if necessary, it eased my conscience somewhat if they didn't need controlling.

I lit as many candles as I could sneak into my small sitting room and positioned them on tables, mantelpiece, and even the floor. The flickering candlelight made the walls and furniture seem as if they were alive, dancing to a rhythm I couldn't hear. I sat in the comfortable armchair and drew in several deep breaths to steady my nerves.

"Estelle Mary Pearson, please come to me here in this world. The spirit of Estelle Mary Pearson, do you hear me?"

A breeze blew out the candles on the mantel and teased my hair. The ribbons of smoke merged with a pale wisp plunging from the ceiling. It streaked toward me. I ducked but wasn't fast enough. The spirit of Estelle Pearson went straight through me and came to a hovering stop near the door.

"My goodness," she said, pressing a ghostly hand to her chest. Her wide eyes took in her surroundings then settled on me. "Is this…am I…?"

"You are in Lichfield Towers, Hampstead Heath, and it's some five months after your death. You're here in spirit form, Mrs. Pearson."

"It's *Miss* Pearson." She spoke as a matter of course, as if it were commonplace to correct people. Considering she appeared to be in her forties or fifties, it was a mistake easily made. I couldn't pinpoint her age more precisely than that. Although the misty appearance of a spirit formed the person's likeness upon death, it was rather like looking at a sketch. There were no colors, making the eyes in particular seem flat. The principle of eyes being windows to the soul didn't apply.

"And you are?" Her tone was crisp but not unkind.

"Charlotte Holloway. I'm a necromancer. That's someone who can raise the dead."

"Clearly." She indicated herself, dressed in her nurse's uniform of white pinafore over a black dress. She wore a cap that hung half off her head, clinging to the wisps of hair by a single ghostly pin, and a long, heavy-looking chatelaine hung from her waist. "Why have you summoned me, Miss Holloway?"

She seemed quite unfazed by the situation, thankfully. A panicked spirit could make my task more difficult. I supposed being a midwife in a lying-in hospital required an unflappable constitution.

"Your name was written in a journal belonging to Lord Harcourt," I told her.

Her eyes widened ever so slightly. "And?"

"And the journal was found in the belongings of his son, who has now disappeared. We're trying to find him."

"We?"

"My friends and I."

She glanced around the room then raised both her brows at me.

"They are not here at present," I said.

"Are they also necromancers?"

"No."

"Then I suppose their presence wasn't necessary. You seem quite unperturbed by what you've just done, Miss Holloway. Your calmness is unexpected in someone so young."

I detected a hint of admiration in her voice, and I smiled. "Thank you, but I've raised spirits before."

"Even so. You would make a good nurse, although I see that you have no need to make your own way in the world." She glanced around the room again. It may be only a small sitting room compared to Lincoln's, but it was intended for the mistress of Lichfield Towers, not a maid. Miss Pearson must have assumed I was somebody important.

I felt compelled to inform her of the truth. "I may, if I ever find myself losing my position here as maid."

She came forward and took a closer look at me. "Yes, I see the uniform now. You do seem like the sort of girl who has had to make her own way in the world for some time—sturdy of mind, confident in nature. Am I correct?"

"Thank you. And yes, you are."

"Now then, about the journal of Lord Harcourt and his missing son. I fail to see the connection between the two."

"There may be no connection, but we must look at every possibility. What particularly caught our attention is that your name appeared in Lord Harcourt's journal, in severe writing, underlined more than once. It was as if your name was very important to him. Do you know why?"

She blinked slowly. "I find it very difficult to converse with you like this, Miss Holloway."

I frowned. "What do you mean?"

"This spiritual form feels odd." She looked down at herself. "Somewhat…insignificant."

"Is that a problem?"

"I am an unmarried woman who has had to find her own way in life as a nurse. More doctors than I care to recall have treated me as insignificant, and so did much of the wider community. Without a husband or a fortune, I was nobody, unworthy of praise or even acknowledgement. My opinions were ignored, sometimes ridiculed, and I was frequently told to stop using my brain. Intelligence is unbecoming in a female, and unnecessary in a midwife who must bow to a doctor's superior knowledge." Her voice slurred into a sneer at the end. "I could have saved more babies and mothers if I had been allowed, I'm sure of it, but some incompetent doctors preferred to use methods they were taught decades ago, rather than listen to me. So you see, Miss Holloway, I would prefer a solid form instead of this faint one, if only for the few moments in which I answer your questions."

I rose from my chair so that I would be eye to eye with her. She was about my height, with a rather masculine face with strong bones and a heavy brow. Her gaze did not waver from mine and she did not back away.

"Are you saying you wish to occupy a body? You do understand that you cannot occupy a living one?" Only a medium could summon a spirit into a living body, so that the spirit overrode the person's conscious. It was known as possession. As a necromancer, I could only direct a spirit into a *dead* body.

"I don't wish to occupy just any body, Miss Holloway. I wish to occupy mine."

I let out a breath. "Oh."

"The thought of being inside a stranger..." She shuddered. "You say this is Hampstead? Then my body will not be far. I made arrangements before my death to be buried at Highgate Cemetery. Do stop staring at me, Miss Holloway, and let's make haste to Highgate."

"I, er, will you answer my questions when you are in your body?"

"Yes."

"All of them?"

"Yes." She lifted her chin. "I give you my word to answer to the best of my ability. I do know Lord Harcourt, and there is a tale to tell. Whether it helps you locate your missing man, I cannot say. But my tale remains with me until I am inside my own body again."

Still, I hesitated. "You understand that it will only be for a brief time."

"A brief time is better than no time. I do so wish to feel the cool night air on my skin again, the breeze in my hair."

"You died five months ago. Your body will have decayed somewhat in that time."

"Are you squeamish, Miss Holloway?"

"No."

"Neither am I. A nurse cannot afford to be. I have seen far more gruesome things than a decaying body in my lifetime, I can assure you. Come along. Let's do it now."

I should be able to sneak out of the house undetected. Lincoln had taken Seth with him to search the remaining gambling dens on his list, so I wouldn't need to worry about him overhearing me leave. Gus and Cook slept in the top floor's servants' bedrooms, too far away to hear the back door open and close. Very well. I would do it, if that's what it took to get Estelle Pearson to talk.

She turned and I had to cover my mouth to smother my squeak of horror. Bile burned my throat at the sight of the back of Miss Pearson's head. The skull had been smashed in. Matted hair and blood formed a dark, sticky mass just above her neck. The top half of her pinafore was also covered with blood. I wondered what sort of accident had inflicted the fatal injury.

"Come along, Miss Holloway." She patted her cap and repositioned it so that it covered some of the wound, but not all.

"Let me fetch my cloak."

* * *

It wasn't a cold night, thanks to the bank of clouds that blanketed the city, trapping in the warmth of the sunny autumn day. The same clouds blocked out almost all light from the moon and stars, and it was left entirely up to my lamp to guide us. I followed the ghostly apparition through the cemetery, my walking stick making a solid *whump* on the damp, dense layer of fallen leaves as I rushed to keep pace. Every now and again Estelle Pearson would stop up ahead and say, "Come along, Miss Holloway," in her no-nonsense yet encouraging tone. I could imagine her speaking in such a way to her patients in their birthing beds.

We stepped around graves and over tree roots, not following any path that I could see. Overhead, bare branches creaked in the breeze and groaned their disapproval at my disregard of Lincoln's order. I had not had any doubts before, but now, in the depths of the vast cemetery in the middle of the blackest of dark nights, I was assaulted with them.

"Are you quite sure this is the way?" I called out to Miss Pearson's ghost. "Perhaps we should turn back."

"Not at all. Look, we have arrived." The mist swirled around the headstone marking Estelle Mary Pearson's grave, then coalesced into her likeness. "Here I am." Her voice had become soft and filled with wonder as she studied the headstone. It was tucked away in a part of the cemetery I'd not visited, where the headstones were more modest and positioned close to one another.

"Do you require a moment to contemplate, Miss Pearson?"

"Certainly not. You're not changing your mind, are you?"

"I… I think I'd prefer it if we don't raise your body after all. The sooner I can send you back to your afterlife, the better."

"Fiddlesticks. We have all night."

"Even so—"

"In for a penny, in for a pound."

Before I could protest further, the spirit sank through the earth covering her grave, and disappeared from sight entirely. I frowned. She appeared to know what to do. Other spirits I'd raised had not.

I lifted the lamp higher. Beyond the whispers of the leaves came the faint sound of thumping. Miss Pearson's corpse, trying to get out of her coffin. Perhaps she wasn't strong enough to do it. The only other body I'd seen emerge from its own grave was Gordon Thackery's, but he was a man. Even though Estelle Pearson would possess superior strength as a reanimated corpse, would it be enough to free herself?

She must have broken through, however, because the earth in the center of the grave bulged. I swallowed and stepped back, preparing myself for the sight of the decaying corpse.

Dirty, skeletal fingers thrust through the soil like spikes. Then came an entire hand, followed by an arm clad in the black sleeve of the nurse's uniform she'd been buried in. Another arm pushed through, dislodging a mound of soil. Estelle Pearson hauled herself out of the ground then stood with her feet a little apart for balance.

"Are…are you all right?" I asked her.

She nodded, an awkward, jerky movement that had her frowning then trying again. She stepped toward me, only to stumble a little. On impulse, I dropped my walking stick and grasped her arm. The bones moved in a way that no living person's arm should.

"It will take a few moments for you to become accustomed to working a dead body," I assured her.

"I know that." Her voice sounded as rough as sand.

"How can you possibly know? Have you done this before?"

"No." She touched her throat, as if self-conscious about her voice. She began to walk off but I still held her so she stopped again and stared down at my hand.

I tightened my hold. "Then how?"

She wrenched free. "Because I know everything there is to know about death, Miss Holloway, and life too, for that matter."

I stumbled backward. "How?" I whispered.

She murmured something under her breath. I couldn't catch the words, but the sounds were guttural, un-English. Dread as heavy as a brick settled into the pit of my stomach.

"Miss Pearson, what are you saying? What are those words?"

She finished murmuring and her entire body jolted as if something had slammed into her. Her chest expanded then fell and expanded again. She breathed.

My God. *She was alive.* I held my lantern higher to get a proper look. She gave me a sympathetic smile that reached her eyes—eyes that should have been empty and soulless.

"Do not be afraid, Miss Holloway, I'm not going to harm you, but I am going to leave you now."

"Y—you can't!"

She walked off, her gait jerky but gaining in steadiness with every step. "I can."

I hurried after her and grabbed her arm again. "But I control you!"

"I have a matter of some importance to see to, now that I am here." Her boney fingers picked off mine until she was free once more. "Do not try to detain me again, Miss Holloway. I do not wish to hurt you." She could have snapped my fingers, but she didn't. She moved away from me with determination and a step that was now entirely steady.

"I release you!" I shouted. "Go! Return to your afterlife!"

She continued to walk on into the night then broke into an awkward run. I hobbled after her but tripped over a tree root. My lantern went out and I was shrouded in darkness.

"I release the spirit of Estelle Mary Pearson! Return!"

"That will not work," she called back to me from somewhere up ahead, where her dark shape disappeared among the trees and tombstones.

I tried again, but this time there was no response. Perhaps I'd succeeded in sending the spirit back after all. I stumbled through the cemetery in the direction she'd gone, but found no body. I crawled on hands and knees, praying I would touch flesh and clothing instead of stone and leaves. I searched for hours, through the rain and increasing cold. I became thoroughly lost in the dark but kept crawling over the ground and graves like a pathetic creature, even after all hope was lost.

By the time the glow on the horizon signaled the start of a damp, miserable new day, my clothes were wet through and my petticoats plastered to my skin. My skirt, stockings and gloves were filthy and torn, and my walking stick missing. I sat with my back to a tomb of a weeping angel and burst into tears.

I knew without doubt that Estelle Pearson's spirit was still on Earth, occupying her decaying body, yet somehow come to life.

And it was all my fault.

CHAPTER 6

Dawn provided enough light for me to find my way out of the cemetery. I limped through the gate and passed a groundsman with his broad-brimmed hat pulled low over his face. If I'd been in a stronger frame of mind I would have checked to see if it was the one with the purple birthmark. That rat had told Captain Jasper where to find me, resulting in my recent abduction. He ought to know what had come of his actions so that next time he would be more careful. But I was in no mood for a confrontation of any kind.

I limped home in the drizzling rain, careful not to put too much weight on my cut foot, even though it didn't feel sore anymore. A small mercy. At least my slow progress gave me more time to think of a way to inform Lincoln of what I'd done. I considered not telling him, but my absence from Lichfield as I searched for Estelle Pearson would be suspicious. Besides, he would need only to look at my face and know something was wrong.

By the time I reached Lichfield's back door, however, I was still no closer to finding the right words. I unlocked the door then relocked it and hung the key on the hook in the kitchen. Despite removing my boots, I left behind damp footprints on the floor and service stairs.

I stopped outside my rooms. The door was ajar. Had I closed it? Light flickered inside, yet I'd blown out all the candles before leaving. Hope flared in my breast.

I pushed open the door. "Miss Pearson, I'm so reliev—"

Lincoln crouched by the grate where a fire blazed. He stood and dusted off his hands as he took in my disheveled appearance. The flickering flames cast deep shadows beneath his eyes and cheeks, and emphasized the downturn of his mouth. He looked exhausted.

It took a long time before I found my voice. I didn't know how to begin, and he didn't make it easier on me by remaining silent. He clasped his hands behind his back, and looked every bit like a king about to pass judgment on his subject.

"You're shivering," he eventually said. "You need to get out of your wet things and warm up by the fire."

"You…you lit it for me."

"When I realized you weren't home, I thought you would get caught in the rain."

"You knew I'd left? How?"

His gaze shifted to the flames. "I…sensed your absence."

"I didn't know you were capable of doing so."

"Nor did I until this morning when I came home."

It was an interesting development of his paranormal capabilities and one that required more thought and discussion, but not now. "You have only just returned?"

He nodded in the direction of my adjoining bedroom. "Go and change, Charlie."

"Will you stay here? I need to talk to you."

He nodded, and I got the feeling he already knew what the discussion would be about, at least in part.

I quickly changed into my nightgown and threw a shawl over my shoulders. I returned to the sitting room and lay my cloak and dress over the backs of the chairs then angled the chair backs toward the fire. I left my unmentionables in the bedroom. Displaying them in front of Lincoln was an extra humiliation I didn't want to endure.

Avoiding looking at him, I knelt by the fireplace and removed the pins from my hair. I tousled the shoulder-length locks with my fingers and tipped my head toward the heat. It felt awkward with him standing there and me kneeling near his feet, the silence stretching and stretching. Why didn't he ask what I was doing out in the night? Was he waiting for me to confess?

"Thank you for starting the fire," I said. "Did you sense me returning? Is that why you lit it?"

"No." His tone had taken on an icy edge that didn't bode well. "I didn't know where you'd gone or when you'd be back. Since you took your cloak, I hoped you hadn't been forcibly taken from the house. Nor were Gus or Cook roused, which would also imply you left quietly. Voluntarily."

I swallowed past the lump in my throat. He'd been through my bedroom and noticed my cloak gone. "I'm sorry if you were worried. I thought I'd be back before you noticed me gone."

"Since it seems I am now able to tell when you are here or not, I would appreciate a note be left when you decide to disappear in the middle of the night. Is that clear?" The icy tone turned positively freezing.

"Yes." I stared into the fireplace, still not able to meet his gaze. "I am sorry."

"You raised the spirit of Estelle Pearson, despite my instructions not to."

I bit the inside of my cheek and nodded.

"And just now you thought it was her in here," he continued. "Why?"

I sucked in a breath and lowered my hands to my lap. I finally met his gaze and shivered. Not even the flames reflected in the black pits of his eyes. "I raised her spirit in here earlier tonight, but she insisted on entering her own body before she gave me answers." I twisted my fingers together. They hurt from the cold, but I didn't care. I welcomed the pain. I deserved it. "She was buried at Highgate, so we went to the cemetery. But once she occupied her body, she said something in a foreign language. Then she just walked away. I called her back, but she didn't return. I ordered her spirit to leave, but it had no effect. I couldn't control her, and she ran off. I don't understand, Lincoln. What went wrong? Did she know a spell to override my necromancy?"

He had been watching me the entire time, that fathomless gaze upon me as if he were trying to see into me. But now it faltered and he turned to the fire. "It seems so. You recognized none of the words?"

"She spoke them quietly, and I don't know any languages other than English. The accent was harsh, throaty."

"Did she say where she was going?"

"No, but she mentioned that she had something she needed to take care of."

He had no more questions for me and seemed lost in thought.

"Is she a witch, do you think?" I asked.

"Perhaps."

"She knew what a necromancer was, and she didn't need instructions on how to re-enter her body. Death and reanimation didn't sicken or frighten her. She seemed quite unperturbed by it all."

He didn't respond, which only made me want to talk more. I needed to talk, to get some things off my chest.

"I should have suspected then. I put her courage down to being a nurse, but looking back now, it's obvious that she understood the supernatural. But I *liked* her. That's the problem. I liked her and trusted her." Tears welled and I sniffed. It felt as if Estelle Pearson had betrayed me, even though the notion was ridiculous. She was dead, for one thing, and we'd only just met.

"You should know better than to trust anyone, by now." He strode to the door, reaching it in a few long strides.

I jumped up and ran to him, catching his arm before he could leave. "What are we going to do?" I choked out.

He removed my hand from his arm then let it go, as if it burned. "You are going to bed and leaving this to me."

"No! I have to do something."

"Do you?" he growled, his lips hardly moving.

I winced. Tears bubbled on my eyelids and I began to shake. I felt so cold, like the ice from his gaze had been injected into my veins. "I need to help fix this, Lincoln. I need to—"

"Stay. Here." He strode out of the room. I pressed my forehead against the doorframe and closed my eyes. It didn't stop my tears from spilling.

* * *

I heard Lincoln pass by my rooms again a few minutes later. I tried to sleep but couldn't. My mind wouldn't switch off and my nerves jumped at every creak of the house. I changed into my maid's uniform and headed downstairs. The others would think it odd if I launched into my housework without seeing them first, so I went to the kitchen. Cook and Gus looked up from where they both stood near the range, warming their hands.

"Mornin', Charlie," Cook said. "Eggs'll be ready soon."

"Where's your walkin' stick?" Gus asked.

Somewhere buried among leaves and mud at Highgate Cemetery. "I no longer need it. No eggs for me, thanks, Cook. I'm not hungry." I gave them both a flat smile, the best I could manage, and left again, but not before I saw them exchange glances. It seemed Lincoln had not informed them of what I'd done.

I dusted and swept the front porch, since it had stopped raining. The cool air felt damp and the clouds hung low on the horizon. It would rain again later today.

The rumble of wheels on gravel had me squinting along the drive to see who visited at such an early hour. It wasn't even mid-morning yet. It couldn't be Lincoln returning, as I hadn't heard a coach leave the stables. He'd either ridden or gone on foot. It must be a committee member, and they were not people I felt up to greeting.

I returned inside and hurried to the kitchen, where Seth was now yawning in the corner armchair. "Visitors are coming," I told them as I passed through. "You'll have to greet them."

"Where are you going?"

"For a walk." I left through the back door and crossed the courtyard. I hadn't collected hat, coat or gloves, and the crisp air nipped at my skin. I passed by the outbuildings, and would have headed for the walled garden or the orchard, but another coach driving toward the house caught my eye. I hid behind a tree trunk and peered round. The coach bore an escutcheon of a snake coiled around a sword—Lord Gillingham's crest.

Damn. What did he want? And whose coach had been the first to arrive? I couldn't quite see the front of the house from my recessed position.

Behind Gillingham came another coach, and another, and finally a rider on horseback, going so fast that he caught up with the final coach. Lincoln.

When they too passed out of my line of sight, I ran toward a shrub, closer to the front of the house, then from there dodged to another, keeping low so that no one could see me. I recognized all four coaches as belonging to each of the committee members. They stood as one, arranged in a wall near the front steps, with Lincoln before them. Gus held the bridle of Lincoln's horse, while Seth stood in the open doorway. None of the visitors or Lincoln seemed inclined to enter.

"…bloody stupid," I head Gillingham say. He smacked the end of his walking stick against his booted foot to emphasize his point.

I strained to hear the snatches of conversation. I had a dreadful feeling that I knew what it was about.

"Where is the witch now?" Lord Marchbank asked, confirming my suspicion.

"I don't know," Lincoln said. "But I'll find her, and Charlie will send her back."

"How?" Gillingham sneered. "She couldn't control her then, why would she be able to control her now?"

I couldn't hear Lincoln's response, because General Eastbrooke spoke over the top of him. "I knew something like this would happen. We should have sent her away months ago."

"We couldn't have known," Lady Harcourt said. "The chances of someone being a witch are small, and the chances that the one spirit we need is a witch are even smaller."

"Need?" Gillingham echoed. "Julia, there was no *need* to raise that witch's spirit yet. The stupid girl took it upon herself to do something highly dangerous—"

"She didn't take it upon herself," Lincoln cut in. "I ordered her to raise the spirit of Estelle Pearson."

I gasped. Lincoln was taking the blame? It was one thing to defend my actions but quite another to let them think it was all his idea.

"Why are you all here?" he went on in the ensuing, stunned silence. "I have work to do. Go inside and have tea, if you wish. I won't be joining you." He took the horse's reins and led it around to the stables.

I watched him go, too stunned to move or think straight.

Gillingham's shouted words roused me. "This just proves that she is a weapon that can be used with the intent of doing good, only to have it backfire."

Lincoln didn't stop. The other three committee members piled into their coaches, leaving Gillingham alone, still shouting at the now empty space where Lincoln had been.

"She's dangerous! She shouldn't be allowed to roam free, even under your guidance!"

"Enough, Gilly," Lord Marchbank said through his lowered window. "Today is not the day."

"Agreed," said the general, also poking his head out the window. "We've confirmed what we needed to know, for now. Returning the spirit must be his priority. We'll tackle the matter of the girl another time, when he's not so busy. I'm only sorry we all made this journey for nothing." He ordered his coachman to drive on, and the carriage rolled away, following Lady Harcourt's.

Marchbank left next, and finally Gillingham climbed into his coach and thumped on the cabin ceiling with his walking stick.

I watched them leave with a heavy heart. I should have owned up to my actions. I should have told them I'd operated without Lincoln's consent; indeed, I had gone against his express order. It wasn't fair for him to take the blame when he didn't deserve it.

Why had I been so cowardly and stayed hidden?

I would fix this, as I would fix the problem of Estelle Pearson. Somehow.

But how? I needed to think, but I didn't want to return to the house. I walked away from it, toward the orchard, and climbed an apple tree. The fruit had all been picked, and only a few valiant rust-colored leaves clung to twigs. I went as high as I could go, lodging my good foot between the V of two joining branches and resting my injured foot lightly. The bark was damp, and I didn't want to get my only dry maid's uniform dirty, so I didn't sit or lean like I wanted to, but just stood, like a sailor clinging to a mast, searching the horizon.

I saw Lincoln approaching well before he reached me, but I didn't descend from my perch until he stopped at my tree.

"You can come down now," he said. "They're gone."

"I'm not up here to avoid the committee."

"Then why are you up there?"

"I…" I wasn't sure, to be honest. I'd just known that I needed to get away and be alone. Sometimes living in a vast house with only four other people seemed more crowded than a small basement hovel with a dozen boys all crammed in together. "I needed some fresh air."

"In a tree?"

I jumped from the lowest branch to the ground, landing so lightly on my feet that my injured foot didn't hurt at all. I used to climb a lot when I pretended to be a boy, but rarely trees. Mostly over fences or low walls and through windows.

"Thank you," I said. "I heard you take the blame."

"I thought so. I knew you were hiding there."

Had he sensed me or had he seen me? "Is that why you did it?"

"No."

"Then why?"

"It was easier."

"For me, yes, but not for you."

He folded his arms over his chest.

"Lincoln, I do appreciate what you did. Very much. I will set it to rights at the first opportunity, and tell them I acted without your consent."

"And give them more ammunition to send you away? No, Charlie. I forbid it, and this time I'm deadly serious. It's better for you if they think I ordered you."

"But—"

"No!" He grabbed my shoulders and shook me, though not hard. "Will you never listen?"

I wrenched away and his fingers sprang apart. He scrubbed a hand across his chin, over his mouth. I blinked at him, my throat tight, my heart trying to punch a hole through my ribs. "If you think it's for the best, then I'll abide by your wishes."

He nodded, calmer. "Good. Now come inside before it rains again."

He held out his hand for me to go ahead. I gave him a sideways glance, which hurt my eyeballs, and saw that he was looking at me too.

"You don't seem as angry with me now as you were this morning," I hazarded.

"You think I was angry with you for raising Estelle Pearson's spirit." It wasn't a question, but I took it as one.

"Aren't you? You did tell me not to, and I went ahead and did it."

He looked up at the gray sky and let out a breath that almost seemed like a sigh. "I probably shouldn't tell you this, but I can't be angry with you for that, since I would have done the same thing if I were in your position."

My step faltered. He stopped and caught my elbow, steadying me, then let go. Neither of us continued on. "You…you would have?" I frowned and thrust my hands on my hips. "Then why order me not to?"

"Because there is always the chance that something will go wrong. Aside from the obvious dangers of having a corpse wandering around the city, you cannot afford to have a strike against your name. The committee, especially Gillingham, will seize upon any opportunity to send you away. It's why I haven't wanted you to help look for Buchanan. It's best if you stay at Lichfield, out of trouble."

"Then why involve me in the Captain Jasper affair? You *asked* me to raise Gordon Thackery and scare answers out of Jasper's men."

"And I came to realize that was a mistake, an almost fatal one." His jaw hardened and a muscle in his cheek jumped. "After your abduction, I concluded that I should not have involved you. Not only for your own safety, but because the committee will use Jasper's interest in you to support their argument and send you away. Lady Harcourt admitted as much to me."

I stared at him. It was a relief to hear that he wasn't too angry with me, but this… It was one thing to dismiss any feelings he had for me, but quite another to exclude me from ministry business. I could not be just a maid at Lichfield. Not ever.

The realization struck me as severely as a blow to the body, knocking the breath out of me momentarily. I pressed a hand to my chest. "But I have to help you fix this, Lincoln. I need to find Estelle Pearson and send her back."

"Only you can send her back, that's true, but I will find her and bring her to you."

"No, I have to help. I *have* to."

"You don't!"

"I would rather risk being sent away than have you face dangers alone because of me. Lincoln, please, if I do nothing..." I shook my head, unsure if I could put into words how I felt. "I won't be able to breathe. I am a necromancer, and I must be allowed to use it to help you or what's the point?"

"This is not open for discussion," he growled, striding off.

I ran after him and caught his elbow. He stopped and did not shake me off, but nor did he look at me. "Stop trying to protect me. You're smothering me. You are not my parent, and I don't need one anyway."

His entire body jerked. "I am not trying to be your parent, I am trying to be your employer, your protector. You are under my—"

"Care. Yes, I know, so you keep reminding me. But I don't want to be *under* your care, Lincoln, I want to be alongside you."

"That's not possible. There's only one leader of the ministry."

"More as an assistant, then."

"I have Gus and Seth to assist me."

I sighed. The conversation had veered in a direction that he wasn't ready to travel down and I wasn't prepared to fight for. Yet. "Let me help you find and return Estelle Pearson. We'll be together, where you can keep an eye on me, and I will only do as you instruct."

"The committee would not want you to be involved," he said, setting off again.

"Since when do you tell them everything?"

He grunted. "I wasn't going to. I was just pointing out that if you want to help, they are not to find out."

"We'll be sure to swear the others to secrecy then." I smiled and almost felt bold enough to slip my hand inside the crook of his arm. Almost.

We reached the courtyard before I thought of another question. "How did the committee members find out that I'd raised Estelle Pearson's ghost?"

"I don't know, but it's something I've been trying to work out since their arrival."

"You didn't tell them?"

"Of course not."

"But no one else knew. I saw one groundsman as I left the cemetery, and a coach or two passed by as I walked home, but that's all."

"Did you recognize any of the coaches?"

"No, but I wasn't really looking. I was too distracted."

"Was the groundsman the one with the birthmark?"

"I couldn't tell."

"I wouldn't put it past them to each have spies planted over the city, including the cemetery, particularly since you came to live here."

"Why do they need spies?"

"To gather information for ministry business, and to be made aware of potential supernaturals for me to investigate."

"If it's ministry business, why not tell you who their spies are? Why keep their networks a secret, rather than incorporating them into your own and making the ministry even more powerful?"

"That, Charlie, is a good question." He pushed open the back door and ordered Seth and Gus to join us for tea in the parlor.

Ten minutes later, Lincoln told the two men what had happened. I kept my hot face lowered, so I didn't see their reactions, but their weighty silence felt like a noose around my neck, condemning me. It served as a good reminder that no matter how lenient Lincoln had been, I was still guilty of disobeying orders and endangering lives.

"Our priority now is to find Estelle Pearson," Lincoln said. "Once Charlie has sent her back, we'll resume the search for Buchanan."

Gus held the delicate teacup between both hands, not even attempting to fit his stubby fingers through the handle. "Can't be too hard to find a walkin' corpse."

"Try parliament." Seth lifted his teacup in salute when Gus laughed.

I giggled with relief that they could make jokes about it. "I think once we find Estelle, we'll know where to search for Buchanan," I said.

"You're convinced her name meant something to him?" Seth asked.

"I am. She promised she'd give me answers about Lord Harcourt. She said she had a tale to tell, and it's likely her tale has something to do with Buchanan's disappearance."

"Why should we believe her? She could have said that so you would take her to her body."

"I'm certain she was telling the truth. The name certainly meant something to her. Her reaction when I mentioned Lord Harcourt was telling."

Gus twisted the cup in his hands and studied the liquid. "No disrespect to your instincts, Charlie, but I don't think we can trust a dead woman. She ain't got nothin' to lose."

"She's the only hope we have at the moment," I said, a little miffed that he wasn't on my side.

"I believe you." Lincoln surprised me with his conviction when Seth and Gus seemed to lack it. "But if she's acting dangerously, we have to send her back before she can harm anyone. Public safety, as well as our own, is paramount."

"Yes, but it won't hurt to ask her for her story first."

He arched his brows. "Did you not just say you will do only as I instruct?"

I bit my tongue. It wouldn't do to argue with him so soon after making up, but I felt my instincts should account for something. I'd met Estelle Pearson—they hadn't—and I didn't think her a bad person. She could have hurt me, but she hadn't.

"Problem is," Gus said, "*how* do we send her back? If Charlie can't force her, and if she don't want to go..."

"We restrain her and remove her from the public," Lincoln said. "As to the rest, we'll simply have to find her weakness."

"But she's bloody strong!"

"A different sort of weakness. Almost everyone has a loved one."

Oh my god! He meant to threaten to harm her loved ones if she didn't comply. The notion made my stomach roll. I set down my teacup. "Do you think we'll find her with one of her loved ones?"

"Perhaps." Lincoln gathered up the riding coat he'd slung over the chair arm. "But it's just as likely that she's gone to the place where she worked and died. We'll begin at the hospital."

* * *

Queen Charlotte's Hospital for Lying-In was located in Marylebone Road, behind a low brick fence topped with iron spires. The five-story utilitarian red-brick building was hardly a pretty sight for expectant mothers but at least it offered a place for poor women to get the care they needed during childbirth.

Gus acted as coachman, and remained with the horses and carriage, while Seth and I went in through the front door, where a nurse greeted us from behind a desk in the sparse reception room. Lincoln had already disappeared around the back of the hospital, where he would sneak in. He wouldn't tell us what he was going to do, once inside. I had a suspicion that he didn't know himself, but I didn't say as much to Seth as I took his arm like a happily married woman.

"Good morning," I said, smiling at the nurse. "I do hope you can help us. We are Mr. and Mrs. Guilford."

Seth tensed beneath my hand. Had I done the wrong thing using his real name?

"How may I help you, sir, madam?" Her crisp tone reminded me of Estelle's, but this woman was younger and her features not as pinched as the spirit's.

"Our housekeeper's niece was a patient here, some six months ago," Seth said cheerfully. "She received excellent care and her boy is now thriving after a difficult, er, time of it."

Good lord, could he not say "delivery" or "birth?" Being brought up to be polite and avoid immodest words might set the upper classes apart from the lower but such politeness and avoidance became a little ridiculous at times. Particularly with a man who'd had to make his way by bare knuckle fighting.

"Our housekeeper mentioned a certain midwife had been wonderful throughout the delivery." I squeezed Seth's arm as he tensed again. "Since our housekeeper is dear to us, and her niece dear to her, we wanted to show the family's appreciation by giving the midwife a token of our gratitude."

The nurse's face brightened, and I knew what to expect next. "How very generous of you. Do you know, the patient sounds familiar. I recall a young woman who gave birth to a boy around six months ago, and she said her aunt kept house for a lovely family. What did you say was the patient's name?"

"Perhaps it was you she was referring to," I said with pleasure in my voice to match hers. "Only you seem too young. The nurse's name is Miss Pearson."

Her face fell. "Oh. No, I am not her." Clearly she didn't think she could lie her way through to the end. "Miss Pearson, you say. That's very unfortunate."

"Why?"

"She died."

I turned to Seth and placed a hand to my chest. "Oh my. Oh, that's quite, quite awful."

Seth patted my hand and frowned deeply. Then he turned his full attention on the nurse, smiled sympathetically and reached for *her* hand. "How tragic for you and her other colleagues here at the hospital. How did it happen?"

If I were the nurse I would have been immediately alerted that something wasn't right by his abrupt question, but she seemed not to notice. She was far too busy falling into Seth's beautiful eyes. He certainly had a way with women.

"She hit her head, down in the basement supply room."

"Hit her head?" he echoed. I was content to leave the questioning up to him since I suspected my interruption would be unwelcome and cause the nurse to close up. He was doing a marvelous job without my assistance. "How? Was she alone?"

"One of the doctors was with her. He witnessed the entire thing. He said she simply collapsed. He tried to revive her, but she lost too much blood from the head wound. The coroner later found that she had a weak heart that gave out on her and caused her to fall unconscious."

"I see. What a tragedy."

"Very much so. Miss Pearson was well liked here, and she was extremely dedicated and clever." She leaned forward and lowered her voice. "Much cleverer than some of the doctors, including Dr. Merton who was with her." She sounded quite pleased about that fact, then her eyes grew sad again. "She's a loss to the hospital. A real loss. If only we'd known she had a heart problem, we would have urged her to take on lighter duties. But she never breathed a word."

A thought took hold and wouldn't let go. A rather sinister thought.

"Do doctors usually go down to the supply room?" I asked. "I thought fetching supplies would be a nurse's job."

"It is." She busied herself with some papers on her desk.

"And yet Dr. Merton was there."

"Yes." The crisp tone had returned, along with a flattening of her lips.

I nudged Seth. If anyone could get her saying more it was him, if he used his charms correctly.

But before he could take her hand again, another nurse bustled up. "Have you seen Dr. Merton this morning?" she asked the midwife on the desk. "He's supposed to have begun his rounds but no one's seen him."

"Have you checked his office?"

"I knocked but there was no answer." She wrinkled her nose. "I suppose I should try again."

The nurses exchanged grim looks then the newcomer bustled off.

"Excuse me," I said to the desk nurse. "I think I'd like to speak to this Dr. Merton." I hurried after the disappearing midwife, dragging Seth with me.

"You can't go through there!" the desk nurse called. "Staff and patients only."

"We'll just be a moment. I'm sure your colleague will show us to his office. There'll be a generous donation given to the hospital when we learn which doctor delivered my housekeeper's baby!"

"Housekeeper's *niece's* baby," Seth muttered as we rushed through the door and caught up to the other midwife. "Keep up."

The nurse eyed us curiously but didn't order us to return to the reception room. It would seem the words "generous donation" had worked their magic.

"I'm glad for your company," she said with a smile that didn't reach her eyes. "Very glad."

We followed her through a ward lined with beds on either side. Each one was occupied by a heavily pregnant woman, some moaning, others lying on their sides, and one who was clearly about to give birth, if her groans were an indication. A doctor and two nurses attended her, and they were obviously about to inspect her *down there*. Beside me, Seth went white and slowed down, gawping at the scene. I grabbed his hand and pulled him along just as the poor woman let out another low groan.

"Are you all right?" I asked him. "Are you going to be sick?"

He swallowed and wiped his brow with his handkerchief. "I think I'll manage."

I patted his arm. "You've been very brave, dear. Well done."

He blanched at my sarcasm. "Thank you, *dear*. I do hope you're taking notes for when we are as blessed as these patients. I'm sure it won't be long before you find yourself in one of those beds, as large as a whale yet somehow still radiant."

"Oh, I won't be confined here. Our marriage bed will do nicely."

He pulled a face, but at least he had his color back.

We followed the nurse along a corridor, her stiff skirts snapping at her ankles with each step, up three flights of stairs then into another corridor with several doors leading off it. She asked the nurses, orderlies, and doctor we passed if they'd seen Dr. Merton, but none had for some time.

"Excuse me," she called out to an orderly dressed in an ill-fitting brown jacket and trousers. He had his back to us and paused with his hand on a door handle. His shoulder-length black hair was tied back in a leather strip.

Lincoln.

He turned to her. He did not look at Seth or me, and he didn't seem at all surprised to see us there. If he was, he was good at hiding it. I wasn't quite so adept. My eyes bulged, but I managed to suppress my gasp before it left my lips. The nurse didn't notice.

"Yes, miss?" Lincoln asked.

"Have you just come from Dr. Merton's office?"

"Is this his office?" He indicated the closed door. "Only I'm new here, and I was sent up to fetch him." His accent placed him directly in London's east end, not at all from Highgate.

"It is," the nurse said. "I've not seen you before. You must be new."

"Just started today, miss."

"And they sent you looking for the doctor alone?" She clicked her tongue then eyed the door with wariness that didn't sit well on her. She'd been energetic and brisk up to this point, but now she hesitated.

I came up close behind her. "Shall we go in?" It was more a question for Lincoln than her, but it was the nurse who answered.

"Of course. There's no reason to delay."

"Let me go in first," Lincoln said.

If the nurse thought his offer odd, she didn't say so. She seemed quite happy to have him open the door. What was she expecting? Her willingness to have Seth and me along, her strange behavior now that she was outside Dr. Merton's office…something was wrong.

Lincoln opened the door and blocked the entrance with his body. None of us could see past him, not even Seth.

"Is he there?" the nurse asked.

Lincoln backed out and shut the door. "No."

She blew out a long breath. "So the search continues. Where could he have gone?"

Lincoln's gaze met mine. I didn't need to be told that all was not right in Dr. Merton's office. The simple fact that he had an interest in Dr. Merton too was enough to make me think I'd been right to be suspicious about the doctor being in the basement with Estelle Pearson when she died.

The nurse headed off again but paused a few steps away. "Are you coming, sir, madam?"

"If it's all right with you, my wife and I will wait for Dr. Merton in his office," Seth said. "Please tell him we're here when you find him."

"Of course." She cast another glance at Lincoln, smiled prettily, then bustled away.

"What's going on?" I asked when she was out of earshot.

"We've found Estelle Pearson," he said.

"Thank goodness. Is she in there?" I felt a weight lift off my chest. I could breathe again.

He nodded. "She is. Crouched beside the dead body of Dr. Merton."

CHAPTER 7

The office smelled like a ten-day old ham had been left in it. Estelle Pearson must have been inside for some time. She squatted on the floor beside the body of the man I assumed was Dr. Merton. Her flaky, bloodless lips moved as if she spoke, yet no sound came out. Perhaps she was praying for his soul. Or hers.

I took a step toward her, but Lincoln's hand flashed out and caught my arm. He had closed the door, leaving Seth outside to keep watch.

"Miss Pearson?" I said. "Are you all right?" Perhaps it was an odd thing to say to a corpse, but she didn't seem at all like the woman I'd met during the night. She looked dazed and the hand that clutched her throat shook.

"Will I pay for this, do you think?" she asked, her voice sounding far away.

I followed her gaze from the feet of Dr. Merton, over his deep barrel chest to his neck. A large purplish bruise formed above his collar, shaped like fingers. I felt the blood drain from my head as if a plug had been pulled. I swayed and Lincoln slipped his arm around my waist.

"Wait outside," he said.

I shook my head and rallied. I drew in a deep breath and felt the blood returning, my nerves settling, and my head clear. "I did this. I must stay and do what I can to fix it."

"You did *not* do that."

Estelle Pearson's head jerked as if I'd slapped her. "He's right, Miss Holloway. This is not your fault. It's mine and mine alone. I killed him. I will face the consequences."

"Consequences?"

She lifted her gaze ceiling-ward. And that's when I saw it.

Dr. Merton's spirit.

The white mist clung to the corner as if he were trying to get as far away from Estelle as possible. His huge eyes flicked between his body and hers, trying to fathom what had happened. He didn't see me staring at him.

"We should go," I said. There wasn't a thing the spirit could do to us now but I would feel better if I couldn't see his shock and the slowly dawning horror at his demise.

Lincoln pulled out a length of rope from beneath his jacket. One end was tied into a loop with an impressive looking knot. Was he going to capture her and tie her up?

"There is no need for that," she said, her hand out to placate Lincoln as if he were a maddened animal. "I'll come with you and return to my grave. I've finished my business here." She cast another glance at Dr. Merton's body. "He'll not harm anyone again."

The spirit twisted and twirled like a pile of leaves caught in a whirling breeze. Then he suddenly whooshed down from the ceiling, straight at Estelle. "You bitch!" he cried. "You raving, maniacal bitch! You killed me!" He crashed into her.

And came out the other side. She'd not felt a thing and didn't bat an eyelash. In her reanimated form, it would seem other spirits were invisible to her. She glanced around the room, as if she suspected his spirit was there somewhere, listening, and one side of her mouth lifted in a bitter, gruesome grin.

"Do you hear me, you monster? You can't hurt anyone now."

He swished around the room, dashing up to the ceiling, down to the floor, left and right, shouting vile words I'd not heard since leaving the slums two months ago. He seemed unaware that I could hear him, and I had no intention of telling him.

"Enjoy your afterlife in hell, doctor." Estelle picked a hat off the floor. It must have come off during a scuffle with the doctor. It wasn't the same hat she'd been buried in, but had a wider brim to cover her face. She also wore a long coat over her dress. "Perhaps we'll meet there, if my actions today outweigh all the good I did in life. If so, it will still have been worth it." She rose. Her knees creaked and cracked, as if her bones were grinding together. "We should go before someone returns. I don't want anyone accused of this."

It was going to be difficult to blame natural causes with a bruise on his throat shaped like hands.

The door suddenly opened and Seth tumbled inside, shutting it behind him then turning the lock. "That nurse is coming back and she has another doctor with her. We need to leave. Now."

"But we'll have to go past them," I said.

Lincoln nodded at the window. "That way."

"It's too high," Seth said. "For Charlie, I mean."

The spirit chuckled from its resting place on top of the filing cabinet. He crossed his arms and watched the proceedings with interest.

I crossed to the window, gratified that Lincoln had faith enough in my climbing abilities to suggest it. "I can manage. There's a drain pipe just there."

"Indoor plumbing," Estelle said. "I'll go down first and break your fall if it comes to that."

Voices filtered to us from the corridor outside. "Go," Lincoln hissed.

Estelle was already through the window and climbing down the pipe like it was something she did every day. It was amazing what a lack of fear could do. She slipped when she was still some feet off the ground and fell the rest of the way. She landed on her back, cracking her already caved-in skull. She got up and signaled for me to hurry.

I hiked up my skirt and petticoat to above my knees, wishing I had some way of securing them there, and slung them up over one arm. Lincoln and Gus helped me through the window, and I let the skirts drop. Climbing down pipes wasn't as easy, dressed as a girl, but at least I could breathe properly since I refused to wear a corset.

I glanced down to see Estelle standing below, her arms outstretched to catch me. She wouldn't be the most comfortable cushion to land on but she would be enough to break my fall. Above me, Seth emerged through the window.

Beyond him, I heard the office door rattle. Thank goodness we'd locked it. Hopefully they would need to fetch a key from somewhere, giving us time to escape.

I glanced up again, but Lincoln had not followed Seth through the window yet. What was he doing? I continued to climb down and reached the ground safely, some considerable distance ahead of Seth, who felt carefully for every foothold.

"Where's Fitzroy?" I planted a hand on my hat and craned my neck back to look up. "He's taking too long."

"What are you doing?" cried the voice of Dr. Merton's spirit.

A gunshot cracked. Birds in Regent's Park squawked and screeched. Seth's hand slipped and he let go of the pipe. Fortunately he was close enough to the ground that he landed without hurting himself.

I opened my mouth to scream Lincoln's name, when he suddenly leapt out of the window, planting his feet on the pipe. As quick as a monkey, he descended. He dropped beside me before Seth had even picked himself up. He grabbed my hand just as raised voices from the third floor window exclaimed in horror.

We ran to the front of the hospital, then walked in a calm, civilized fashion toward Gus and the waiting coach. "Was that a gunshot?" he asked.

"Yes," Seth said, assisting me up the steps and into the cabin. He practically shoved me inside at the last moment. "Fitzroy shot a dead man."

Seth handed Estelle up behind me, his fingertips barely touching her boney ones, then he and Lincoln followed.

"Highgate Cemetery," Lincoln barked. Gus had the horses away before we'd even shut the curtains.

"You shot him?" I asked as we rounded a sharp corner.

Lincoln nodded. "In the throat, with a gun and bullet I found in the drawer. I placed the gun near his right hand where it would have landed if he had fallen. A competent coroner will know he was shot after death, but an incompetent one might miss it and declare suicide. A corrupt one certainly will."

Estelle snorted. "The one from this jurisdiction is certainly corrupt. My death certificate says I suffered a heart attack. I lingered in spirit form long enough to hear Merton and his crooked crony planning it. For a fee, of course."

"Oh, Estelle, I am sorry." I laid a hand on her arm, gently so as not to disturb what was left of her decaying skin and wasted muscle beneath the layers of clothing. "Are we to understand that Dr. Merton killed you?"

She bowed her head, but not before I saw sorrow shadowing her eyes—eyes that weren't dead, but weren't quite alive either.

"Tell us how it happened."

She clasped her hands in her lap and lifted her chin, once more the no-nonsense woman I'd first met in spirit form in my sitting room. "Dr. Merton is the worst kind of man. He preys—preyed—on women, particularly the young and vulnerable. I was neither, so I avoided his notice until I confronted him over his misdeeds."

"He hurt the other nurses?"

"Yes, Miss Holloway, he hurt them. Two midwives under my supervision came to me after he'd raped them in that same basement storeroom where I came to my end."

"Bloody hell," Seth muttered. "The man deserved his death then."

"That's why the nurse didn't want to go to his office alone," I added. "She was happy for us to go with her rather than face him on her own."

"There were other stories too, of attempted rape and indecent acts," Estelle went on. "I brought them to the attention of both the hospital board and the local constabulary. Unfortunately, the poor girls were frightened of him and of the effect a trial would have on their reputations. They refused to testify, and it all came to naught." She shook her head. "It sickens me that they would have suffered if he was found innocent."

"How would he be found innocent if they testified?" I asked. "Surely a judge would believe their accounts."

"Your faith in our justice system is misguided, Miss Holloway. Dr. Merton would accuse them of being loose women and claim that they approached him in the storeroom, not the other way around. I knew he would stop at nothing to protect his reputation from this sort of scandal, but I had no idea that he would resort to murder. I was gathering evidence against him, you see. I talked to the girls and had almost convinced them to take the witness stand, but they only agreed to do so if there was an iron-clad case. That involved speaking to all the nurses at the Queen Charlotte, as well as those not associated with the hospital. It's possible there were other victims, you see, ones that we didn't know about. I checked inventory records for the storeroom, and cross-checked the dates and times of his signature in the dispensary book with the reported incidents. I was developing a solid case."

"So he killed you," I said, "then paid the coroner to cover it up by blaming heart failure."

"There's nothing wrong with my heart. My health was extraordinarily robust when I was alive."

"You appear to be alive again," Lincoln began, with his usual dark intensity. "How is that possible?"

Estelle bristled and regarded him down her nose. "I don't believe we've been introduced."

"My apologies," I muttered. "My manners are a little rusty. This is Mr. Lincoln Fitzroy and Mr. Seth Guilford. I work with them."

If Lincoln noticed me say "with" and not "for," he gave no sign. "Miss Holloway said you spoke some words in the cemetery before coming to life. Was that a spell?"

"You're an earnest man, Mr. Fitzroy, and quite unperturbed by the notion of spells, necromancers and the like."

"Answer the question."

Good lord, sometimes he had as much subtlety as a room full of dancing elephants. "We belong to an organization that wishes to keep the supernatural from harming the public," I assured her. "As you can imagine, having a corpse with incredible strength come to life is a worrying incident."

"Of course it is, and I'd like to assure you that I will return willingly to my afterlife." When Lincoln opened his mouth to speak again, she added, "Besides, I am not alive. Not exactly. I merely have the appearance of life. As to your question, Mr. Fitzroy, you are correct. I spoke a spell that my female ancestors have used for centuries to give consciousness to the dead, albeit for a brief time. It makes them act and look alive, but they are not. There is no air in their lungs, no blood pumping through veins, and the vital organs don't work. If there was, I would have died all over again when I fell from that drainpipe. In a way, it's similar to necromancy. I suppose that's why the spell overrode your orders, Miss Holloway. Perhaps you and I are two branches of the same ancestral tree."

Seth and I exchanged confused glances, but Lincoln's gaze didn't waver from Estelle's. "You're a witch."

"My ancestors were accused of witchcraft on occasion, so yes, I suppose I am. It's why I'm so good at what I do." At our blank looks, she elaborated. "Stillborn babies are common in my line of work, sadly, as is the death of the mother during childbirth. That spell allows me to buy them some time on this mortal coil. In some cases, only a few hours, in others, they continue on for a day or two."

"But…why?" Seth asked. "What's the point of giving a baby or mother a few hours of something that is not even a life? Why prolong the death and the pain?"

Estelle clicked her tongue and shook her head. "So that the mother can hold her child, Mr. Guilford. Just for a little while, and look into her baby's eyes, and know a mother's love. It's better to die in the arms of a mother than in her womb. On a more practical level, there is time to baptize the child and have other family members see the baby. In all cases, it's clear that the baby is sickly and will pass on, so I'm not giving false hope. The same in the cases of the deceased mothers. They know they only have a short time in which to continue, but I think they would all claim that is better than nothing. Some have older children they wish to hug one last time, and then, of course, there are burials or other matters to discuss with husbands."

"But you're playing God," Seth said. I was surprised to hear him say such a thing when he'd never shown much interest in religion. He never went to church, whereas Gus and I made the occasional effort on Sundays.

"If that is how you think, then I'm unlikely to change your mind," Estelle said stiffly. "I've never used my witchcraft on anyone outside childbirth until myself, this morning. When you raised my spirit, Miss Holloway, you unwittingly presented me with an opportunity for vengeance that I couldn't pass up. My decision to kill Merton was spur of the moment, but I don't regret it. Even if I have damned myself, I will face the consequences, not run from them. I do not shy away from my fate."

"I admire you for that," I told her.

She blinked in surprise at me, then smiled. "Thank you, Miss Holloway. You're quite an admirable young woman yourself. You weren't afraid of escaping through the window, for instance."

"Years of practice," I said, laughing.

"Did anyone at the hospital know about your witchcraft?" Lincoln asked.

"No, nor outside it, either. It was a family secret."

"No one? Didn't Lord Harcourt discover it?"

She shook her head. "I don't believe he did."

"He must have," I said. "You see, the late Lord Harcourt belonged to our organization. When he learned of something supernatural, he reported it to Mr. Fitzroy, here. Oh." I suddenly saw the hole in my logic. "He never brought this case to your attention, did he?"

Lincoln shook his head. "Why was your name in his journal, Miss Pearson?"

"Because he discovered I was the nurse who delivered his grandchild, and he had some questions for me."

"Whoa," Seth said, hands up. "The present Lord and Lady Harcourt are childless."

"She gave birth to a stillborn boy, five years ago. The birth was difficult, and we almost lost her too. I managed to give the little boy an extra day, through my spell, but that was all. As with every resurrection, the family was never aware that it was my magic that kept him on this realm a little longer."

"So why did old Lord Harcourt need to see you about it?" I asked. "And why was he angry with you? Are you quite sure it wasn't because he found out about your witchcraft?"

"He never mentioned it when he met with me, a few years later. He wasn't angry with me, you understand, he was angry with his son and daughter-in-law. The couple had been married only four months when I assisted with the birth, yet I delivered Mrs. Buchanan, as she was known then, of a full-term baby. You see, when she announced her pregnancy, everyone assumed she'd fallen in on the honeymoon.

Including her husband. However, she was already well into her pregnancy by the time she married. Some five months, in fact. She must have hidden it well."

"She told you this?" I asked.

"I learned it after the delivery. One cannot hide the difference between a full-term baby and a four-month old fetus."

"Why were you summoned to deliver the child?"

"She'd heard of my skill." Estelle straightened, but did not puff out her chest or sound in the least boastful. "I have a reputation, you see, and I've often been asked to assist in home births in good households. Mrs. Buchanan knew she was going to deliver a full-term baby and, by asking for me, I'm quite certain she hoped the baby would survive. Despite her lie, she wanted that child very much."

"How sad," I murmured. "The poor thing died."

"Very sad. She was distraught, but the extra hours I gave the baby helped, I believe. She held him every moment until he finally slipped away a second time."

I dabbed at the corner of my eye.

"It was then that Donald Buchanan discovered his wife's lie?" Lincoln asked.

She nodded. "It was impossible to hide."

"How did he react?"

"Confused, shocked."

"Was the baby his?" I asked.

"I don't know. He never suggested otherwise in my presence, and never spoke harshly to his wife or questioned her. Of course, that could have been because she was distraught and weak. She only had eyes for her son. He never said a word to anyone about the baby being full-term, I do know that much. As far as the outside world knew, she was delivered of a stillborn fetus at four months gestation. The baby never had breath to cry, so it never made a sound, and aside from Mr. Donald Buchanan, myself and the local parson, who christened the baby, no one entered that bedroom. The servants and villagers were all told that Mrs.

Buchanan needed to be alone to recover and mourn. Her husband and I took care of everything."

"Villagers? So this happened on the Harcourt estate?"

"They lived up there after the wedding," Seth said. "Old Lord Harcourt preferred London. He liked the theater too much to live far away from it."

The theater and its delights in the shape of Julia Templeton.

"Old Lord Harcourt must have discovered the truth," Lincoln said. "That's why he came to you, to have it confirmed."

She nodded. "It was a few years later. He was angry, as I said, with both his son and daughter-in-law. He somehow heard a rumor that the baby was full-term, and he thought he had a right to know. I don't know how he found out, but I was able to confirm that he was correct. I'm not a liar, and it was the first and only time anyone has ever asked me directly about that baby."

"He was quite the controlling father, so I heard," Seth said. "I can imagine having this kept secret would anger him. It was, after all, his first grandchild, not merely a fetus. He probably would have liked to see him and hold him too before he died."

Lincoln shifted the curtain aside. "We are almost at the cemetery. Miss Pearson, did Andrew Buchanan ever ask these questions of you too?"

"No, just Lord Harcourt." She peered out the window as the coach rolled to a stop. "I've told you everything I know about the situation. May I go now?"

"Of course."

Seth opened the door, climbed out, then helped us ladies to alight. He remained behind with Gus, while Lincoln and I escorted Estelle to her grave. We continued past it, however, when we spotted a groundsman lingering nearby. Someone had raked over the disturbed soil to make it seem as if the body were still inside, so as not to alarm the public, but the groundskeeper watched us carefully. I did not recognize him.

Estelle kept her hat low over her head and her thin, knotty hands in her coat pockets until we were out of sight.

"We'll have to do it here," Lincoln said, stopping at a large tomb bearing a cross. It and the other tombs kept us hidden from the groundsman, but still I looked around anxiously. Fortunately the drizzling rain kept visitors away.

"When they find your body here, they'll know it's yours and return you," I assured Estelle.

She nodded. "No doubt they'll assume it was boys having a lark."

I hoped so. "How does this work? I can't send you back while you're like this."

"My strength is rapidly waning, but a reversing spell will speed up the process. You will notice the moment I've died again, so to speak, and then you can return my spirit. But first, I wish to thank you, Miss Holloway. Dr. Merton deserved justice, and because of you, I was able to deliver it."

My stomach rolled. I wasn't as certain that I'd done the right thing. What he'd done in his lifetime was heinous, however I didn't like being judge and jury—or playing God, for that matter.

She laid a hand on my shoulder and peered into my eyes. "You have helped save the lives and reputations of several young women today, but ultimately, his death is on my conscience, not yours." Without waiting for me to respond, she spoke some foreign words in the same harsh accent as earlier. At the end, she staggered a little then her eyes went dead. She remained standing, however, and her cracked, colorless lips stretched into the semblance of a smile. "There," she said crisply. "I am done. Now you may say your piece." She clasped her hands in front of her and tilted her chin. "Goodbye, Mr. Fitzroy."

Lincoln gave a shallow bow. "Farewell."

"Goodbye, Miss Holloway."

"Goodbye, Miss Pearson. Thank you for your assistance. I'll not trouble your spirit again. Please return to your afterlife now, Estelle Pearson. Leave this realm and go back."

The mist rose like a thin wisp of smoke from her chest. As the last of it left, the body crumpled, landing awkwardly on the grave. Lincoln righted it, propping her up in a sitting position. The mist formed the shape of Estelle, smiled at me, then whooshed up into the clouds.

"She's gone," I said on a sigh.

"We must leave before we're discovered." He took my hand, only to let it go again almost immediately. He stepped away from me and indicated I should walk first. "I'm sorry, I didn't bring an umbrella."

"The rain doesn't bother me."

"Even so."

We wound our way through the cemetery, keeping our heads bent against the light rain. I was in the midst of thinking through everything Estelle had told us when Lincoln spoke again, just as we headed out through the gate.

"How is your foot?"

"It no longer hurts, and I gave it every reason to do so today."

"You had no trouble descending the drainpipe?"

"None. Thank you for not doubting my ability to do it. I appreciate your faith in me."

"There was no other choice."

I gave him a withering glare. "Thank you for pointing that out."

He arched a brow and slowed, but I continued on. He caught up and reached past me for the coach door. "Your nimbleness and speed were never in doubt, Fleet-foot Charlie," he murmured in my ear.

I turned my head to see if he was smiling, since I swear I could hear a smile in his voice. But his mouth was as firm as ever, his face a mask, and his eyes hooded.

He opened the door and helped me inside. We drove back to Lichfield Towers, where Cook dished out soup and plied us with questions. We told him what we'd learned, then discussed what to do next.

"This is all very interesting," I said, "but I fail to see how any of this would matter to Andrew Buchanan."

Gus slurped his soup, drawing everyone's attention, then licked his lips. "He'd be angry, like his father. No one told him he had a nephew, and he never got to meet him."

Seth shook his head. "He wouldn't care."

"He might, if the child had lived," Lincoln said. "With his brother childless, he remains heir to the estate, but a son changes that."

"Do you think the child lived after all?" I looked at him in horror. "But that's not possible, according to Estelle. She cannot give life, just the appearance of it."

"Miss Pearson may not know everything about her gift. But you are correct, it's unlikely the baby came back to life. I assume they buried him. However, we now know that Lady Harcourt is capable of having children. If she did so once, she can do so again. That might worry Buchanan."

"But it's been years, and she hasn't been with child again."

"It ain't an exact science," Gus said, with all the authority of Estelle herself. "Some women just fall pregnant if you look at 'em—"

"I'm pretty sure that's *not* how it works," Seth said, with a roll of his eyes.

"And some women can't have babies for years, and then suddenly, they have dozens."

"Dozens?"

"Shut your hole, Seth. What do you know about it? You ain't got brothers and sisters."

"I didn't know you were an only child," I told him.

Seth shrugged. "Did Miss Pearson say she spoke to Andrew Buchanan?"

"She never met him, but that doesn't mean he didn't learn that she was a midwife, after seeing her name in the journal, then put two and two together."

"I don't know if he's bright enough to work it out."

"Either way, it's obvious what has to be done next." Lincoln rose, and we all waited for him to elaborate. He didn't.

"Mr. Fitzroy?" I prompted as he headed for the kitchen door. "What are we going to do now?"

"You're not doing anything. I'm going to confront Lord and Lady Harcourt."

I exchanged glances with the other men. "He bloody well is not doing this without us," I muttered so that Lincoln couldn't hear.

"Go after him," Gus said, shooing me with his hands. "Tell him Cook wants to bake something special for fancy guests. Get him to invite them for dinner tonight so's we can listen in."

"Good idea. Even better, Seth, why don't you take an invitation to Harcourt House now, that way Fitzroy can't refuse."

The gazes of Seth, Gus and Cook drifted to the door behind me. All three turned pale then found their bowls of soup of utmost interest. I winced. Lincoln and his damned instincts.

I turned to see him leaning against the doorframe, his ankles and arms crossed as if he'd been there all along, waiting for me to walk into a trap.

CHAPTER 8

"I'll write them an invitation now," Lincoln said, pushing off from the door. "It seems Seth will be delivering it, as plotted." He left again.

I stared at the empty space where he'd been standing.

"Did I just hear what I think I heard?" Seth asked.

I raced after Lincoln and caught up to him at the base of the main staircase.

"Yes?" He stopped on the lowest step. "Is there something you need to confess?"

"What makes you say that?"

"It seems to be the order of the day, lately."

I crossed my arms. "That's not true." I lowered my voice and stepped up next to him, then went a step higher again. I was still shorter. "Besides, why do I need to confess when you can predict what I'm about to say and do?"

"I can't. I have instincts only, and they're not that well-defined."

"I think your instincts are growing stronger. First, you know when I'm not in the house, and now you seem to know what we're planning as if you overheard every single word."

"I did overhear you. I decided to come back and suggest the same thing only to hear you already giving orders as if you were the ministry's leader."

I bit the inside of my cheek and tried on an innocent smile. His scowl deepened.

"I thought you might somehow try to find out the details of my conversation with the Harcourts," he went on. "Since that would mean getting one of the Harcourt House staff on your side, I thought it much easier to swim with your tide, Charlie, instead of against it, and question the Harcouts here."

"I…I'm not sure how to take that."

"You're a force of nature, and not one I can control."

"Oh. No mincing words, then."

"I never do." He sighed and looked to the ceiling. "I can't believe I am suggesting you eavesdrop on our dinner tonight. Just be sure not to get caught."

"Why are you involving me at all? Aside from the force of nature part, that is. You could banish me to my room and lock me in."

"There will be no more locking you in your room," he snapped. "I thought I'd made that clear."

"It was just a joke."

He turned and headed up the stairs. "I've decided. That's all you need to know. If you question me further then I might change my mind."

I pressed my lips together and managed not to say anything else. He'd given me permission to listen in, and that was all I needed to know. For now.

"Thank you," I called up.

He didn't respond.

I returned to the kitchen, beaming. "You look like the cat that got the cream," Cook said.

"I'm the girl who got what she wanted. Fitzroy is actively encouraging me to listen in to the dinner conversation tonight."

Seth clapped me on the back as if I were his little brother. "Good show. Now, there's a pile of dishes in the scullery that need cleaning. Your foot's better, so there'll be no getting out of it."

"I don't want to get out of it. However." I turned on the same sweet smile I'd used on Lincoln. "Would you mind helping me? There's something I want to ask you. In private," I added in a whisper.

His face brightened. "Intriguing. Come on, then. I've got a few minutes before Fitzroy will be ready with the invitation."

He helped me fill the tub with warm water then picked up the cloth to dry as I washed.

"In the hospital earlier, I introduced us as the Guilfords. You seemed not to like that. Did I do the wrong thing? Should I have used a false name?"

His hand slowed as it circled the base of the plate. "No. Theoretically, you should have used my title. You all call me Seth, but out in the big wide world, I'm Vickers. Guilford is my family name but I haven't gone by that since my father died. It sounded odd to my ear, that's all."

I dangled my hands in the water and gaped at him. "You have a *title*."

One side of his mouth lifted. "I thought you knew."

"Perhaps I should have, but I've just put all the pieces of the puzzle together. It never occurred to me that *you* were a lord. Nobody treats you like one."

"I prefer not to use the title among friends. Besides, it only serves to remind me of how far I've sunk." He held up the plate and cloth with a shrug.

"Oh, Seth, I'm sorry."

"Don't be. It is what it is.

"What's your rank?"

"Just a baron, like Harcourt."

"So you are Lord Vickers, and you outrank us all here at Lichfield."

He snorted. "Not in this household. It's the most egalitarian in England, I'd wager. Where else does a housekeeper call her employer by his first name?"

I blushed. He'd heard that? "And where else does a baron do the dishes?" Or, for that matter, where else would an illegitimate son of a gypsy have more power than the three lords and one lady on the committee of a secret organization?

* * *

Lincoln didn't invite the dowager Lady Harcourt to dinner. At first I thought his manners poor, until I remembered that she'd invited Mrs. and Miss Overton to dine with her in the hope that Lincoln would join them. He'd refused, but she could only get out of it now if she pleaded ill.

Which, as it turned out, she did. "My stepmother postponed her dinner, claiming a headache," Lord Harcourt said, as Gus took his cloak and I accepted his wife's. "Otherwise Marguerite and I wouldn't have been able to come tonight. We were expected to dine with her guests."

"Please pass on my best wishes for a speedy recovery," Lincoln said. "And are you feeling better, madam?"

"Call me Marguerite." Lady Harcourt fluttered her fan against her pink cheek and eyed him over the top of it. On most women, it would have been flirtatious, but Marguerite seemed to be genuinely taking his measure. I wondered what she thought of him tonight, dressed in his dinner suit.

"Only if you call me Lincoln." He bowed graciously, and once again I admired how this man, who seemed to abhor formality and pomp, could perform as adequately as any gentleman in the appropriate setting.

She giggled. Perhaps she was flirting after all. I scrunched her red and black velvet cloak in my fingers and stood meekly by the wall, where I had no trouble disappearing; not because it was dark—an impossibility with all the candles in the chandelier blazing—but because Lord and Lady Harcourt took no notice of me. To them, I was invisible.

That was as it ought to be, but it galled nevertheless, particularly when Lincoln and the others at Lichfield never treated me that way.

From there I could watch them. Both gentlemen looked dashing in their dinner suits, although Lincoln was by far the more handsome man, his mysterious and serious air enhancing his looks in a way that most women would find intriguing without being able to explain why. Lady Harcourt—Marguerite—looked very pretty in a red wine silk dress with black beading at the cuffs, collar and down the front skirt panels. The bustle was large, compared to the neat one her mother-in-law wore, but it suited her figure. It was quite high at the throat so she wore no necklaces, but her ruby earrings commanded enough attention that no other jewelry seemed necessary. She'd added black beads to her hair, but they got a little lost in the brown locks that were once again arranged in ringlets that framed her face.

She took Lincoln's offered arm and together they walked ahead of her husband into the parlor. I followed discreetly behind and remained outside the door. It was at times like these when I wished the drawing room on the first floor was in use. Using the parlor for such illustrious guests seemed inappropriate. I didn't care what they thought of me, but Lichfield Towers was an important manor house on the edge of London, and Lincoln ought to socialize with people of rank more. Perhaps it was time to discuss furnishing it properly.

I waited only a few moments then departed, but not before I heard Lady Harcourt lament how difficult it was to find good footmen these days and her husband respond with: "I'm surprised you have the same difficulty here in London, Fitzroy. I would have thought the unemployment problem would insure a steady supply of good staff."

"Oh, Donald," his wife chided. "Let's not discuss such vulgar things."

I wondered what else she considered too vulgar and how Lincoln would navigate through the minefield of inappropriate topics. He wasn't very adept at small talk.

I retreated to the kitchen and helped Cook and the others with dinner. He rarely got to show off his culinary skill, so he liked to turn even a small dinner party into a marvelous dining experience for the guests. Tonight he'd prepared no less than five courses.

Lincoln had left it to Cook to decide on a menu, something that would ordinarily be a hostess's duty. He claimed not to care what was served. Cook had shaken his head in disgust then taken preparations in hand.

"This be Lichfield's first dinner that ain't a committee one," he'd said. "We be doin' it proper."

This pronouncement was followed by a mad flurry of activity, since the day grew late. Seth and Gus had been dispatched to butchers, grocers and other shops, while Cook instructed me on the dishes he would serve. Involving me in the planning had seemed odd at first, when Cook had done it for the few committee dinner parties held at Lichfield, but now I was used to it. I didn't dare offer suggestions, however. My knowledge of fine cookery was very slim, and Cook was a master, as good as any French chef, according to Cook himself.

"There is going to be an awful lot of food left over, even after we take our share," I said, as I carefully poured soup from the pot into the silver tureen.

Seth placed the lid on and picked up the tureen. "Maybe your orphan friends can have it."

I wouldn't call Stringer and the other gang members I'd lived with, prior to being kidnapped by Lincoln, my friends, but they would certainly be grateful for the food. "You can deliver it to them tomorrow." I would not join them. I'd left that life behind and had no desire to go back. Besides, they'd known me as a boy, not a woman, and if they recognized me, we would all feel awkward.

Gus had already announced that dinner was ready, so the three of them were seated when Seth and I entered. Seth deposited the tureen on the sideboard, and I ladled soup into the bowls. We placed them in front of the guests and Lincoln.

Lord Harcourt eyed Seth as if he was trying to work out where he'd seen him before. I couldn't be certain if he'd remembered by the time Seth left, but the frown never quite disappeared from his lordship's brow.

I remained in the dining room to listen in, as planned. I wasn't sure how Lincoln would approach such a delicate matter with his guests—a matter that was absolutely inappropriate for the dinner table—however, my curiosity was answered when he simply stated: "There has been a development in the search for your brother, Harcourt."

Lady Harcourt swallowed her mouthful of soup too fast and coughed delicately into her hand. "Have you found him?"

"Not yet."

Her face fell. "Oh."

"Don't fret, my dear." Her husband lifted his hand as if he would reach across the table to take hers, but the distance was too great and he let it drop to the white damask table cloth. "What's the nature of this development, Fitzroy?"

"It is a matter of some delicacy." With only the briefest pause to allow his guests time to digest that news, yet not allow them to avoid discussion, Lincoln added, "Do you recall me asking you about the woman known as Estelle Pearson?"

Lady Harcourt paled. She set her spoon down, her soup unfinished. I drew a little closer in case she fainted again. It would be messy if she ended up face-down in her soup.

"What about her?" Lord Harcourt snapped.

"We learned that she worked as a midwife at the Queen Charlotte Hospital for Lying-In." His use of "we" warmed my heart. He was no longer thinking of himself as the sole person within the ministry, something that he used to do even with Seth and Gus as his only employees. He was now talking as if we were a team. "We were able to ascertain that she delivered you of a baby boy, Marguerite, five years ago."

A kittenish mewl came from Lady Harcourt's throat. She pressed her fingers to her lips and appealed to her husband.

"Don't fret, my dear," he said again, more gently. "I will deal with this." He turned to Lincoln, and his face darkened. He looked as if he would leap out of his chair and attempt to thrash his host. "What is the meaning of this?"

Lincoln remained calm, seemingly unperturbed that he'd offended his guests. "Only that we wish to find Buchanan, and Miss Pearson's name was of possible interest to him. We want to know why."

"Miss Pearson and her visit to Emberly Park have nothing to do with my brother! Do you understand me? This is outrageous."

"Donald, please." Lady Harcourt whimpered into her napkin, instantly silencing her husband. He sat back in his chair and regarded his wife with sad, troubled eyes. "If answering Lincoln's questions will help him locate Andrew, then we must answer them."

"But my dear," he said with what appeared to be considerable effort. "It clearly upsets you."

"I'm stronger than I look."

I admired her fortitude. I filled up her wine glass and offered her a sympathetic smile. She wasn't looking at me, however, and didn't notice.

To Lincoln, she said, "What precisely did Miss Pearson tell you?"

"Estelle Pearson is dead." She gasped, but he spoke over the top of it. "It was a close relative who informed us of her association with you."

"But she promised not to tell a soul!" Lady Harcourt wailed. "How *could* she?"

Lord Harcourt finally got up and went to his wife. I took the opportunity to nudge Lincoln in the shoulder and urge him with a nod. It was important to strike before they decided to leave. Lady Harcourt might be keen to help, but if her husband got his way, they would walk out before the main course arrived.

"Your secret is safe," he assured her. "We know your baby was full-term, Marguerite, and that he only lived another day after his birth."

Lord Harcourt took his wife's limp hand in his own and patted it. "That's enough, Fitzroy," he growled. "No more questions. Can you not see my wife is distressed?"

But Lady Harcourt no longer looked distressed. She fixed her watery yet defiant gaze on Lincoln and said, "Hector. That's the name we gave him."

I opened my mouth to tell her it was a lovely name, but shut it again. She didn't want sympathy from me. Any kind of acknowledgement from a servant would only embarrass her, so I kept quiet and pretended I wasn't listening. I hoped Lincoln would say something kind to her, but he didn't.

"I believe Lord Harcourt, your father, somehow learned the baby was full-term, not premature. He went to Estelle Pearson to find out the truth and she confirmed it."

"How *could* she," Marguerite said again, the words tearing from lips twisted with bitterness. "I trusted her. She came highly recommended."

"Did he confront you?" Lincoln asked them.

"That's none of your bloody business," Lord Harcourt ground out.

"If you want your brother found, it is."

"Yes, he confronted us," Marguerite blurted. She winced as her husband's hand tightened on her shoulder. "We told him Hector was full-term but sickly, and he hadn't lived long. That was the end of that. He never mentioned it again." She accepted her husband's handkerchief and dabbed at her eyes. "Do you think that will be of use in finding Andrew?"

"Everything is of use."

Lord Harcourt grunted. "It's more likely his disappearance has something to do with this damned supernatural order Father belonged to."

I froze.

"What order?" Lincoln said, none too smoothly. From Lord Harcourt's smug face, I thought it too late to pretend innocence anyway.

"Don't play the fool, Fitzroy. I know you're very far from it. Father mentioned it to me, years ago, when I was still at university. He didn't tell me much, but I was led to believe I would inherit some important position upon his death. Clearly that didn't happen, and I forgot about it until my stepmother told me there were books about the occult found in Andrew's rooms."

"She mentioned that," Lincoln said flatly.

"She did. It prompted my memory so I asked her about it. She told me what the order—ministry—does and that *she* inherited Father's position." The baron shook his head and muttered, "Old fool."

"I don't understand." Marguerite had gone pale again, her lips as bloodless as any corpse. "What is this ministry? Is it dangerous?"

Lord Harcourt gathered her hand in both of his and bent to her level. "Don't fret, my dear," he said gently. "It's nothing for you to worry about. Andrew will turn up. He always does. You know what he's like."

She bit her lip and nodded down at the cold bowl of soup. "Yes, of course. You're right, Donald. You always are."

His wife's faith seemed to inflate him a little. He angled his chin at Lincoln. "If I were looking for a reason behind Andrew's disappearance, then I would change direction and leave my wife out of it. I don't care a whit for this ministry of yours, nor do I care that I was overlooked for a position in favor of my stepmother. However, it is the sort of thing that would annoy Andrew. God knows, he has enough reasons to resent our father, and this just adds to the pile."

I wondered if he was referring to Andrew having his sweetheart stolen by his father, or whether he merely meant having his inheritance—Harcourt House in Mayfair—bequeathed to Julia instead.

"Now, if you'll excuse us, my wife has a headache. She's in no fit state to continue with dinner." He pulled out Marguerite's chair as she rose then escorted her to the door, where he paused and raised his eyebrows at me.

It took me a moment to remember that it was my duty to fetch their cloaks. I passed Seth near the door, carrying a tray of oysters and shrimp. "Take that back to the kitchen," I whispered. "Inform the Harcourts' coachman to bring the carriage around."

He shot a glance over my head then departed without a word.

"Your footman looks familiar," Lord Harcourt said, as I handed him his cloak.

"He's not my footman," Lincoln said. "He's my assistant. Lichfield Towers is short-staffed, and he sometimes performs other duties."

I helped Lady Harcourt on with her cloak and bobbed a curtsy. She turned away and thanked Lincoln, apologizing for her delicate health. Her husband too, thanked Lincoln, and he accepted it. It was an odd dance of etiquette. After the tension in the dining room, I expected them to storm out without a word, but they were acting as if none of that had happened. Toffs were strange indeed.

The coach wheels crunched on the gravel, and I opened the door, bobbing another curtsy as they left. Lincoln walked them out and Seth, who'd traveled around on the coach from the stables, held the cabin door open and assisted Lady Harcourt up the step.

"Well that was the height of rudeness," Seth said, shutting the door after they'd gone. "Was it the soup?"

"Fitzroy's questions."

Seth's mouth formed an O.

"I can't blame them for walking out," I said. "I would have too, if confronted with such impertinence. Perhaps you should have waited until dessert."

The corners of Lincoln's eyes crinkled, almost as if he were smiling. "One course in their company was enough."

"It wasn't even an entire course! Nobody finished their soup."

He strode in the direction of the dining room. "As I said, that was enough."

"You really ought to master the art of small talk."

"And responding without actually listening," Seth added, following us. "It saves one from boredom. Just nod at key moments or utter general sentiments that could be applied to any topic. It's a trick I learned back when I had to endure dull parties peopled with dull debutantes searching for a husband."

"There will be even more food left now," I said, collecting the soup bowls. "Such a shame when Cook went to all that effort. And the dining room has never looked more magnificent." I'd spent more than an hour getting it just right, setting out the best silver and china, following Seth's instructions on which forks, spoons and knives went where. Folding the napkins had taken an age in itself, although I'd given up trying to make a swan and simply formed them into a peak. The lack of color in the autumn garden meant the center of the table wasn't as pretty as I'd have liked, but the pineapples Gus had brought back from the costermonger gave it an exotic flavor.

"You're right, the room shouldn't go to waste," Lincoln said. "We'll dine in here all together."

All of us, including Cook, sat at the long mahogany table and feasted on the oyster and shrimp appetizers, followed by a sorbet to clean our palettes. I'd never heard of sorbet before coming to live at Lichfield, but the lemon flavored dish had quickly become a favorite. With palettes suitably refreshed, we helped ourselves to the roasted sirloin and chicken, with sides of lobster salad and vegetables. I wished

I'd saved room for dessert when Cook and Gus brought in the apple pie, sweet cakes, frozen creams and cheeses.

"There'd better be some left for me tomorrow," I said, watching Gus shove an entire cake into his mouth.

"There is enough food left over in that kitchen to feed half of London," Seth told me. "You won't miss out."

"So, what'll we do next?" Gus asked. "About Buchanan, I mean. Don't know as we're any closer to findin' him than before."

Lincoln had told Gus and Cook of our confrontation with the Harcourts as we ate, but he had gone quiet since then. Perhaps he was contemplating exactly the same thing as Gus.

"I think Harcourt is correct," Seth said, dabbing his mouth with a napkin. "His brother's disappearance is most likely due to his sudden interest in the supernatural, not the baby. We don't even know if he learned anything about Estelle Pearson and her visit to Emberly Park. It's not like he could summon her spirit and ask her."

Gus stretched his legs out under the table and leaned back, his hands clasped over his stomach. "I agree. He prob'ly read about the ministry in his father's journal, then found all them other books and charms. That got him more interested and he dabbled with forces he don't understand then disappeared." He belched. "Gawd, me stomach hurts."

Seth pulled a face. "You're a pig."

"You ate just as much as me."

"But you don't see me making disgusting noises at the dinner table."

"Disappeared how?" I asked before they could come to blows. "And where?"

"If we knew that, we wouldn't be sittin' hear stuffin' our faces."

"Mr. Fitzroy?" I prompted. "What are you thinking?"

"That if I were Buchanan, and had found some references in my father's journal that piqued my curiosity, I would try to find out more from someone with a better knowledge of him than me."

"His wife," I suggested.

"Or brother," Seth said.

"Neither mentioned speaking to him about the ministry."

Lincoln shook his head. "I meant he would sneak into their rooms and search while they weren't there, or intercept mail, question servants, that sort of thing."

"Or he could have just asked them directly," I said.

His left eyebrow kicked up. "We don't know if Buchanan would behave more like you or me, or a combination of both."

"How do we find out?"

"I'll question them in the morning."

"If they will speak with you now. You're unlikely to be on their list of favorite people."

* * *

The dowager Lady Harcourt saved Lincoln the trouble of visiting her when she called at Lichfield the following morning. Dressed in full black again, her hair pulled back severely beneath her small hat, and her face pinched, she reminded me of a raven about to swoop on an unsuspecting mouse.

But Lincoln was no mouse. He met her at the door and invited her into the parlor, where I'd just finished cleaning out the fireplace. She greeted me with a curt nod, but no smile, and waited for me to leave. I did, but I hovered on the other side of the door, out of sight. Lincoln wouldn't mind if I eavesdropped, surely. Not after allowing it the previous night. Anyway, if he wanted privacy, he ought to walk with her in the garden.

"What got into you last night?" she asked, her voice pitched somewhere between incredulous and curious. "Donald and Marguerite told me you posed some very impertinent questions, and now they think you vulgar. You must call upon them and apologize immediately."

"I was merely trying to ascertain the whereabouts of Buchanan."

"Andrew's disappearance has nothing to do with Donald or Marguerite!"

"How do you know?"

"Because...because..." She clicked her tongue. "You're being deliberately provoking. Of course they don't know where he is."

"I didn't imply that they know, just that he may have discovered their secret and disappeared in the course of finding out more."

"What secret?"

"Julia, you know I can't tell you."

"You can, you just won't." After a moment, in which neither spoke, she sighed. "Everyone has secrets, I suppose, but I am surprised that Marguerite and Donald do. They're so...ordinary. Dull. I wonder..."

"Wonder what?"

I leaned closer to the door.

"I wonder if you may be heading in the right direction."

"About Buchanan's interest in their secret?"

"I'm not sure if this is important or not but, in light of what you've just said, perhaps it is. My coachman informed me yesterday that Andrew wanted to be driven to Paddington Station on the morning of his disappearance."

There was a pause then Lincoln said, "The Greater Western Railway trains leave from Paddington and go through Oxfordshire."

"Precisely. There is a station not far from Emberly Park."

I pressed my lips together to suppress my gasp. We were finally getting somewhere.

"Did your coachman not understand the importance of this information earlier?" Lincoln asked.

"No, because he never took Andrew anywhere. He was busy driving me that day, you see, and thought no more about it. He said he forgot the conversation entirely until yesterday."

"It's possible Buchanan took a hackney instead."

"I agree; it's possible, even likely. But he cannot have reached Emberly Park or Donald and Marguerite would have said something."

"Unless they don't want us knowing."

Lady Harcourt's throaty chuckle had me picturing her taking Lincoln's hand and batting her eyelashes. "You're so suspicious of everyone. Or *almost* everyone." The laughter died, and her voice became clipped. "Your own employees seem to escape your suspicions."

"Do they?" he said lazily. "You know my mind?"

His accusation stung her to silence.

"Please convey my apologies to your stepson and his wife," he went on. "But, I can assure you, my questions were necessary."

She sighed. "Why not apologize to them personally? Dine with us tonight at Harcourt House."

"I doubt my presence would be welcomed."

"Nonsense. *I* welcome it. Isn't that what matters?"

Silence.

"Come to dinner, Lincoln. Please. You can ask Donald directly, in the billiard room afterward, if Andrew ever reached Emberly."

"If he has kept silent until now, I doubt more questions will produce results."

"Come to dinner and try anyway. I'm sure you'll know if he's lying or not. You have a knack for that."

What was she up to? A moment ago, she'd been appalled at Lincoln's poor manners during dinner, and now she was encouraging him to question Lord Harcourt further, over yet another dinner. Worse, she was advising him to accuse Lord Harcourt to his face of hiding his brother's visit to Emberly. Why?

"What time?" Lincoln asked.

He was agreeing?

"Eight-thirty. We'll dine at nine." Her skirts rustled, and I dashed across the entrance hall and slipped into the corridor leading to the service area.

I waited until her coach drove off then intercepted Lincoln when he returned inside. He didn't seem surprised to see me. "She's up to something," I said. "I could hear it in her voice."

"I know." He went to walk off, but I caught his arm.

"If you think she has an ulterior motive for inviting you to dinner, then why are you going?"

He looked at me like I was a fool. "To find out what that motive is."

"Oh. Yes. I suppose." I let him go. "Why didn't I think of that?"

"I don't know." He headed up the stairs, but not before I saw his lips twitch at the corners. "Devious methods of gathering information are usually your specialty."

CHAPTER 9

I awoke at dawn the following morning, but Lincoln was already in the kitchen when I went down, cooking bacon and eggs. The man required very little sleep. I'd not heard him return after dinner, but I'd still been so tired from the night I'd missed sleep altogether, that I slept soundly.

"Are you going to eat all of that yourself?" I asked, peering past him to the five rashers of bacon sizzling in the pan and the three boiling eggs.

"Not anymore."

I fetched another plate and eggcup then allowed him to serve me. I chose the side of the table closest to the warm range and he sat on the other. He didn't seem to feel the cold. When I'd first met him, he'd seemed more machine than human, with his lack of emotion and few needs, and sometimes I still felt as if I didn't know the man behind the mask. At least I now knew he wore a mask most of the time.

"How was the dinner?" I asked.

"Adequate. Cook's a better cook."

"You should tell him that. It would mean a lot to him."

He considered this a moment then nodded.

"I was actually referring to the conversational aspect of dinner. Did you get an opportunity to ask Lord Harcourt whether Buchanan arrived at Emberly Park?"

"No. I wasn't seated near him at dinner and he avoided me afterward."

"But you were the only two gentlemen there. Weren't you alone with him in the billiard room?"

He shook his head as he cut through a bacon rasher. "Another two were invited to make up numbers."

"But you were already two gentlemen and two ladies, an even, if somewhat small, number."

"Four ladies, four gentlemen. Julia invited the Overtons—Mr. Mrs. and Miss—and an elderly fellow by the name of Matthews."

I'd been slicing off the top of my egg, but his news caused my hand to slip. The egg and cup toppled over, spilling gooey yolk on the table. I quickly righted the cup, stuffed the egg back into it, and reached for a cloth to mop up the yolk.

Lincoln watched me from beneath long, thick lashes. "I was as surprised as you are. Julia didn't warn me."

Probably because she knew he'd refuse to go. "She seems very keen for you and Miss Overton to…become better acquainted."

"I noticed."

"And did you become better acquainted last night?"

"No."

"Surely Lady Harcourt contrived to sit you next to her."

"She did, with her mother on my other side. They soon learned that I make a terrible dinner guest and gave up attempting to converse with me."

"Did you even try to have a proper conversation? Or did you sabotage it deliberately?"

"I don't give away my secrets." His eyes gleamed like polished jet.

I couldn't help a smile, although it vanished just as quickly as it rose. "Poor Miss Overton. Do you think she will give up now and set her heart on someone else?" Or was she so smitten with him that she would continue to throw herself in his path? It was a distinct possibility. I certainly couldn't imagine setting aside my affections to consider another man.

"I don't think it's up to Miss Overton but her mother. And perhaps Julia, to some extent. She hasn't accepted that I am a hopeless case, unfit for marriage."

"You're not, Lincoln. Not in the least." I raised my fork as he opened his mouth to protest. "Can we discuss something else? Please? I don't wish to go over old ground with you again. We only seem to end up fighting, and I don't like it when we do."

"Nor do I." He rose. "Tea?"

"Yes, please. So we've hit a dead end again in the search for Buchanan."

"Not quite," he said as he checked the kettle. "I'm catching a train to Emberly Park straight after breakfast." He cast an eye at the clock on the sideboard. "Seth or Gus will drive me to the station even if I have to drag one of them out of bed."

Seth chose that moment to enter, hand over his mouth, smothering a yawn.

"Speak of the devil," I said.

Seth blinked sleepily. "Huh?"

"You're driving Mr. Fitzroy and me to Paddington station this morning. Come on, eat up or we'll be late. What time does the train leave?" I asked Lincoln.

"It's inappropriate for you to join me," he said darkly.

It was not an outright refusal. I took that as a positive sign. "It's inappropriate for me to live here with four men, and yet I do. Lincoln," I said, deliberately calling him by his first name, even though Seth was listening, "let me be involved. I think I'll be of use in questioning the servants, which I'm assuming was on your agenda." At my arched brow, he nodded. "We all know that I'm better with people than you."

After a loaded silence in which his gaze didn't waver from mine, he finally gave in. "Don't make me regret it."

"Thank you," I said, in the most dignified manner I could muster, when I really wanted to let out a *whoop* of victory.

"Pack for an overnight stay in the village. You'll act as my sister."

"We look nothing alike. No one will believe it."

"My ward, then. It's close enough to the truth."

I hadn't thought of our relationship like that. I was an adult in my own eyes, if not that of the law. I wouldn't gain my majority until I turned twenty-one. But it threw up an interesting question—who was my legal guardian? My real father was dead, and if I had living male relatives, I didn't know them. Anselm Holloway might have been given legal guardianship when he took me in, but he'd disowned me so was that still relevant? And did it really matter if I didn't have a guardian anyway? All my needs were taken care of by Lincoln, and I owned nothing, not even the clothing I wore.

"Can we simply say I'm your assistant?" I said.

Lincoln blinked, which I took as ascent.

Seth sighed. "It seems you're going to be doing more ministry work, Charlie, and that means less time for your maid duties."

"Don't worry," I told him. "I'll only leave you the dirtiest tasks. I know how you love them."

He groaned.

* * *

The train to the village of Harcourt in Oxfordshire took a little under two hours, and we both read most of the way, although I regularly peeked to see if Lincoln was looking at me. He wasn't.

We secured rooms at The Fox and Hound Inn, a short walk from the station. The bedrooms were separated by a private sitting room that could be accessed from each bedchamber. Lincoln had asked for entirely separate rooms, that were not joined in any way, but the proprietor had said there were none. If we wanted a sitting room, then those were the only two bedchambers available. I'd quickly accepted them before Lincoln could announce that we were going to try another inn.

"My foot's a little sore," I lied. "I don't wish to traipse all over the village in search of another place to stay. Besides, The Fox and Hound is charming." I smiled at the innkeeper as I said it, and he smiled back, handing me a key.

"That it is, miss. The Fox is the oldest and best inn for miles. You won't get a fireplace as cozy as the one in the dining room, and our beds are clean, unlike some places I could mention. Be sure to dine with us this evening and enjoy our cook's special. You won't be disappointed."

"I look forward to it."

He led us up the narrow staircase, worn smooth in the center from centuries of trampling boots. Lincoln had to duck as we passed from the ground level to the next, and the top of his head almost skimmed the thick, black beams holding up the corridor ceiling. The innkeeper showed us into our rooms, then left. After fifteen minutes, Lincoln tapped on the door leading to the sitting room.

"Ready?" he called.

"I'll fetch my cloak and gloves."

A few minutes later we were outside, hailing a cab to take us to Emberly Park, a few miles west of the village. The term "cab" could only loosely describe the vehicle. It wasn't the hackney variety that crowded London's streets, but a crude wagon that happened to be going to the big house to deliver sacks of flour, tea, sugar and other supplies.

I sat on one side of the squinting, stooped driver and Lincoln sat on the other. Fortunately it was a lovely sunny autumn day, albeit a cool one, and we didn't require protection from the weather.

"Does Lord Harcourt own this village?" I asked as we drove along the main street, lined with shops that seemed to be a mixture of old and new. Three of them were the narrow black and white Tudor type, all leaning drunkenly to the right. "It's very pretty."

"He owns a few buildings here and there," the driver said.

"Is he a good landlord?"

He shrugged. "Don't know, don't care. He ain't *my* landlord."

"Have the Buchanan family lived here long?"

"Long as anyone alive can remember, and well before that."

"The baronetcy was named after the village when it was awarded to the Buchanan family, a little over a century ago," Lincoln explained. "They lived at Emberly Park for two centuries before that, however."

"You know their history well."

"I know the history of every noble family in the British Empire. My tutor on the subject made sure I memorized family trees."

"That sounds horrible."

"It wasn't."

Probably because he possessed an excellent memory. "Does the baron's brother come here often?" I asked the driver.

"Wouldn't know."

"Do you know if he was here recently, say about a week ago?"

"No."

We'd already asked the stationmaster, but he claimed not to know what Buchanan looked like, never having met the fellow in the year since he'd moved to the village. We couldn't rule out Buchanan having arrived by train. Not yet.

I fell into silence as we drove past thatch-roofed cottages, over a stone bridge that crossed a gently babbling stream and out of the village. I was too in awe of the beauty of the countryside to bother attempting conversation with two of the poorest conversationalists in England. Sunshine speared through the remaining autumn leaves clinging to the elm trees, turning them a fiery gold. Beyond the trees, green hills rolled into the distance, as smooth as carpet, with only some sheep and the occasional hedgerow to break it up.

I breathed deeply, drawing the cleanest air I'd ever known into my lungs. It was so clean that it even *tasted* different to the London air. The colors were much brighter than in the city too, as if someone had dipped trees, grass and sky in the same dyes used to color silk gowns and waistcoats. I'd thought the Lichfield Towers grounds were pristine—and they were, compared to London—but *this* was magical. If fairies existed, they would surely make their homes here.

"You've never been to the countryside," Lincoln said quietly.

The driver glanced at him then returned to concentrating on the horse and road.

"Not this far outside of London," I said. "Is the rest of England like this?"

The driver snorted, and I instantly regretted asking. I sounded so unworldly. Lincoln had been to the continent and perhaps further. He must think me childish. The driver certainly did.

"The countryside changes, depending on a variety of factors from the weather and soil, to the proximity to the sea, mountains and other natural landmarks."

I breathed deeply again and watched a little bird take a bath in a shallow puddle by the side of the road. "One day I'm going to go to the seaside."

I thought he hadn't heard me, but then he suddenly spoke in a rush. "I'll take you."

I glanced at him over the driver's head, but he quickly looked away.

He nodded up ahead. "There's Emberly."

I followed his gaze to the large building situated on the rise, its soft gray stone wings stretching out like a dancer's slender arms. Beyond the iron gate, the driveway circled the lawn. No smoke rose from the dozens of chimney pots, and the curtains were drawn across the arched windows. No footman greeted us either. The house seemed empty.

Lincoln jumped down from the cart before it stopped completely and came to assist me, as if I were a lady. I needed to remember to act my part and not to fall into habits picked up from living with boys' gangs. While my accent had returned to the middle class one of my childhood, over the last two months, other habits weren't so easy to adopt, like walking with a small, neat step and keeping my hair tidy.

The cart driver drove away just as the front door to the house opened. A silver-haired man dressed in a tailcoat emerged. The thrust of his chin and clear, direct gaze gave him an air of authority, but it was undermined somewhat by the ruddiness of his cheeks and his heavy breathing. He must have run to the door.

"Good afternoon, sir," he intoned in the plummiest of toff accents. "May I offer you assistance?"

"I'm Lincoln Fitzroy, a friend of the dowager Lady Harcourt's, and this is my assistant, Miss Holloway. You are?"

"The butler, Yardley. I'm afraid Lord and Lady Harcourt are in London."

"We know. I dined with them last night. We're not here to see them, we're here to speak to you."

"Me?"

"And the other servants. We're looking for Andrew Buchanan."

"He's not here, sir." The poor man looked terribly confused, and Lincoln wasn't explaining himself at all well.

"Have you seen him recently?" he asked.

"Not for a year or more. He rarely comes to Emberly."

"Are you sure? It would have been a week ago."

"Quite sure, sir," Yardly said.

"May I question the other servants?"

The butler's jowls shook with indignation. "I'm afraid not, sir. Not without his lordship's permission."

"He's not here." The steeliness in Lincoln's voice was a sure sign that his frustration was rising. "Don't you have authority in his absence?"

"Y-yes, but—"

"I'm trying to locate his lordship's brother. Are you attempting to stop me?"

"No!"

I looped my arm through Lincoln's. "It'll only take a few moments, Mr. Yardly," I said quickly. "And then we'll be on our way. We do hate to trouble you at such a time, but this is very important and his lordship is most anxious to have his brother return to the family bosom. We simply want to ask the staff some questions. One of them may have seen him."

"I doubt it," he said, but he suggested we follow him anyway.

He ushered us into a spectacular drawing room, furnished with spindly chairs and sofas upholstered in pale blue, with paintings of country scenes on the walls. The white marble mantelpiece was the largest I'd seen, but it would have to be to warm such a vast space. There were ornaments everywhere, mostly vases of differing size and design. Lady Harcourt must collect them. Filling some with flowers would have given the room a little more interest, however. As it was, it felt like a museum rather than a home.

The butler opened the curtains and bright country sunshine flooded the room, burnishing the gilt frames. It helped give the room some life, but I still felt uncomfortable in it, like I didn't belong.

"We shut the place up when his lordship and ladyship are away," Yardly said. "Mr. Edgecombe doesn't mind."

"Mr. Edgecombe?" I echoed.

"Her ladyship's brother. He lives here."

"Oh. I had no idea."

Going by Lincoln's narrowed gaze, neither did he. We both eyed the door, expecting him to walk in at any moment, but no one came. The house felt empty.

"Is Mr. Edgecombe at home?"

"He's in the garden. I'm afraid he's not well enough to receive callers, however."

"But if he's in the garden, surely he's not *unwell*."

"I'm afraid so, Miss Holloway." He tugged on a bell pull and stood like a soldier with his back to the wall, his hands behind him. I wondered if he didn't want to leave us alone in case we were, in fact, opportunistic thieves. I admired his loyalty.

Lincoln sat in an armchair, looking very much out of place in the feminine room. It made me realize how masculine the Lichfield parlor was. Our furniture was more blocky and sturdy than slender and curvy, and the colors were bolder. The vases, statuettes and other knickknacks were rather pretty here, however I didn't like the paintings of cows. There were an awful lot of them.

A footman entered, took orders from the butler, then left again. Mr. Yardly didn't introduce us.

"Andrew Buchanan disappeared about a week ago," Lincoln informed the butler. "Are you sure you haven't seen him here?"

"I'm sure. Mr. Buchanan hasn't been to Emberly for a long time."

"Have any strangers come to the house recently?"

"No, sir."

"Have there been any disturbances?"

"No, sir."

A few moments ticked by in which I could hear the clock on the mantel ticking. "What about rumors?" Lincoln eventually asked.

"What about them, sir?"

"Have you heard any about Mr. Buchanan?"

"I couldn't say, sir."

"What about the baby Lady Harcourt gave birth to a few years ago?"

The butler's mouth dropped open. A red patch crept up his throat and over his cheeks.

I shook my head at Lincoln, and he arched his brows in return. We weren't going to find out anything useful from this man. He was much too loyal. Or perhaps he simply knew nothing.

The footman returned, after what felt like a painfully long time, and Lincoln asked him the same questions, omitting the final one about the baby. The footman glanced at the butler before answering each time. Intriguing. If he had nothing to hide, then why check with the senior member of staff?

I thought for a moment Lincoln wouldn't let him go after he served us, but he dismissed him with a nod as if he were the lord of Emberly Park. "I wish to speak to the other servants," he told Yardly.

"Their answers will be the same, sir. Mr. Buchanan wasn't here a week ago."

I cleared my throat before Lincoln lost his temper. "Yardly, can you point me in the direction of the powder room, please."

"Certainly, miss."

He gave very precise directions, but even so, I was sure I would get lost in such a large house. It was fortunate that I wasn't looking for the powder room but the service area. I might have better luck getting answers without Yardly there to frighten the other servants into silence with his glare.

After a few minutes, I despaired of finding the service area, however. The doorways must be hidden. I was about to begin tapping walls when I passed through a music room that overlooked a paved terrace and garden. A man sat with his back to the house, gazing out across the low shrubs, potted flowers and lawn. It must be Mr. Edgecombe, Marguerite's brother.

I quietly unlatched the door leading out to the terrace then closed it again behind me, so that my voice couldn't be heard by any servants passing inside. I approached the figure who sat a little slumped in what I'd thought was an ordinary chair, but now saw had wheels attached.

I cleared my throat. "Mr. Edgecombe?"

The man jerked and twisted. He pushed back his cap and peered at me from beneath droopy eyelids patterned with red spidery lines. It was difficult to determine his age. The brown hair poking out from beneath the cap bore no gray, and he had smooth if somewhat slack skin except beneath his eyes, where it was dark and puffed. If he was under thirty, he wasn't aging well.

I smiled but he didn't smile back. "I'm sorry to wake you—"

"You didn't." His top lip curled up in a sneer. "I was just sitting here, enjoying a drink and doing nothing, as usual." He lifted his empty glass. Going by his slurring, it wasn't his first. "Who're you?"

"Charlie Holloway." I came forward and stood where he didn't have to twist to see me. "I'm an acquaintance of the dowager Lady Harcourt's."

"Charlie's a boy's name."

"It's short for Charlotte."

"Prettier." He appraised me, but I bore his scrutiny and didn't duck my head like I wanted to. He lifted his glass in salute, and went to take a sip, but remembered at the last moment that it was empty. He muttered something under his breath that sounded very much like a crude word I hadn't used in months. "The dowager isn't here," he said. "She never comes here. If you were an acquaintance of hers, you'd know that."

"I didn't say I was calling upon her."

His back straightened, and he grunted as he gave me yet another appraisal, this one quicker. It didn't leave me feeling like I needed to bathe.

He adjusted the blanket over his lap, pulling the edge up to his stomach. Neither it nor the blue and gold striped smoking jacket hid his paunch. "Why are you here?"

"The dowager has asked my employer to look for her stepson, Andrew Buchanan. He has disappeared."

"So I heard. Marguerite and Donald have gone to London to help with the search. Not that they'd be much help," he added with a mutter.

"I've met them. And you're right, they've been of very little assistance."

He gave me a rueful smile and a nod of approval. "I don't know why the fuss. Buchanan's a grown man and a rakehell at that. His shoes are probably parked under a whore's bed, or in an opium den. Perhaps a whore in an opium den. Does that shock you, Miss Charlotte Holloway?"

"No. I've been to opium dens. In fact, I smoked opium once." It was perhaps more accurate to say I'd accidentally inhaled the smoke of others' opium pipes, but he didn't need to know that.

His brows rose. "Is that so? It seems you're more worldly than me, and I got up to a thing or two before my accident." The grim smile softened his appearance and tugged at my heart. So he hadn't been born with legs that didn't work.

"What sort of accident?" I asked.

"You're bold, for a mere slip of a thing."

"So I've been told. You don't have to answer it if my question upsets you. I was simply curious."

"Curiosity can get a girl into trouble."

"So I've discovered," I said with a wry twist of my mouth that he matched with one of his own.

"Riding accident. I fell off my horse at home. My home, not this one."

"But you live here now?"

He nodded. "Have for a year or two. What month is this?"

"Late October."

"Then it's been one year and nine months. The days all blend into one, when you've got nothing to do but sit in this contraption and watch the world pass by out the window." He smacked the arm of his wheelchair then dragged the same hand through his hair, knocking off his cap.

I picked it up and handed it to him. He snatched it from my grip and slapped it back on his head.

"Don't you have something better to do than stand there and talk to me?"

"No. I'd like to ask you some questions, if I may. Since all you do nowadays is sit and peer out windows, I think you may be of help to me."

He barked a harsh laugh. "Glad to know you've found a use for me." He lifted his empty glass. "Fetch me a drink and I'll answer one question. Fetch an entire bottle, I'll answer a dozen."

"Where?"

"Billiards room, through the music room on your right."

I took the glass and headed back inside. No one had come searching for me yet, but it wouldn't take long before the butler grew suspicious or Lincoln became worried. I wondered if he was enjoying his tea while the dour Yardly watched on.

I grabbed the first decanter I could find from the sideboard in the billiards room and returned to the terrace. "Will this do?"

"Nicely."

I handed back the glass and poured an amount that I'd seen Lincoln drink at a time. Edgecombe waggled the glass until I poured more. He then downed it in one gulp and held the glass out again. I hesitated.

"Don't pretend you care, Miss Charlotte Holloway. Just fill the damned glass. And be quick about it. My assistant will be back soon, unless he's forgotten about me. He's stupid enough that he may have."

"Why hire a stupid man to assist you?"

"I hired him for his brawn, not his brain."

I poured another then set the decanter down. "I've fulfilled my side of the bargain, now you fulfill yours."

He wiped his mouth with the back of his hand. "Of course. A gentleman doesn't renege on a promise."

I swept aside my skirt and sat on the terrace step that led down to the lawn. I twisted so that I could see him. "Andrew Buchanan disappeared a week ago. We have evidence to suggest that he wanted to come here on the morning of his disappearance, but no firm proof that he took the train. The stationmaster doesn't remember, and the butler said he never called at the house. I rather think he's lying, however. Do you remember him coming here?"

"No, but I don't come downstairs often. It's not easy when one has to rely on an assistant who'd rather be in the kitchen with the maids. My previous fellow wasn't quite so bad as Dawkins, but he very inconveniently died, and I had to hire the fat-headed Dawkins in rather a hurry. As you can probably guess, I can't manage the stairs without him."

"Your sister didn't mention Buchanan calling?"

"No."

"Your brother-in-law?"

"We rarely talk."

"May I ask why?"

He hesitated. "I don't like Donald, and he doesn't like me."

"Yet he allows you to live under his roof."

"Yes." His brittle chuckle sent a chill down my spine. "Yes he does."

I smoothed my hands over my skirts then clasped them over my knees. While I felt some sympathy for Edgecombe's plight, I was very glad that he couldn't reach me from his wheelchair unless he rolled it forward. I suspected I could leap out of the way faster than he could move. "Did you see or hear anything unusual a week ago? Did the servants act strangely, or was there more activity in the house than usual? Anything?" My desperation was getting the better of me, and I spoke more harshly than I meant to. I suspected Buchanan had made it to the house, but time was running out to find proof.

"A week ago, you say? Yes, I suppose there was something out of the ordinary." He pointed at a low rise in the distance, well beyond the formal garden and parkland. There seemed to be a small folly built on it, but it was difficult to tell from a distance. "Do you see that mausoleum?"

"Mausoleum?" I squinted at what I'd thought was a folly. "Who's buried up there?"

"Everyone who matters, according to Donald. All the Buchanans, going back centuries. But that structure itself is new. It was built only a few years ago."

"Five years ago?"

His eyes turned cloudy. "So you know?" he said quietly.

"About Marguerite's baby? Yes." But how much did *he* know? According to Estelle Pearson, no one outside of herself, Marguerite and Donald knew the baby was full-term. I decided to take another risk and said, "Marguerite told me she had him christened Hector before he died."

"After our father." He lowered his glass and stared toward the mausoleum. "Marguerite told me he was full-term. Not at the time, but later, when she was…upset. She never quite got over the baby's death, you see. It affected her greatly." He tapped his temple. "Up here. It hasn't helped that she doesn't seem to be able to have more children. She's taken her barrenness very hard. And *he* hasn't helped."

"Lord Harcourt?"

He nodded and drained his glass. He held it out for me to refill. I did. Whatever was in that decanter had loosened his tongue nicely.

"What about the mausoleum, Mr. Edgecombe?" At his frown, I added, "You implied that something happened up there."

"I can see it better from my rooms." He pointed up. "Third floor. Great view." He snorted. "With nothing else to do, I sit in this bloody chair all day and stare at the same bloody scenery. One evening, about a week ago, I saw two figures up there. The full moon was out, I remember, because I could see them quite clearly. They appeared to be fighting."

"Any idea who they might have been?"

"None."

"Did you ask your brother-in-law or the servants about it?"

"No. Why would I?"

Because it was something different, something interesting. But I didn't let him see my frustration at his lack of curiosity. "Thank you, Mr. Edgecombe. I appreciate you telling me. But may I ask, *why* are you telling me? No one else seems to want to admit that Buchanan might have been here."

"It may not have been him."

"True, but it may well have been too."

"Perhaps no one else saw the commotion. Perhaps they don't sit by windows all day and all night. Or perhaps they're protecting the great lord and master." He drained the glass again, his fingers white around the tumbler.

"Do you hate him?"

He sucked air through his teeth. "Do you know my sister spent time in Bedlam?"

I gasped. "The lunatic asylum? Because she was so upset about the baby?"

He nodded. "He had her committed. By law, he can. By law, he's the only one who can get her out again, other than the doctors, but why would they when she brings in a tidy sum as a patient?" He drifted off as his eyes turned cloudy, dark.

"When was this?"

"About a year or so after the baby was born. She was troubled but not insane. She shouldn't have been put in there."

"Lord Harcourt came to his senses and got her out, though."

His lips twisted and his back teeth ground together. "Only because I demanded he do so. That place…what they did to her…it was inhuman. I dragged him there one day, and showed him what it was like. He'd only seen what the doctors wanted him to see before that—the relaxing garden, the gentle massages—but I forced my way through and showed him the cold bath room, the manacles on the beds, and the degrading things the so-called patients had to endure. He signed her out immediately, thank God, but I never forgave him. She did, but I haven't forgotten and I never will."

"Is that why he allows you to stay here?" I asked quietly, aware that I was treading on rocky ground. "Because he feels guilty?"

"Guilt?" He snorted. "No, he allows me to stay here because he's afraid I'll tell people what he did. He doesn't care too much for society convention, but even he knows how humiliating it would be for them both if it were discovered she spent a few weeks in an asylum. He had let everyone believe she'd gone to the seaside for some rest, you see, but I found out the truth. I'm the only one who knows the truth."

Dear lord, poor Marguerite. I knew little about asylums, except that the boys in my gang thought they were haunted. Edgecombe didn't paint a very nice picture. Manacles and cold baths didn't sound like they could cure much, let alone deep sorrow.

"Thank you," I said rising. "I appreciate your honesty."

His hand whipped out as I passed him and he grabbed my arm. "My brother-in-law would not like to know that I told you that."

"I won't tell him."

His fingers tightened. "I wish my sister had never married into this fucking mad family." A drop of spittle landed on his lower lip and he wiped it off with the hand that held his empty glass. "She was always a little simple, but now…" He shook his head. "They've got secrets, and not just the one about the baby. For one thing, the late Lord Harcourt was a blind fool for not seeing your friend, the dowager, for the gold digger she is."

"She's not my friend."

"No, I suppose she wouldn't be." Once again his gaze raked over me, and this time it was openly lewd. "She would never befriend a younger, prettier woman."

The door to the music room opened and Lincoln charged out, the butler on his heels. While Lincoln's glare was sharp enough to tear Edgecombe to pieces, Yardly's eyes went wide as he seemed to realize that I'd been questioning him.

Edgecombe let me go and held up his hand in surrender. His gaze flicked from Lincoln to me then he chuckled into his glass again. Discovering it empty, he went to pick up the decanter near the wheel of his chair, but Yardly was faster than he looked. He got to it first.

"I'll fetch Dawkins to take you back inside, sir." Yardly held out his hand for us to walk ahead of him into the house.

I went first, followed by Lincoln and the butler who shut the door on the sorry figure of Mr. Edgecombe cradling the glass to his chest.

"Thank you, Mr. Yardly," I said in my sweetest voice. "We'll trouble you no further." I hurried ahead of them to the front door, eager to get far away from Emberly Park and its occupants.

CHAPTER 10

Yardly didn't offer us the use of one of the Harcourt carriages to take us back to town, and Lincoln was not too pleased about it.

"My assistant has only recently recovered from a foot injury," he said. "We require a ride back to the village."

"It's quite all right, sir," I said before Yardly could respond. The poor man looked as if he didn't know what to say anyway. Manners dictated that he should offer us the use of his master's coach and driver, but he didn't seem to trust us, particularly after catching me plying Edgecombe with drink. "I can walk, and the day is lovely. Thank you again for your warm hospitality, Mr. Yardly. Lord Harcourt will hear of it."

As Lincoln and I walked along the drive, I told him everything Edgecombe had told me. I'd finished by the time we were out of sight of the house.

"If we head that way, we'll reach the family graveyard," I said, nodding to our right.

"You think we'll learn more there?"

"I don't know, but we should take a look." I set off across the grass, and he soon fell into step beside me.

"Your foot?"

"Is perfectly fine, thank you. What did you and Yardly talk about while I was gone?"

"Nothing."

"You sat in silence the entire time?"

"It was the longest fifteen minutes of my life. Next time, I'm not going through the front door and making idle chatter with servants."

"Why do so this time?"

"I didn't want to leave you on your own."

I rolled my eyes. "I would have been perfectly all right. In fact, separating works well, as we proved in the hospital. I question people while you sneak about."

"You had Seth with you then. You would have been alone here."

"Yardly doesn't look dangerous. I think I could have managed him on my own."

We fell into silence, and I hoped he was considering my suggestion. The more I thought about it, the more I liked the idea. By separating, we could attack on two fronts, each of us doing what we did best.

"Did Edgecombe say whether he or anyone else told the late Lord Harcourt about the baby?" So much for him considering my suggestion.

"I never got a chance to ask. It's possible, I suppose. Or perhaps he saw the mausoleum too and realized that fetuses aren't given proper burials in such grand style."

"It's difficult to miss."

The square building with classical columns marking the entrance reminded me of a miniature version of the British Museum. It occupied one corner of the small graveyard and commanded a spectacular outlook toward the house. I wondered if Mr. Edgecombe was watching us from his window or the garden terrace. I resisted the urge to wave.

"There are signs of a scuffle." Lincoln pointed to some divots in the grass near the base of the mausoleum step.

"They could have been made by anything, at any time."

He crouched and inspected a dark stain on the stone. "Blood."

I crouched beside him. "Are you sure?"

"Moderately."

"Wouldn't it have been washed away if it was from a week ago?"

"Not entirely, if the rain wasn't heavy and there was a lot of blood." He moved away and, keeping low, brushed his fingers through the ankle-deep grass.

I followed suit, heading in the other direction. Not three feet away, I found a silver button. "From a gentleman's jacket or waistcoat?" I asked, showing it to him.

"Possibly."

"It's quite distinctive. Look, something's been engraved on it."

We bent our heads closer. Our arms pressed together and our faces were only inches apart. Being so close to him scrambled my senses and clouded my brain. I fought to clear it and focus on the button.

After a moment, I could make out the inscription. "The letter B," I said. "For Buchanan?"

Lincoln cleared his throat and shifted his weight which moved him a little further away from me. "I…yes, it is."

I opened my reticule and placed the button inside. "This proves that Buchanan was here and knew about the baby."

"Agreed."

"I think it also proves his disappearance is related to that discovery, and nothing to do with the occult."

He shook his head. "It proves nothing, except that he knows his sister-in-law gave birth to a full-term baby and he got into a fight up here. We don't know who with or why."

"Surely with his brother."

"Perhaps. But we also don't know what happened to him after the fight."

"I'll put money on him being dead."

His face darkened. "You are *not* going to summon his spirit."

"I wasn't going to. However—"

"No."

He walked out of the graveyard, back down the slope. I picked up my skirts and ran after him. "Come now, Lincoln, it will prove one way or the other if he's alive."

"You're suggesting that, after what happened with the Pearson woman's spirit?"

"Andrew Buchanan doesn't have magical powers."

"He might have learned some through the books."

"Lincoln," I said, walking fast to keep up with his long strides, "you've read the same books. Did *you* learn any new magic tricks?"

My logic had silenced him for almost a mile when I decided to break it. "Do you have a better idea?" I asked defiantly.

"Yes. We'll question the local doctor. It's likely he sought out medical assistance to tend the wound."

"If he was alive."

We walked another mile, and I finally conceded that his idea had merit. "But if we learn nothing, may I then summon his spirit?"

"No. And for once, I would appreciate you doing as I ask."

"I would," I muttered, "if you actually asked me instead of telling me."

A muscle bunched in his jaw. It remained bunched until we reached the village. The day was still sunny, and I'd enjoyed our walk. While he'd walked on in anger, I'd soaked in the fresh air and sunshine, and the pretty scenery. I wasn't ready to head inside, even though I was a little hungry.

"You can go ahead, if you like, and find the doctor," I said. "I want to walk alongside the stream." I picked up a brown leaf and dropped it over the side of the bridge. I counted the seconds as it floated to a large tree with giant roots clinging to the bank like claws. I picked up a smaller leaf and timed it too.

"I'll walk with you," he said.

I turned to see him watching me, his eyes clear and not as dark as they usually appeared. It must be an effect of the bright sunshine. I smiled at him. I couldn't help it. He was so dashingly handsome, standing there with his hands resting on the stone bridge. It was so tempting to kiss him and see if he kissed me back.

But I didn't want to risk ruining the moment.

I clamped a hand on my hat and trotted along the bridge. "Come along then."

We descended a set of crude stone stairs to the path edging the bank. Small fish flashed silver in the water, darting over pebbles and between reeds. I removed my glove and dipped my fingers in near the school. They scattered but a moment later returned to investigate the strange objects in their midst. They kissed my fingers before once more swimming off to find something to nibble. I stood and shook off the icy droplets.

"I can't believe how clear this water is," I said. "The Thames is a cesspit by comparison."

When Lincoln didn't respond, I glanced at him. He leaned one shoulder against a tree trunk, his arms crossed, and watched me from beneath lazy lids. I'd never seen him quite so relaxed before. The countryside agreed with him.

We walked a little further but my growling stomach reminded me that it was growing late and we hadn't eaten luncheon. "Hungry?" I asked.

"Very." His quiet purr made my stomach flutter.

We ate a hearty lunch at The Fox and Hound then headed out again, following the innkeeper's directions to Dr. Turcott's rooms. We waited while the doctor finished with a patient, using the opportunity to question his wife who sat at the front desk and managed his schedule. She claimed that her husband hadn't seen any patients fitting Buchanan's description a week ago. The doctor confirmed this when he finally spared a few moments for us.

By the time we left his rooms, the shadows had grown longer and the air cooler. I pulled the edges of my cloak together.

"What now?" I asked.

"Now you should rest your foot. You've walked far today."

"It's fine, Lincoln. Besides, I'm not going to sit down while you continue to question villagers."

"You are if your foot hurts."

"It doesn't."

"If the wound reopens, it could become infected and take much longer to heal."

"Thank you for your concern. I'll certainly stay off it if it does reopen but, for now, it's perfectly all right. So who shall we speak to next?"

"Buchanan must have stayed somewhere overnight, but our innkeeper claimed he wasn't there. I've seen two more inns in the village. We'll ask at those."

"What about boarding houses?"

"Those too, if the inns prove futile."

It was almost dark by the time we'd finished questioning the innkeepers and all the houses where a gentleman might board for the night, including the one where a rakehell like Buchanan would prefer to stay, thanks to its more dubious delights of gambling and women.

"Edgecombe witnessed the fight in the evening, but Buchanan didn't stay at Emberly, or in Harcourt," I said as we walked back to The Fox and Hound. "The trains don't run that late, and he had no private means of transport. Unless he found a farmer willing to give him a ride on his cart, then he couldn't have left, and the likelihood of a farmer traveling on country roads at night is slim. Lincoln, I don't think he made it out of there alive."

"It's now a distinct possibility."

I hunkered into my cloak, but it didn't smother the chill skittering down my spine. Lincoln removed his jacket, and I protested as he placed it around my shoulders.

"You'll need it," I said. "It's much too cold to be wandering about in nothing but your shirt and waistcoat." Not to mention uncivilized.

"I don't feel the cold."

We'd stopped beneath one of the few streetlights already lit by the lamplighter. The warm glow toyed with the planes of Lincoln's face, softening the sharpness of his cheeks but throwing his eyes further into shadow. The warmth and heaviness of his coat was a comfort, but the closeness of his hands to my jaw as he arranged it played havoc with my nerves. Every part of me felt aware, alive and tight with expectation.

Without really knowing what I was doing, I reached up and cupped his cheek. I didn't see him move, but an ever so slight increase of pressure on my hand proved that he had. We stood like that for what felt like eternity. Despite the poor light, and the darkness of his eyes, I knew he was watching me with pinpoint focus. I could *feel* his gaze on me.

I whispered his name so softly that it was little more than a breath. His throat moved with his swallow. His lips parted by the tiniest of margins. He placed his bare hand over my gloved one and drew it to his mouth. With deft fingers, he undid the button at my wrist. I waited with my heart in my throat for that moment when his smooth lips met my achy skin.

The kiss did not disappoint. Where before I was cold, I now felt hot. Everywhere. Blood thrummed along my veins to an erratic beat and rushed between my ears. I could hear nothing except my own pulse, see nothing except Lincoln's bent head. Feel nothing but his lips and my body, throbbing now with the heady thrill of desire and the knowledge that he desired me too.

"Avert your eyes, Emmaline." The curt voice of a passing woman punctured my thoughts and wrenched me out of the moment.

Lincoln dropped my hand and snapped to attention as the family hurried past. The severe downturn of the mother's mouth marked her displeasure at our very public display. It was quite a rude reminder that we were not alone. A cart rumbled past, and two men stopped to speak with the lamplighter, now working on the other side of the street.

Lincoln, with his back to me, said, "We must go." He walked off then remembered his manners and waited. I caught up, but did not take his arm as the other couples did.

We were not a couple.

Not yet, the small voice inside me piped up. I walked quickly to keep up with him as we headed back to The Fox and Hound in silence. I wanted to say a thousand things to him, but nothing sounded right in my head. Everything was too pathetic or childish, and that wasn't how I wanted him to see me.

Once inside, Lincoln asked the innkeeper to have supper brought up to our rooms. Once upstairs, I handed him his coat and asked him to come inside to wait for supper.

"I think it's best if we part here," he said outside my door. He didn't meet my gaze, and he kept a few feet of floor between us. But if he was disturbed by what had happened outside then he didn't show it. He looked as calm as ever.

"But we must discuss the situation."

"It was a mistake. There's nothing to discuss."

"I meant the situation with Buchanan."

He blinked slowly, as if flicking a switch to alter the course of his thinking. I almost smiled. I liked that he was thinking of the kiss still. But my smile never broke free.

It was a mistake.

"Buchanan is most likely dead," he said. "There's nothing more to discuss."

"Nonsense. I'm going to freshen up then I'll be in the sitting room. I would very much like your company."

"I don't think that's necessary."

I huffed out a breath. "I don't care. Come into the sitting room. Please. Unless, of course, you're afraid I'll ravish you."

His eyes flared ever so briefly. "In part."

I grinned in spite of everything. I hadn't expected him to admit it. "I promise I won't try to kiss you again. But if you don't come, I might just summon the spirit of Buchanan without you."

With my announcement still ringing in my ears, I opened the door and entered the room. By the time I'd turned to close it again, he was already unlocking his own door.

Some fifteen minutes later, I entered the sitting room and warmed myself by the fire that he must have lit in the grate. He wasn't there now, however. I opened the door at the maid's knock and stepped aside as she placed the tray on the table. She bobbed a curtsy, then left. I tapped lightly on the door leading to Lincoln's room.

"You'd better join me if you don't want me eating your share of supper." No answer. "Andrew Buchanan's ghost sends his regards."

The door opened faster than I could blink. His eyes narrowed and his lips pressed together. "That was a joke," he said flatly.

"No, it was a ruse to get you out here. It worked."

I sat at the table and poured wine into the glasses. I handed him one. "Let's say a toast."

He took the glass. "To?"

"To working together." I sipped, but he didn't. "What's wrong?"

He set the glass down. "I'm not sure it was a good idea to collaborate on this investigation." He held up a hand as I began to protest. "But we are, and there's no going back. Let's not discuss us working together, but rather what we know."

I sighed. "You're so stubborn, Lincoln."

"You say that as if you're not."

I lifted the platter lid to reveal a selection of cheeses, nuts and fruit. "In what way?"

"For one thing, you've continued to call me by my first name even though I forbade it."

"You call me by my first name."

"That's different. You work for me, not the other way around."

"I think people who kiss one another ought to be on first name basis, don't you?"

He had no response and we ate without speaking for several minutes. Even though I'd won a point, I felt as if it hadn't been worth it. I preferred to talk to him instead of sit in silence.

"I think we ought to summon Buchanan's spirit," I finally said. "We need to know for certain if he left Emberly Park alive."

"Agreed."

"Really?"

"I see no other option, now. You can summon him after supper." He pointed at the bowl of nuts. "Eat."

I picked up an almond, somewhat stunned that he'd changed his mind about calling Buchanan's spirit. He'd been so against it before. "I think he's the baby's father. The rumors Seth heard were probably true, and Marguerite was the woman Buchanan put 'in the pudding club,' as Seth called it. There's that, and now the scuffle at the baby's mausoleum…it's too much of a coincidence."

He didn't seem surprised, so it must have occurred to him too.

"Marguerite also seems to be fond of him," I added. "Too fond for a sister-in-law, if you ask me."

"I hadn't noticed." He nodded slowly, however, as if he thought the idea had merit.

"Buchanan must have recently learned that the baby was full-term. He then came here to find out for certain, and confronted his brother about it. Why not Marguerite, I wonder?"

"We don't know that he didn't. They may have spoken prior to the argument."

"What a tangled family," I said. "Marguerite was, and probably still is, in love with Andrew, yet Andrew was in love with Julia. And Julia is in love with you."

He flinched. I picked up my glass and sipped, watching him over the rim. He met my gaze. "Charlie...Julia's feelings are irrelevant."

"Not to her."

He spread his fingers out on the tablecloth. "That's not what I meant."

For a self-assured and articulate man, he had a lot of difficulty expressing himself when it came to matters of the heart, both his and others'.

"Julia and I are no longer, and never will be, together. She was a mistake I will not repeat."

I snatched up my glass and stood. "Ah, yes, mistakes," I bit off. "You said that kissing me was a mistake. At least I am in illustrious company with the lovely dowager." I spun away and marched to the hearth. Damn him for making me feel this way, like a pathetic, silly girl with an inappropriate infatuation. I hated him for it, yet I hated myself more for allowing him to affect me so.

I lifted the glass to throw it into the fireplace, but found my hand enclosed in Lincoln's. He stood close behind me. His breathing sounded ragged, like my own.

My heart stopped beating.

"Different mistakes," he murmured. "Very different."

I angled my face to look up at him. His stubbled jaw was very close to my eye. It was hard as rock. I kissed his throat above his collar and felt the throb of his blood against my lips, the tiny shudder ripple across his skin.

"This is not a mistake, Lincoln," I murmured. "You don't feel—"

He wrenched himself away. "Don't pretend to know what I feel."

Hot tears stung my eyes as he turned his back to me. "I know you better than you think," I whispered. "I felt your body respond to me. I saw the heat in your eyes."

He dashed a hand through his hair. "It doesn't matter what I feel," he growled. "Don't you see that?"

"No."

"We cannot be together."

I crossed my arms, wishing that could somehow keep the pieces of myself from fracturing. I didn't want to shatter in front of him. If I did, and he walked out, I couldn't bear it. "But you want to be with me," I said, without conviction. I wasn't entirely sure of his feelings, despite saying so. A few small signs might prove he desired me, but he was a man and I was a woman and we were alone. Of course his body would respond to my attentions. It was only natural. But anything more…I didn't know.

"Yes." His voice cracked.

My heart soared. Giddiness swamped me. "Then be with me, Lincoln. Lie with me."

He spun round. There was no heat in his eyes, no sign that he cared for me or wanted me. Only anger, cold and fierce and raw. "No. It would mean the end of our friendship, of working together. Of this."

I rubbed my arms. "It doesn't have to be."

"It will, whether we want that or not. This will pass, Charlie, this…need. I'll see to it."

I spluttered a harsh laugh. "You'll *see* to it? There is no switch to turn feelings off and on, Lincoln. That is absurd."

His back straightened. His nostrils flared. Had I offended him? Angered him further? It was difficult to tell. "Don't suggest we act upon these feelings again. There is a line between us. Do not cross it if you want to continue to help me investigate Buchanan's disappearance."

I watched as his face slowly lost its hardness and his fists unclenched. My own temper also dampened, making way for confusion. I wasn't even sure my feelings were hurt. He did, after all, admit that he desired me. That was something, a base, of sorts. But I was no longer certain how to act on that desire. It seemed that forcing him to do so was a sure way of awakening his temper.

"Raise him," he said shortly. "Then we'll part for the evening and return to London tomorrow."

I nodded and sat by the fire. "Afterward…" I swallowed. "After I raise Buchanan's spirit, will you continue to want me to work with you? Or have I destroyed all chance of that now?"

He rested his elbow on the mantelpiece and stared down into the glowing coals. "Your necromancy comes in handy, from time to time, and I admit that your questioning of Edgecombe today was inspired. You think and act quickly, and you're good with people, whereas I'm not. We work well together." His fingers twisted around one another and he glanced at me before once more staring at the fire. "I'd be a fool to shut you out of the investigation now, and any future ones."

"Thank you," I said, smiling, despite myself. "I appreciate it."

"Buchanan's middle name is Myron. Let's begin."

I blew out a breath and dragged my thoughts away from Lincoln to the task at hand. "Andrew Myron Buchanan, do you hear me?"

No white mist rushed out to me. The air in the room didn't shift and the only sounds came from a dog barking in the distance. I set my glass down on the table and tried again.

"This is a message for the spirit of Andrew Myron Buchanan. Please come to me here in this room and talk to me. I need to ask you some questions." Still nothing. I shrugged at Lincoln.

"Try again," he said.

"I wish to speak to the spirit of Andrew Myron Buchanan. Can you hear me? There is nothing to fear. I just want to talk." I waited then shook my head. "He's not here."

"Then he's not dead."

CHAPTER 11

The train left early the following morning. We had the compartment to ourselves. I thought Lincoln might demand we find one that had other passengers in it, to insure we weren't alone, but he didn't. He sat with his newspaper raised so I couldn't see his face.

I tried to concentrate on my book but ended up looking out the window while we sped through the countryside. I liked it immensely and didn't particularly want to return to London yet. While the city would always be my home, I wouldn't mind visiting Oxfordshire again. Or perhaps going to the seaside next time. Lincoln had even said he'd take me. I wondered if he now wished he'd kept his mouth shut, or if he even remembered making such a promise. He certainly wouldn't keep it. After our discussion the night before, such a journey would be too inappropriate.

"Lincoln," I said and waited until he lowered the paper. "You may regret bringing me along, but I want you to know that I'm glad I came."

He folded the paper and set it on the seat beside him. "I don't regret bringing you. I told you last night, we work well together. I don't want to lose that." He turned to the window. "I do regret not insisting Seth or Gus come. Having others around might have kept us from…indulging."

"Perhaps." I wasn't so sure. I think we would have stolen a few moments away from the others to *indulge*, as he'd put it. Some things were inevitable, like time ticking forward or the ebb and flow of the tide. There was no way to stop them. "Anyway, I just wanted to say thank you. Despite our unfortunate exchange last night, I've enjoyed being in the countryside."

He picked up the newspaper. "I noticed."

My face heated. Thank goodness he wasn't looking at me. I opened my book but couldn't concentrate on the words. "You must think me foolish," I mumbled. "It's just grass and trees, after all."

He unfolded the paper and began to read again. I'd thought the conversation over, until he said, "It's not just grass and trees. Not anymore."

I puzzled over what he meant for the rest of the journey home.

* * *

Cook made a special celebratory cake for our return, decorated with little cream swirls piped onto the top through a calico bag. "House was quiet without you, Charlie," he said, finishing the final swirl with a flourish.

I set out four plates, cups and saucers on the kitchen table, and another on a tray for Lincoln. He'd gone straight to his rooms upon our return, and I doubted we'd see him for the rest of the day. "That's sweet of you to say so," I told him. "This cake looks far too lovely to eat."

"Speak for yourself," Gus said, holding out a plate for the first slice.

Cook placed it on another plate then handed the plate to me. "Ladies first."

Gus rolled his eyes and waited for the second slice. "Seth, you take afternoon tea up for Death. I've been mucking out stables all morning."

"And I've been in here helping Cook." Seth poured cups of tea then returned the teapot to the tray. "I want to hear all about Emberly Park when I get back."

He was saved from footman's duties by the entrance of Lincoln, carrying a letter. He looked refreshed after our journey, his hair loose, his tie, coat and waistcoat discarded. I found it difficult to meet his gaze. So much had happened between us since we left Lichfield, and I wasn't yet certain how to proceed.

"I'll join you all," he said, handing me the letter. "Charlie, this concerns you."

"You're receiving letters about me?"

He hitched his trousers at the knee and sat opposite. "It's from an orphanage in France."

"France?" I scanned the letter and passed it back to him. "It's in French. What does it say? And why are you receiving letters from French orphanages?"

"I wrote to several charitable organizations there and asked for names and addresses of orphanages, poor houses and lying-in hospitals for unfortunate women. I then wrote to each of those, inquiring about a woman known as Ellen who gave birth to a daughter eighteen years ago and gave her up for adoption to an English couple. I included as many details about Holloway as I knew."

I stared at him. He'd done that? For me? Or for himself? "When did you begin your inquiries?"

"Two months ago."

When I first came to live at Lichfield. So perhaps not for me, but to find my mother on the ministry's behalf. Still, he was telling me now when he could have kept the information to himself.

I wasn't the only one stunned into silence by Lincoln's admission. The other three had stopped what they were doing to stare at him.

"France," Seth said with a slow nod. "That's why the Calthorn woman found the information to give to Frankenstein. He took advantage of her self-imposed exile to

Paris and asked her to do exactly what you did—make inquiries at orphanages and the like."

Lincoln accepted the slice of cake from Cook. "It seems likely he already knew to look in France, perhaps because Ellen was French. The response in this letter also explains why Frankenstein didn't know precisely where to look for you in London." He pointed to a line on the letter that I couldn't understand. "The matron explains here that the baby she suspects is the one I'm interested in was adopted by a vicar based in London. There was a fire some years ago and all records were lost, but she remembered you."

"Why?" I gripped my teacup harder in both hands. I felt like my eyes were huge as I stared at him, holding my breath as I awaited his answer. "They must see hundreds of babies."

"The matron states that Ellen Mercier was unlike the other mothers who are forced to give up their children. She spoke well, with an educated accent, and her clothes were well made and of good quality, although they were old and worn. Matron suspects Ellen was from a good family but had fallen on hard times, perhaps as a result of her pregnancy."

"She did not marry Frankenstein," I whispered.

"No. As an unwed mother, doors would have been closed to her."

"Perhaps even the door to her father's home."

He nodded as he watched me. After a moment, he turned the letter over and pointed to the small, neat writing near the top. "She describes Ellen Mercier's appearance here. 'Small in stature and figure, with features to match except for her large eyes that one couldn't fail to notice.' Like you."

"Yes," I whispered.

"But her eyes were brown."

"Mine are blue, like his." I wished I'd found out more about my mother from my father, before his death, but there'd been so little opportunity, and now he was gone. "Does the letter say what happened to her?"

"The matron notes that Ellen left in something of a hurry. She was upset at having to give you up, but she felt certain it was for the best. It was very hard for her to walk away, but she was very sick and knew she couldn't look after you. The matron says Ellen begged her to give you away to a nice, respectable family, one who desperately wanted a child of their own to love. When the Holloways came to them a few days later, wanting a daughter, she didn't hesitate to give you to them. You were a good baby, content, and the right age. The matron suspects your mother probably wouldn't have lived very long. She was too ill."

He watched me very closely, his gaze never leaving my face. I wanted him to hold me, comfort me, but I knew I would get no affection from him now. He'd made his stance clear.

"Why were the Holloways in France looking for a baby?" Seth asked.

"Aye," said Gus. "What's wrong with an English one?" Seth smacked his arm, spilling some of Gus's tea. "What's wrong with that question?"

Cook swore under his breath, gave me a pointed look, and smacked Gus's other arm.

"The matron doesn't know for certain," Lincoln said, "but she implies that the Holloways wanted to pass the child off as their own, after an extended tour of the continent. Apparently it happens frequently. Holloway claimed their decision to 'save a poor French babe,' as he put it, was made on a whim the day before, but matron said it can't have been. They already owned a perambulator and some baby clothes. With the previous day being a Sunday, they couldn't have purchased anything. They must have been planning an adoption for some time."

"Blimey, this matron has a good memory."

"She asks how you are, Charlie," Lincoln went on. "She's very interested to know how you turned out. If you'd like to write to her, I can translate for you."

I nodded dumbly, even though I couldn't think of a single thing I wanted to say to her at that moment. Thank you, perhaps?

"There is one final thing she notes. Your mother left something, with the stipulation that it would remain with you, but the Holloways wanted nothing from your past. She asks if I want it sent over."

"Yes," I said quickly. "Yes, please, tell her to send them." I rose, hardly knowing what I was doing. I just wanted to be alone with my thoughts. The woman who'd given birth to me seemed more real now, not an unknown, vague figure. And she had loved me enough to do what was best for me.

"Excuse me," I said with a weak smile for them all. "The cake was lovely, Cook, but I'm not hungry. I'll finish it later."

"You ain't started," Gus noted.

"Shut it," Cook hissed.

I left and headed…somewhere. I hardly knew where to go. Outside, perhaps. I needed some fresh air. But Lincoln caught up to me before I reached the front door.

"Charlie, a moment."

I stopped and looked up at him. I was very aware of my full eyes, my tight throat. My emotions were close to the surface. Close to spilling over. Speaking with Lincoln might not be the best thing for my tender nerves at that moment.

His fingers brushed mine so briefly that I wondered if I'd just imagined it. "I'll take you." The words tumbled from his lips. I'd learned that he spoke that way when he said something on a whim, without much forethought.

"I'm not going anywhere in particular." I waved in the general direction of the front door. "Just outside for a walk."

"I mean to France."

"France?" Surely he wasn't serious. And yet he looked so earnest, so sincere.

"After we've found Buchanan, we'll travel to Paris together and retrieve your things from the orphanage."

I became aware that I was staring at him rather stupidly, my mouth ajar. "Lincoln...don't say things you'll regret later."

He clasped his hands behind his back. "Hopefully before winter comes, when the crossing is rougher. Sea voyages are unpleasant at the best of times."

"I wouldn't know." I waited for him to retract his offer, but he didn't. He simply stood there, as if he were waiting for me to speak. "Lincoln, I...I don't know what to say."

"There's nothing to say." He turned and marched off. His fingers twisted together at his back, the knuckles white.

I wanted to run after him, take his face in my hands and kiss him. But instead I simply called, "Thank you."

He stopped at the base of the stairs but did not turn around. He rested a hand on the balustrade. After a moment, he finally said, "My pleasure." Then he took two stairs at a time and disappeared from sight.

* * *

I didn't stay outside for long after it began to rain. Upon returning inside, Lincoln found me as I headed to my rooms.

"You're here," he said simply. "Good. Collect your coat and gloves if you want to come with me to Harcourt House."

"We're going to confront Lord and Lady Harcourt?"

"Yes."

"What if the dowager's there? You wanted to shield her from what we'd learned about her. I don't think we can do that if we reveal what we know."

"We can't, and it was a futile and misguided suggestion on my part. I should have listened to you." He gave a stiff nod. "You said there might be a link between her, The Alhambra and Buchanan's disappearance, and you've been proven right. I'm sorry I doubted you, Charlie."

He strode past me, leaving me staring at his back. I wasn't sure which shocked me more—that he was wrong or that he admitted it.

I hurried up the stairs. The cool air outside had cleared my head. I no longer felt stunned to stupidity by the news in the letter; I was energized by it. I felt more whole—complete. Before, it was as if I were reaching into the dark and finding emptiness. Now I felt like I carried a small lamp and could see a person nearby, almost within reach. I very much wanted to go to the orphanage with Lincoln. It spurred me on to find Buchanan and finish our business faster. Confronting the Harcourts was a good place to start.

Seth and Gus both drove us since they claimed to have nothing better to do. I suspected they simply wanted to get away from the housework and gardening. I traveled in the cabin with Lincoln and pretended not to feel awkward as he watched me from the opposite seat.

"You're happy," he hedged when we were almost at Harcourt House.

"I am."

"Because of the news from France?"

I nodded, smiling.

"You didn't seem happy when I told you in the kitchen."

"It came as a surprise, that's all. It took some time to sink in."

"Good." He hooked the curtain with his finger and tugged it back as far as it would go. He peered out at the elegant Mayfair houses. "I was afraid my actions had been thoughtless and made you unhappy."

I frowned. He seemed genuinely concerned that he'd upset me by seeking out information about my mother. "Lincoln, you've given me quite a number of gifts. This cloak for one thing, gloves and hats. The chatelaine most recently too."

He let go of the curtain and gave me his attention.

"But none of them are as special as the gift of that letter."

He returned to looking out the window and our gazes locked in the reflection. "It cost me nothing," he said, breaking the connection.

"It would have taken you considerable time to write all those letters to France. That's not nothing."

"The information is from the matron, not me. You can show her your gratitude when you meet her."

I shook my head and smiled. "You're impossible."

"And you're not like any female I've met."

I laughed. "Then you need to go to more balls and dinners."

"I doubt I'll find another there."

The coach slowed to a stop. It dipped as Seth jumped down. He opened the door and held out his hand for me, but I didn't take it straight away. I angled myself so that my body blocked the doorway then quickly kissed Lincoln on the cheek.

"The best gifts come from the heart," I told him, "not a jeweler's shop or the dressmaker's. Thank you for writing the letters and offering to take me to Paris. It's very sweet of you."

I had the very great satisfaction of seeing him stunned. His eyes had never been so wide, nor his jaw as slack. I stepped out of the coach, with a smile for Seth, and waited on the pavement. It was a long time before Lincoln emerged, his bland expression once more in place.

Millard, the butler, opened the door to us and almost stumbled backward in aghast at seeing me alongside Lincoln. The last time I'd called at Harcourt House, he had pointed out that maids should enter through the service entrance.

He recovered enough to bow and step aside. "Mr. Fitzroy, sir. How good to see you again."

"And you." Lincoln presented me as if I were a debutante and Millard the queen. "You remember Miss Holloway."

"Of course." The bow he gave me was considerably shallower than the one he gave Lincoln.

"Is his lordship at home for callers?"

"Not at present. Lady Harcourt and the dowager Lady Harcourt are both here, however."

"Please inform them I'd like to speak with them both."

"Of course, sir. If you will wait in the drawing room."

Despite being smaller, the drawing room was even more spectacular than the one at Emberly House with its soft green velvet curtains, and crimson and gold carpet. Where Emberly's walls were covered with paintings of cows and countryside, this drawing room was more elegantly decorated with pictures of women and children. I assumed they were family members, but it was odd that there wasn't a single man in any of the paintings. Each one was framed in heavy gold, as were the three mirrors, and gold leaf decorated the mantelpiece, ceiling and much of the furniture. The dowager's tastes ran to less clutter than her daughter-in-law's, making the room appear large and airy. I liked the room considerably more for it.

Lady Harcourt—Julia—sailed in, a surprised smile on her face. It turned hard when she spotted me. It would seem Millard hadn't thought me important enough to announce. "Lincoln, Charlie, how lovely to see you." She greeted Lincoln with a kiss on his cheek. "To what do I owe this pleasure?"

"We need to speak with Lord and Lady Harcourt," he said.

Her gaze shifted to me then back again. "What about?"

"We learned some things at Emberly Park that need clarification."

"We?" she echoed, once more eyeing me. "Lincoln, what is going on? Why is Charlie here?"

Marguerite took that moment to enter. Unlike her mother-in-law, she didn't so much glide into the room, but rather she padded with heavy feet and swaying hips. She greeted Lincoln cordially but frowned through his introduction of me as if she couldn't quite place me.

"Tea, m'lady?" Millard asked.

Julia lifted her brow at Lincoln, but he shook his head. "No, thank you, Millard," she said. "You may go. Please close the door."

He bowed himself out and shut the double doors.

"Madam," Lincoln began, but stopped when Marguerite lifted her hand.

She hadn't taken her eyes off me since sitting down. Now she sat forward and pointed at me. "That's your housemaid."

"Miss Holloway is my assistant."

"She looks very much like your maid."

Julia arched her brow at him, but he paid her no mind. I suddenly wished the sofa would swallow me up. I didn't know why I had thought this would be a good idea. Of course both ladies would find it abhorrent that I sat in their drawing room, let alone pried into their private matters. Lincoln should never have included me on this excursion.

Then again, it was precisely what I'd wanted him to do. I'd wanted to be his partner in investigations, to be more than a maid within the ministry. It wasn't fair that I thought him wrong now for doing exactly as I requested. Nor should I feel awkward in the presence of these ladies. I might be beneath them in situation, but I was Julia's equal in birth and at least Marguerite's equal in intelligence. I wouldn't want to be in either woman's position now.

"Miss Holloway and I returned from Emberly Park this morning."

Lincoln's declaration was met with a gasp from Marguerite. Her hand fluttered to her chest and she looked to the closed doors. Wishing her husband was present, perhaps? "Why did you go there when you knew we were here?"

"To find out if your brother-in-law visited the house or not."

"My husband told you he did not. Was his word not good enough?"

"No."

Marguerite's lips pinched. "This is outrageous!"

"Lincoln didn't mean it like that, Marguerite." Julia gave Lincoln a withering glare.

He ignored them both. "It seems that Buchanan did go to Emberly that day, after all." I eyed him carefully, but if I'd not known he was stretching the truth to test her, I wouldn't have guessed. "He was seen in the grounds."

"He was not!" She flattened her hands over her lap, stretching her fingers. "He couldn't have been, since he wasn't there."

"Mr. Edgecombe saw him from his window."

"John! B-but you cannot believe everything he tells you. H-he's…not quite right in the head. Ever since the accident…" She put out a hand to her mother-in-law.

After a long moment, Julia took it. "He was in a riding accident, a year or so ago," she said. "He changed after that. He drinks heavily, for one thing. Are you sure he wasn't mistaken?"

"He must be," Marguerite blurted. She shot another longing glance at the door.

"It's difficult to say," Lincoln said.

"Did the servants see him?" Julia asked.

"No, but they were lying."

"How do you know?"

Lincoln's gaze slid to her. She pressed her lips together.

Marguerite looked as if she would burst into tears at any moment. She continued to glance at the door, but I began to wonder if it was because it was her only escape route and not because she hoped her husband would walk in and rescue her.

"Mr. Edgecombe told me that Mr. Buchanan fought with a man in the family graveyard on the rise," I said. "Near the mausoleum."

Marguerite's face drained of color. Her hands shook. Julia frowned. "Is it necessary to bring up old wounds?"

"We believe the baby is integral to this investigation," Lincoln told her.

She scoffed. "Don't be ridiculous. How can that be?"

"Marguerite, may we speak with you alone?"

Julia's back straightened. "Are you throwing me out of my own drawing room?"

Lincoln's glare at Marguerite didn't waver. I wanted to warn him to scale back his sternness, for the sake of her nerves, but I couldn't catch his attention.

"Perhaps you could fetch tea for Lady Harcourt," I said to Julia. "She might need it."

Julia went rigid. "I do not *fetch* anything, Charlie. That is what Millard is for."

"My apologies," I mumbled as my face heated. "I just thought she might like some privacy."

"Oh, for goodness' sake, she might as well stay now." Marguerite dabbed at her eyes with her pinky finger. "Everyone else seems to know, even the maid. Hector was full-term," she told Julia. "He lived only a day then died in my arms."

Julia patted her hand. "Oh, my dear. I am sorry. But it happened over five years ago."

"Can I not still mourn him?" Marguerite spat. "It may not be the done thing in your circles, Julia, but he was my *son*." Despite her dabbing, a tear escaped. Lincoln handed her his handkerchief.

"That isn't what I meant," Julia said quietly. "Of course you still mourn him." She appealed to Lincoln.

"Marguerite, I'm sorry to have to ask you this," he said. "It's a delicate matter regarding the baby's father."

Julia retracted her hand as if it had been slapped away. She stared at Marguerite, who'd gone very still. Even her tears had stopped.

"Is it Andrew Buchanan?"

"How do you know?" Marguerite whispered.

"The fight at the mausoleum, his interest in Estelle Pearson, some gossip…we joined the pieces together."

"No." Julia shook her head over and over. "Surely not. *Andrew*?"

Marguerite nodded.

"But he…he…" Julia slumped back on the sofa as if she'd been pushed, unconcerned that she was crushing her bustle. "He never breathed a word."

"You think he tells you everything?" Marguerite bit off. "He doesn't, you know."

"How long had Buchanan known?" Lincoln asked.

"I told him when I first discovered my state," Marguerite said. "But he…he refused to do anything about it."

"That sounds like Andrew," Julia said on a sigh.

"It was not his fault." Marguerite fired back. "Indeed, it was yours!"

"Mine?"

"His father gave Andrew's inheritance to you." Marguerite growled like a dog protecting her cubs. "Andrew had no money, no house, nothing. Of course he couldn't support a wife or family. It is grossly unfair!"

"He could have found work. He went to university, for goodness' sake. He's not an imbecile."

"It may be very well for schoolmasters' daughters to tread the boards at The Alhambra, but not for barons' sons!"

Julia's face flamed, her eyes flashed. "You foolish girl. If you think Andrew refused to marry you because he had no money, then I am sorry to inform you of your mistake. There was a stipulation in my husband's will that if Andrew marries, he receives a generous annuity from the estate."

Marguerite's mouth flopped open.

"Andrew knew that. So did Donald." Julia sat upright again and rose. "I've had quite enough grubbiness for one day. I no longer wish to be a part of this conversation."

"Stay," Lincoln said quietly. "You are the one who brought this to my attention and asked me to investigate. You'll remain to hear all the details."

She hesitated then sat again. I wasn't sure I would have been so acquiescent if Lincoln had spoken to me the way he spoke to her. It seemed most unlike her to put up with it. Perhaps she really did want to hear more grubby details, and her attempted storming out was for show only.

"Marguerite," Lincoln said, "did your husband know the baby wasn't his?"

"Yes, but not until after the birth." All the fire she'd displayed in her defense of Buchanan had gone out of her and she was once more a pale, forlorn figure. "It was obvious that Hector was full-term, and I admitted everything. He was angry, at first, but then he realized we hadn't even begun courting when Andrew and I…when it happened. Our marriage was a hasty one, you see, at my request. We'd known one another for some time, of course, and he had asked to court me but I'd always refused. When I acquiesced, we married almost immediately."

It aligned with what Estelle Pearson had told us so it must be the truth. However I wondered if Marguerite really knew her husband's thoughts on the matter. How many men would be so understanding upon discovering their younger brother had fathered their wife's child? And did he know that his wife still held a torch for Andrew?

"I think this throws water over your theory that Andrew was at Emberly recently," Julia said. "If he has known about the baby for years, why stir up old wounds now?"

I looked to Lincoln as a small frown connected his brows. "Unless his visit had nothing to do with the baby, after all," I said.

"You must be mistaken," Marguerite said with an unladylike sniff. "Andrew wasn't there, fighting with anyone on my baby's grave. Either it was someone else or John got confused. It happens, from time to time."

The double doors suddenly burst open and Lord Harcourt strode in, looking like thunder. "Fitzroy," he barked.

Lincoln stood and met him in between the two sofas. He held his arms casually at his side, whereas Harcourt's fists pumped. "I'm glad you're here," Lincoln said. "I have questions for you."

Marguerite rose and took her husband's arm, pinning herself to his side. Her bottom lip was thrust so far forward in a pout that it looked as if a bee had stung it. "Darling, he's been asking questions about Hector again. And…and about Andrew."

"Out!" Harcourt exploded. "Get out!" Then he did a very foolish thing. He stepped up to Lincoln and swung his fist.

CHAPTER 12

Lincoln caught Harcourt's fist a mere inch from his face. He didn't flinch. "Not in front of the ladies," he said.

Harcourt spluttered a garbled protest and looked as if he would wind up his other fist.

"Donald, *please*," his wife begged. She batted his shoulder with the hand that still clutched Lincoln's handkerchief, her face pale and pinched. "Don't fight him."

"Not here," Julia said, briskly. "I don't want blood on the sofa. Come now, everyone sit down and be friends again. This will not do."

I admired her determination to keep the meeting civilized. I wasn't sure I could have stepped between them like she did. While she shooed Harcourt with one hand, she placed her other on Lincoln's chest. Ah. *Now* I saw why she had stepped between them.

I folded my hands in my lap and kept my head bowed as Lincoln returned to the sofa beside me. I kept my gaze on my linked fingers.

"Explain yourself, Fitzroy," Harcourt snapped. "What is the meaning of your inquisition this time?"

"Your brother was seen fighting with someone at Emberly Park on the evening he disappeared. It was the last time he was seen."

I lifted my head when Harcourt didn't respond. All the bluster leached out of him as we all waited, watching. "Seen?" he asked.

"Only by John," Marguerite told him.

"Fighting with whom?"

"Presumably with you," Lincoln said.

Harcourt's brows rose. "Do you have proof?"

"Of your involvement? No. However, a button engraved with the letter B was found at the mausoleum, as was some blood. Your brother hasn't been sighted since."

Julia's narrowed gaze pinned me. "Is he… That is to say, do you think he has met with…?" She fingered the black choker at her throat.

"We believe he's still alive," I said before she could accidentally divulge my necromancy to the Harcourts.

Her eyes fluttered closed. She breathed deeply. "Thank God."

"Pray that you're right," Marguerite said weakly.

"Harcourt," Lincoln prompted. "It's time you explained what happened."

Lord Harcourt, however, had just registered my presence. "Why is your maid here?"

"She works for me as an assistant now. Everything you wish to say to me can be said in front of her."

"I think not."

Lincoln's small sigh probably couldn't be heard by anyone except me. He was frustrated, and I felt guilty at being the cause of it.

"Donald, please, just tell us what happened," Marguerite whined. "Where is Andrew?"

"I don't know," he said tightly. "And that is the truth. We met around dusk as I was out riding. He'd seen me as he approached the house and hailed me. We talked for a long time. It became heated and we fought. I'm afraid he did hit his head and lost some blood. He was quite groggy for several minutes, but then he got up. I can assure you, he walked away. I told him to call in at Dr. Turcott's house and have the wound seen to."

"He never saw the doctor," Lincoln said. "We don't think he made it back to the village."

Harcourt scrubbed his face. "My God. Where is he?"

"Why didn't you invite him to dine with us?" Marguerite asked. "If you had, none of this would have happened?"

"I did. He refused."

"But why? It's been so long since he's been to Emberly. To have come so far and not dine with his family…I don't understand it."

"My dear, did you not hear me? We fought."

"Yes, but I haven't seen him since your father's funeral." Tears hovered on her eyelids. She dabbed at them again with Lincoln's handkerchief.

Julia's gaze was the first to slip away, then Harcourt's. As the realization slowly came over Marguerite that Andrew was likely avoiding her, her face fell further.

"What did you fight about?" I asked in an attempt to distract attention from her so she could recover. "The baby?"

"Money," Harcourt said.

"Money?" Julia lifted her shoulders. "But I give him a monthly sum to live on."

"It's not enough according to him. Andrew's tastes are expensive, Julia, you know that. No matter how much you give him, it will never be enough, because he'll gamble it all away." To Lincoln and me, he said, "He told me his debts have become too high and that his creditors are requesting payment."

"Oh, Andrew," Marguerite muttered.

"Our fight had nothing to do with the child. That matter was laid to rest years ago, along with Hector."

"So you refused to give him money and he became violent," Lincoln said.

"In a nutshell, yes. Andrew threatened to blackmail me when I first refused. He said he would make it known that I wasn't the baby's father. I think that's why he insisted on speaking to me at little Hector's grave. My brother has always enjoyed theatrics." This was said with a pointed look at Julia.

She pretended not to notice.

"I refused to give in," Harcourt went on. "I reminded him that he could get his hands on his annuity if he married. He said he'd rather gouge his eyes out, and declared that it was my responsibility as the elder brother and current baron to assist him. Once again, I refused. Then he brought up the order you belong to."

"Ministry," Lincoln corrected.

Julia sat forward. "What do you mean?"

Harcourt sighed. "He very recently discovered Father's link to your ministry through the journal he finally got around to reading. He must have been bored one night to open up that old thing and Father's other books. He said it took him several weeks of following up names, places and dates noted in the journal, but he worked out what Father and the others were up to. He told me that if I didn't give him money, he would tell the newspapers about the supernatural gibberish Father was involved in. As I already told you, I refused to give in. I don't care a whit whether Father was mad, or whether the world thinks he was. That's when we fought."

"That's what prompted him to go to Emberly," I said. "He'd only just pieced together the puzzle and decided to use it to his advantage."

Lincoln nodded. "So he left the estate in the dark, on foot, with a bleeding head wound. Not to mention that he was disappointed in your refusal to help."

"Oh, Donald," Marguerite said on a sigh. "Why didn't you go after him and give him some money? He's your brother. He *needs* you."

Harcourt lifted his chin. "He's hopeless."

"Yes, but we must make allowances for him being the younger brother. He was never given the same responsibilities as you, or the same opportunities."

Harcourt snorted. "He was pampered by our mother."

"As was my brother. John is so like Andrew. At least, he was before the accident. And yet you've given John a home and comforts."

Harcourt gave another snort. "You are right there. They are very much alike. I cannot support them both. It's unthinkable. Besides, Julia is supporting Andrew." He flashed a hard, cold smile at her. "Our dear stepmother is more than happy to help her beloved stepson. Aren't you, Julia?"

Marguerite's nervous gazed shifted between them. Julia returned Harcourt's smile, but with more softness. "Of course I'm happy to help," she said smoothly. "Andrew and I are company for one another."

"How pleasant for you both," Harcourt sneered.

"Did Buchanan mention where he was staying that night?" Lincoln asked.

"No, but I do know where he was planning to go next. My brother is such a fool. After I refused to support his gambling habit, he declared that he was going to consult a seer and win some ready for himself."

"A seer?" the rest of us echoed.

"He says he found her name in Father's journal then cross-checked it against some ministry archives you keep in the attic, Julia. I told him the idea was absurd, and that he'd lost his mind, but he was determined to find her and use her so-called foresight to learn the winner of an upcoming boxing match. If it worked, he would use her again to place strategic bets all over the city, culminating in next spring's racing carnivals." He snorted. "I told him he was a fool and he laughed in my face. He said I was the fool and always had been."

Marguerite tucked her feet underneath the sofa and wrung her hands together. She did not meet her husband's gaze, even though he didn't stop looking at her.

"Do you remember the seer's name?" Lincoln asked.

"Leah, Lill, something foreign. Do you think that's where he went?"

"It's possible."

"I don't know if this supernatural business is real or not, nor do I want to know. If I can't see it or touch it, then I want no part of it."

"How fortunate that your father gave me the responsibility of being on the committee then," Julia said with a smile that didn't disguise the sting in her tone.

"You'll get no argument from me, but you might from Andrew. He seemed put out that he wasn't even informed." Harcourt slapped his hands down on the arms of his chair and pushed himself to his feet. "Christ, I need a drink."

Lincoln and I rose as Harcourt poured himself a glass of brandy at the sideboard, but Julia didn't let us leave immediately. Or rather, she didn't let Lincoln leave. She hung onto his arm. "We are all grateful that you're looking into Andrew's disappearance, Lincoln. You've done a marvelous job so far."

"Marvelous," Marguerite echoed as she tugged on the bell pull. "Do continue to keep us informed. We're most anxious to have Andrew return to the family bosom. Aren't we, Donald?"

"Of course," Harcourt muttered, lifting the glass to his lips. "I just wish it required less turning over of old stones."

"The stones have only been turned over in private," Julia assured him. "Mr. Fitzroy is a gentleman and won't reveal anything told to him in confidence."

"And her?" Harcourt pointed his glass at me. I felt like he was poking me in the shoulder in the hopes of picking a fight.

"Miss Holloway can be trusted to keep silent," Lincoln said.

Harcourt's top lip curled. "We all know what gossips the servants can be."

Millard, who'd entered at that moment, stiffened, which was quite a feat since he was already rigid. Julia finally relinquished her grasp on Lincoln's arm and Millard showed us to the front door.

Outside, Seth lounged on the driver's seat while Gus leaned back against the coach, one foot resting on the step behind him. He came to attention when we joined him, and opened the door.

"You're supposed to give her your hand, you Philistine," Seth said, from the edge of the driver's seat.

Gus rolled his eyes and I smiled back. "I can manage," I assured him.

He held out his hand anyway. "What's a Philistine?" he whispered as I stepped past him.

"I don't know," I whispered back. "Handsome cove?"

He grinned a somewhat sinister grin thanks to his broken teeth, but the humor dancing in his eyes softened it considerably.

"I'm sorry I wasn't much help in there," I said to Lincoln as the coach rolled away. "I was probably more of a hindrance."

"They'll grow used to you."

I pulled a face. "I hope not, only because I wish never to see the Harcourts again once Buchanan is found. Except the dowager, of course. I can't avoid her."

"I'll shield you from the committee members as much as possible."

"Thank you, but I don't wish to be shielded. If I am to work with you—"

"*For* me."

"If I am, then I must be prepared to face them, from time to time, across cups of tea."

"They will come to accept you. I'll see to it."

I didn't know how. Centuries of tradition and prejudice couldn't be wiped out with a few choice words, even if those words were spoken by someone who was not easily trifled with.

"Do you recall the name of a seer in the journal?" I asked. "Leah, I think Harcourt said."

"Lela. It appeared in the first few pages."

"You have a good memory."

"Yes."

I suppressed a smile. He wasn't shy about his many abilities. "Can a seer really predict which horse will win a race?"

"It doesn't work like that, as far as I am aware."

"Buchanan will be disappointed when he discovers it. So how does it work?"

"Since I am the only seer I know, and my talent is limited, I cannot be entirely sure. I have vague feelings, impressions if you like, and only about people I am close to. You, Seth and Gus, for example. I know when you are about to seek me out, and occasionally the gist of what you are about to say, if not the exact words. I can also predict when you are about to slap me, for instance."

Was he trying to make a joke? Yes, I think so. His eyes danced merrily and his features lifted a little. "That's because it usually comes immediately after you've admitted doing something worthy of a slap. I hardly call that a fine example of your talent."

"Granted, your temper is easy to predict."

I laughed. "What's put you in such a fine mood? I feel positively wretched after spending time with that family. They aren't particularly supportive of one another. There is even an undercurrent of dislike between Lord and Lady Harcourt, although outwardly he seems to dote on her and she depend on him."

"I hadn't noticed."

"For a seer, you're quite blind at times. Don't you think it's odd that you are aware when I am not in the house, yet you don't understand other people at all?"

He shifted on the seat, and I wondered if my observation had made him feel inadequate. He was so used to being competent that this failing might bother him. "As I said, my talent is limited. I couldn't tell you if we were about to have an accident, for example, or who will win a boxing match."

"I wonder if this Lela can."

"We'll find out tomorrow, when we visit her."

"Where will we find her? We should have asked the dowager if we could look through the archives too, like Buchanan did."

"No need. I've made copies of them and stored them in the attic at Lichfield. The records are catalogued by name and cross-referenced to an index of supernatural talents. There are not many seers listed. It won't take long to find Lela."

"Why am I not surprised that you're so organized?"

"We'll check the records together. It's time you became familiar with them. Once you are, you can create a new entry for Estelle Pearson, and update the one about yourself."

Oh. Of course I would be listed in his catalogue. I wasn't sure whether to be pleased or disconcerted, however. Perhaps a little of both. It was, after all, nice to be worthy of being catalogued yet troubling for the same reason.

* * *

Lela lived in a van on Mitcham Common on the southern edge of the city. She was a gypsy, and we were fortunate that it was coming up to winter or she and her family would have been traveling through the countryside, picking fruit. The cold weather brought the Romany gypsies back to London, and its numerous commons, where they squeezed what small fortune they could from selling their crafts or pushing grinding barrows through the streets to sharpen scissors, saws and knives.

I'd never been to Mitcham. My haunts were north of the river, in the familiar territory of my childhood. It took us some time to drive from Highgate to the city's south, but at least the weather was fine. It would have been difficult going if the unmade roads near the common had been muddy. As it was, Seth had a devil of a time avoiding potholes, much to Gus's annoyance.

"You think you can do better?" I heard Seth growl when Gus once again swore at him for not maneuvering around a rough patch that caused me to almost bounce off the seat. "The landau's not as nimble as the brougham."

Thankfully we soon reached the common and the jolting came to an abrupt stop. There was only a rough track ahead, so we would have to walk through the gypsy camp to inquire after Lela. The common really was little more than a campsite. Tents and vans huddled around smoky fires, their flaps and awnings fluttering in the breeze. Horses grazed on the open grass and several dogs lazed beneath the carts and vans. Some fifty or so dirty faces watched us through eyes the same deep black as Lincoln's. If I'd not known he was part gypsy already, I would have guessed now.

Seth and Gus jumped down from the driver's seat. Gus's jacket flipped open, revealing the bone handle of a gun tucked into his trousers.

"We'll wait here," Seth said, keeping a watchful eye on an advancing group of children.

"Oi, get back," Gus growled at him.

"They're only looking at the horses and rig," I told them.

"Don't be so sure, Charlie. They're thieves, the lot of 'em."

"As was I," I said. "But I wouldn't of stealed a horse from under your nose now, would I?" I let my slum accent come through, playing it up a little to remind him that I had been no different to those children only a few short months earlier.

Gus was too busy watching the children to notice.

"How up to date is the information about Lela?" I asked Lincoln as we followed the track into the camp.

My first glimpse at the ministry's archives had been a revelation. Centuries of investigations had been meticulously recorded, with anyone suspected of possessing a magical talent noted down and filed away. It wasn't just names and addresses, but also the type of magic they possessed, the names of immediate relations, and a note on how harmless they were deemed to be. Most of the records were old, the subjects deceased, but Lela's entry had been added relatively recently.

"It's several years old," Lincoln said, as he scanned the crude dwellings.

"Do you think she still lives here through the winter?"

"Gypsy groups follow the same pattern of travel every year, going to the same farms in the summer and returning to the same camps in winter. If Lela's still alive, she should be here."

"And if she's dead?"

"We'll have to look for Buchanan elsewhere."

A group of burly men emerged from between the tents like a slow moving tide and blocked our route. They wore long coats that had probably once been black or rich brown but were now faded to gray and a muddy dun. Some were hatless, one wore a cap and another a broad brimmed hat more suited to a farmhand. Bushy moustaches and beards did nothing to hide their angular cheekbones and the undisguised challenge in their eyes.

I shuffled closer to Lincoln and glanced over my shoulder at Seth and Gus. They watched us from the coach, hands hovering near their waistbands where their weapons were stowed.

"We're looking for a woman known as Lela," Lincoln said. He opened his palm to reveal several coins.

One of the men reached for the money but Lincoln snapped his hand closed. He arched a brow in lazy inquiry.

"What d'you want wiv 'er?" the man in the cap asked in a thick accent.

"My friend is missing and I have reason to believe he came here to speak with her."

"He ain't here."

"I know, but I wanted to find out if he ever made it or got lost along the way. You are not under suspicion."

The man spoke to his companions in a foreign language. I wondered if it was one Lincoln understood. He gave no sign that he did, however, and waited for them to address him again.

"Old Lela be tired," the man said. "Come back tomorrow."

Lincoln dipped into his waistcoat pocket and pulled out more coins.

One of the hatless men scooped them up and the one in the cap jerked his head toward a wagon. "In there."

The large wagon was one of the sturdiest and certainly the brightest in the camp. Crimson curtains covered the windows and the door was painted to match. Panels along the side bore a swirling pattern in deep green with hints of yellow that appeared golden in the beams of sunlight filtering through the clouds.

I stood behind Lincoln as he knocked and felt my skirts shift in a direction opposite to the breeze. Without looking, I thrust out my hand and caught the wrist of the little thief.

"You have to do better than that," I told the lad. He was no higher than my waist with black hair sticking out at all angles from his head and serious eyes that held no fear, only defiance.

"How'd you know?" he asked.

"It takes a thief to catch a thief."

The eyes widened and I winked at him. His jaw dropped and he eyed me up and down as if he were seeing me for the first time. "You never."

The door to the wagon opened and a stooped woman, wearing a faded red scarf over gray hair, regarded us. Even though she stood four steps above Lincoln, she was still only his height. She regarded him closely. At least, I think she did. Her eyes were hard to see, lost as they were amid deep wrinkles.

One of the men who'd followed us said something in the foreign tongue, but Lincoln interrupted him in the same language. The woman, who I assumed was Lela, chuckled so hard her entire body shook. She stepped aside and indicated for him to enter.

Lincoln spoke again and I caught my name amid the sharp consonants and throaty vowels. Lela nodded then disappeared inside the wagon. I followed and Lincoln stepped up behind me.

The wagon wasn't a simple farmer's cart that had been covered over. It was a home with a table, a small faded blue sofa and two chests bearing the same pattern as the outside of the wagon. A large crimson curtain hid the far end from prying eyes, and a thin gray-green carpet deadened our footsteps. Throws and tasseled cushions in jewel colors covered the sofa and chairs, and several charms hung from the ceiling so that Lincoln had to duck. Both of the Harcourt ladies would have a fit at the mish-mash of colors, although Marguerite might like that the interior had a cluttered, close feel to it.

Lela indicated we should find somewhere to sit. The man who'd followed us remained near the door, his arms crossed and his feet a little apart. Her bodyguard, I suspected.

Lincoln spoke again in the foreign language and Lela glanced at me.

"I try," she responded in a heavy accent, and I realized he'd asked if she could speak English for my benefit.

I smiled. "Thank you."

She did not smile back but instead turned her focus toward Lincoln. She studied him closely and even reached over and fingered his hair. The web of wrinkles bracketing her sunken mouth drew together. She nodded slowly and said something in her own tongue.

"Half Romany," Lincoln answered.

Lela glanced at me. "Her know?"

"Miss Holloway knows."

She nodded again, this time in what I guessed to be approval, but whether that was because she approved of him not keeping his heritage a secret, or because she approved of him being half gypsy, I couldn't tell.

"Your friend?" Lela asked. "His name?"

"Andrew Buchanan." Lincoln described him, right down to his snobbery and dissoluteness.

Lela shook her head. "He not come to me." She arched thin, patchy brows at the man standing by the door, but he shook his head too.

Lincoln thanked her and stood, knocking one of the multi-faceted pendants hanging above his head. "Charlie," he said when I didn't move.

"Miss Lela," I said, "are you a real seer?"

"Some say yes, some say no." She shrugged.

"What do *you* say?"

She broke into a grin that revealed more gum than teeth. "I say I know things you do not."

"Like what?"

"Charlie," Lincoln warned.

"Like he is son of great man."

Lincoln went very still, but he did not show surprise, only apprehension.

"How great?" I asked.

Lela shrugged. "I cannot see through shadows. So many shadows. But you..." She suddenly grabbed my hand, causing Lincoln to step forward, a move that in turn made the bodyguard shift closer. "You have no shadow. You clear, bright." She let me go and traced my outline from my head to my waist without touching me directly. "You chase bad shadows away."

Lincoln grabbed my elbow and hauled me to my feet. A glare at the bodyguard caused him to step aside.

"Er, thank you, Lela," I tossed back as Lincoln directed me down the wagon steps ahead of him, not altogether gently.

She said something in her own tongue that had Lincoln's hold tightening on my elbow as he marched me through the camp. Lela's chuckle followed us on the breeze.

"What did she say?" I asked, repeating her words as best as I could.

His hard gaze didn't waver from the coach, up ahead, where Seth and Gus were surrounded by gypsy men. "Nothing."

"It wasn't nothing. She thought it was amusing, but you did not."

There was no opportunity to question him further. The small crowd gathered around our horses and coach looked angry. Sleeves had been rolled up to reveal strong forearms, and one or two men danced on light feet, fists raised in Gus's direction. He stood between Seth and the horses and looked very relieved to see Lincoln.

"What's going on?" Lincoln growled, finally letting me go with a little shove in the direction of the children who stood out of the way.

"Bloody Gus thought it would be a good idea to take up the challenge of a dice game with these…fellows," Seth said. "He lost."

"They cheated!" Gus cried.

"You didn't have to accuse them! Now you've offended their honor or something."

"But they cheated!"

"Shut it," Seth hissed.

Lincoln reached into his inside pocket and pulled out a small pouch filled with coin. The gypsy men lowered their fists and one snatched at the pouch.

I bent down to the little boy next to me, the same one who'd tried to pick my pocket. "What does *fara scapare* mean?" I whispered in an accent I hoped was close to Lela's.

The boy wrinkled his face and I worried that his Romany might not be very good or that my accent was atrocious. "No escape," he said after a moment then held out his hand for a coin.

I turned out my empty pocket to show him that I had nothing to give. His face fell. I bent closer to his ear. "Allow me to pass on something I learned when I was only a little older than you."

He looked at me dubiously, perhaps regretting that he hadn't asked to see a coin first before translating.

"When picking a woman's skirt pocket," I said, "move with the breeze, not against it."

"Charlie!" Seth shouted. "Hurry up."

I kissed the top of the boy's greasy head then took the hand that Lincoln held out for me and climbed into the cabin.

No escape.

CHAPTER 13

To my dismay, two of my least favorite people were waiting for us upon our return to Lichfield. I groaned as I recognized General Eastbrooke and Lord Gillingham's coaches and horses.

"What are they doing here?"

"Either Julia or Harcourt has informed them that we've made progress in our search for Buchanan," Lincoln said.

"But why do they need to come here to discuss it?"

"Perhaps they're not here to discuss the developments, but my methods."

I frowned at him until it dawned on me what he meant. "Oh. You mean my involvement."

"I'll tell them it was necessary for you to summon Buchanan's spirit as a test. They'll see reason."

"I doubt it," I muttered.

The coach slowed at the top of the drive instead of taking us around the back as Lincoln usually preferred. He rarely stood on ceremony, but his visitors would expect him to heed propriety and enter through the front door.

"I should come with you and talk to them, since it involves me," I said.

"That may not be wise."

"No, but it's cowardly for me not to."

He leveled his gaze on me. "You are not a coward, Charlie."

I gave him a grim smile, and decided that I would act as maid and bring in refreshments. It would give me a legitimate excuse to be among them, and Lincoln couldn't send me away.

As it turned out, I had to act as maid anyway. Seth and Gus remained in the stables to tend to the horses. I suspected they remained outside purposely to avoid our guests.

Cook was already assembling teacups on a tray when I entered the kitchen. "'Bout bloody time," he muttered, shoving the tray at me. "Thought I was going to have to wait on 'em myself." He shooed me away with a flick of his apron and some grumbled words of which I only caught "Gillingham" and "prick."

I hurried along the corridor to the parlor at the front of the house. The general's blustery voice drifted clearly out to me before I reached it.

"...doesn't justify your methods, Lincoln."

"He's a peer of the realm, for God's sake!" Gillingham exploded. "That alone puts him above reproach."

"Not to mention he's Buchanan's brother. He's hardly going to clock him, is he?"

"Your accusation was made doubly humiliating by having your maid overhear it all, Fitzroy. For God's sake, man, what were you thinking?"

Ah, yes, there was the slight against me that I expected. It didn't bother me, since I cared nothing for Gillingham's opinion, and I entered the parlor without any anxiety.

"I wasn't accusing him of anything," Lincoln said, as he took the tray from me with a nod of thanks. "And Charlie had every right to be there. She's assisting me. Tea, General?"

Eastbrooke muttered something incomprehensible that I suspected was a protest about a number of things—Lincoln serving tea, and me being involved in the investigation, chief among them.

"You are being deliberately provocative, Fitzroy," Gillingham said, looking down his nose at me. "Her involvement is unnecessary and inappropriate."

"I think not." Lincoln's bored dismissal disguised an undercurrent of frustration, which I suspected only I noticed. "Involving Charlie is effective. We now know Buchanan is alive."

"Use her necromancy by all means, under supervision, but do not invite her into Lord Harcourt's drawing room!"

Lincoln handed Gillingham a teacup then looked to me. "Tea, Charlie?"

"Yes, thank you." I sat on a chair, well away from the two visitors who were both still standing. The general glanced at the sofa behind him, as if he didn't know what to do, and Gillingham set down his cup on a table.

"Very well," he said on a sniff. "If you insist on remaining here, child, I cannot be responsible for the things you'll overhear."

"I'm sure you *can* be responsible," I countered, "but you choose to say them anyway. Go ahead. I doubt my sensibilities are as delicate as those of other ladies."

"No doubt you will have heard worse in the sewers." He picked up his teacup again and addressed Lincoln. "You're too lenient on her, Fitzroy."

"Agreed," the general said, eyeing me with a frown as he sipped his tea.

"Raising the witch proves she is a danger—"

"That matter has been resolved." Lincoln's voice was as sharp as cut glass. "Estelle Pearson has been sent back."

"I didn't know she was a witch," I told them.

Gillingham didn't look at me. I might as well not have spoken. "By taking her to Harcourt House yesterday, you have exposed Lord and Lady Harcourt to an indignity they should never have had to endure."

"I'm quite sure Marguerite's illegitimate child had nothing to do with Charlie."

I smiled into my teacup, only to jump when Gillingham stamped the end of his walking stick into the floor. "This is not a joke! She is your *maid*, Fitzroy, and a gutter rat at that. Can you not see the harm you do to your reputation, and that of Lichfield—"

"My reputation is *none* of your concern."

The earl recoiled at Lincoln's low, vicious snarl. "General?" Gillingham turned to his friend, his face a patchwork of pink splotches. "Surely you have something to add. Or is it up to me to rein in your man? Again."

But the general was still staring at me over the rim of his teacup, as if he were trying to go unnoticed. Despite my conviction not to let it bother me, I felt my color rise.

"My God," the general murmured. He lowered his cup and turned to Lincoln. "You've developed feelings for the chit."

I dropped my teacup into the saucer so hard that a small chip flew off. My face flamed. My heart thumped. I wanted to hear Lincoln's answer a little too much for my own comfort.

"Charlie is living here under my protection." Lincoln had gone quite still. Even his lips hardly moved as he spoke. "My feelings for her are as a guardian toward his ward."

My teacup rattled in its saucer. I set them down on the table and studied my hands in my lap. My guardian. So that's how it was for him. It was all very proper and respectable, considering the circumstances. And yet I didn't want proper and respectable. I wanted him to be very improper with me.

"I've never known you to allow anyone as much leeway as you give her," the general protested. "There's no other explanation."

"She is my employee," Lincoln ground out, delivering every word with a blunt, brutal edge. "To imply otherwise is inappropriate."

"Since when have you cared about what is appropriate? Anyway, you just said she is like a ward to you. So which is it? Ward or employee?"

Lincoln's answer was an ice-cold glare that forced even the formidable general to sway back a little.

"If this is true," Gillingham said, glancing between them, "she cannot stay here! Once she has you dancing to her tune she'll use her necromancy and unleash chaos!"

"That is ridiculous," I said.

Gillingham's head jerked round to look at me, but Lincoln got in before he spoke. "Charlie's right. This entire conversation is absurd. If you're quite done, then see yourselves to the door. We have work to do."

"Hear him out," Eastbrooke said.

Gillingham nodded his thanks at the general. "I know how women work, particularly women of her ilk."

"There is no ilk where Charlie is concerned," Lincoln said in that quiet, commanding voice of his.

The general shook his head sadly. "And you tell us you have no feelings for her," he muttered. "It is quite obvious that you do."

My heart lifted, and I frowned at Lincoln, trying to determine if there was any truth in the general's observations. But he merely scowled harder than I'd ever seen him scowl.

He strode to the door. "Good day, gentlemen."

The general shook his head sadly and followed, but Gillingham remained where he was. "Good lord, use your head, man! You must see that she has far too much power over you now."

"All I see is a man who is not listening to a thing I'm saying. Get out of my house before I throw you out."

Gillingham stalked past Lincoln, his walking stick barely hitting the floor. "This is not over."

Lincoln followed the two men, and I slipped through the far door that led to the unused music room to avoid him. In something of a daze, I made my way outside, desperate to escape the house. And Lincoln.

I needed a few moments alone to think. I ruled out hiding in the orchard. Autumn had stripped the trees of coverage, and he would look there first. The stables were now quiet except for horses munching on their feed. Seth and Gus had finished their duties. I climbed the ladder to the loft and picked my way past a rusty wheel, some tools, and a cracked leather saddle, to the bags of feed piled into a pyramid. I sat with my back to them and swiped at the tears dampening my cheeks, willing myself to stop being a pathetic fool.

But I couldn't dislodge the memory of Lincoln's face as he denied General Eastbrooke's accusation most vehemently. It had been one of stone-cold fury. If ever I needed proof that he had no feelings for me, that look was it. And, of course, his denial. Our kiss had merely been a heat-of-the-moment thing, hastily done and just as quickly forgotten. Eastbrooke had been wrong. Lincoln wasn't in love with me.

I didn't want to rejoin the household and face him just yet, so I stretched out my legs and rested my head against the rough calico. It smelled of oats and horse, a surprisingly comforting smell that lulled me.

I sat forward as I heard footsteps pause near the door before moving closer. The top of the ladder shook with the weight of someone climbing it.

I wasn't surprised to see Lincoln's unruly, dark hair appear. He remained on the ladder and regarded me through eyes still dark with the remnants of his anger. "This looks more comfortable than the orchard."

"How did you find me?"

He tilted his head to the side and regarded me with an arched brow.

"Oh. Yes, of course. I suppose I'll never truly be able to escape you." It was meant as a joke to lighten the mood, but his face fell.

"I know I'm not the easiest person to work for, but I hope you don't wish to escape me altogether."

"That's not what I meant. Of course I don't wish to go away. I'm happy here." I bit my lip to stop myself saying something that would make this moment even more awkward.

"I'm glad to hear it."

"But if the four committee members get their way…"

"Pay Gillingham and Eastbrooke no mind. I'm not going to banish you, and they have no power to force me. Not because of…that, anyway."

That? What was "that" precisely?

"You know how things lie between us, don't you?" he asked tentatively. "You understand my…position?"

"You made it very clear to me."

His eyes clouded at my snippy retort. "Then come inside. It's cold out here and your presence is missed."

By him or the others?

We crossed the courtyard together and headed into the house through the rear service doors. Seth and Gus were in the midst of recounting the events from the gypsy camp to Cook who listened with an amused smirk.

"We were lucky we got out of there with our lives," Gus said, shaking his head.

"*You* were lucky." Seth lounged in the corner armchair and propped his booted feet on a stool. "*We* were perfectly fine. Charlie, I saw you whispering with one of the snotty-nosed little brats before we left. What about?"

"He was not a brat, nor was his nose dirty," I said.

Seth waited for an answer with an expectant air. So did Lincoln. He stood by the door, his mild gaze on me, his hands behind his back.

"He acted as interpreter, that's all."

Lincoln continued to watch me. His lips parted and he drew in a small breath as if he were about to say something, but he must have thought better of it and closed his mouth again.

"For free?" Gus asked.

"I paid him with knowledge. I told him how to be a better thief."

"Charlie!" Seth threw his hands in the air and let them fall on the chair arms. "You can't go around doing that."

"He's only a little child. I would rather he escaped the clutches of the constables than wind up separated from his family…and worse."

"Then he should stop thieving altogether!"

I rolled my eyes as Lincoln retreated from the kitchen. I didn't know why I expected him to remain after he'd fetched me. We had nothing more to discuss for now. Our investigation had once more hit a dead end, and we were no closer to finding Buchanan. Perhaps he would come up with a plan of action if we were alone.

The afternoon wore on and I continued to perform the duties expected of me as a maid, since there was no one else to do so. Nor did I particularly mind. I would rather work than sit around and sew something I neither wanted nor needed. As I was helping Cook mix the bread dough at dusk, Seth came up to me with the chatelaine box.

"I forgot," he said. "I fetched this from your room when you first asked me, but I haven't returned it to Death yet. Are you sure you still want me to?"

I shrugged. "Why wouldn't I be?"

His mouth shifted from side to side. "What is your education in the classics like?"

"The classics? As in old books?"

"Ancient Greek and Roman myths."

"Non-existent. If it wasn't Christian, Anselm Holloway didn't want it in the house. If it wasn't in the house, I didn't learn it."

"That explains it then."

"Explains what?"

"Why Fitzroy gave this to you. He knew you wouldn't understand the meaning behind it."

"Show me," Cook said, looming over my shoulder.

Seth opened the lid and the silver chatelaine winked in the light from the lamps. My breath caught. I'd forgotten how pretty it was, and how finely worked. Perhaps I'd been too hasty in asking Seth to give it back to Lincoln. Hasty and cowardly. I ought to do it myself.

"He gave it to me because it's a practical gift for a housemaid," I told Seth.

Cook looked at me. "If he wanted practical he would of given you one made of tin, and plain. This ain't no practical gift."

"No indeed." Seth pointed to the figure of the woman looking out to sea from the balcony. "Do you see the dolphin?"

"Yes," I said, peering closer. "What of it?"

"And the vine? Also, she's holding a dove."

"I didn't know it was a dove. So?"

"So, this woman is Aphrodite, a Greek goddess."

"I see. Well, it's a pretty piece, if not a practical one. I suppose Fitzroy thought I might like it. But it's much too expensive for me to accept."

And yet parting with it suddenly seemed unnecessary. I wouldn't want to offend him by returning it. I held my hand out and Seth handed the box to me with a frown.

"What do you know about Aphrodite?" he asked.

"Nothing except what you just told me. That she is depicted in artwork with dolphins and doves. You're very clever to have worked that out. I thought she was just a fine figure."

"You really don't know anything about classical symbolism, do you?"

I snorted. "Stringer and the others weren't very well versed in Greek mythology. Most of them couldn't even read."

"Put it on," Seth said before I could ask him what Aphrodite and her animals meant in Greek myth.

"Not sure that be wise," Cook said. "It be too good for kitchen work."

I hesitated only a moment then removed the chatelaine from its velvet bed. I pinned it to the waist of my skirt and let it hang loose against the dark gray fabric, where it looked even shinicr.

Seth took the box from me. "When you get a chance, you ought to learn about the Greek gods and goddesses. They're very interesting."

"Not now," Cook cut in. "That dough won't mix itself."

Seth smirked. "I'll return the box to your room, if you like."

I thanked him and decided to investigate Lincoln's library for books on classical myths later.

* * *

Unfortunately, I had no opportunity for reading that night, as the men insisted I play cards with them. Lincoln didn't join us.

Early the following morning, we had two surprise visitors—Marguerite and her brother, Mr. Edgecombe. They refused to get out of the carriage, and it wasn't until I noticed the blanket over Edgecombe's lap that I remembered why. A man like him would find it an indignity to be carried where others could see.

"May Miss Holloway and I join you?" Lincoln asked instead.

Marguerite's gloved hand tightened on the window frame. Her mouth turned down. She did not look at me.

"Very well," Mr. Edgecombe said. Unlike his sister, he didn't know me as a maid, only as Lincoln's assistant. "Come sit by me, Miss Holloway. Unless my crippled state disgusts you."

"No, sir, it does not." I climbed into the spacious cabin. "But your manner sometimes does."

Marguerite gasped. "I beg your pardon! How dare you speak to my brother that way?"

But Edgecombe only chuckled. "She has reason to, Sister." He patted the seat beside him and I sat, careful that not even my skirts impinged on his space.

Lincoln settled opposite, his knees touching mine. "I didn't think you left the house, these days, Edgecombe."

Edgecombe turned a sour gaze onto Lincoln. "You try getting in and out of carriages, up and down stairs, without the use of your bloody legs."

"John, really, do you *have* to embarrass me like this?" Marguerite muttered.

Edgecombe's brows shot up his forehead. "Embarrass you? My *dear* sister, I came all this way to London, exposing myself to ridicule if any of my old chums see me, and you accuse *me* of embarrassing *you*? You don't even know what embarrassing is until you can't perform in the bedroom like you used to."

Marguerite's face flushed scarlet.

Edgecombe reached under the seat, opened the storage compartment and pulled out a bottle of whiskey. He took a swig then wiped his mouth with the back of his hand. "Sorry, Fitzroy, but there's only enough for one."

"You came here for a reason," Lincoln said flatly. "It must be important."

"Ah, yes. I got to thinking about Buchanan after you left Emberly the other day. I'm quite sure he's dead."

Marguerite spluttered a short sob. Lincoln handed her a handkerchief and she held it to her nose.

"He's not," I said.

Lincoln gave his head a slight shake. "We don't think so."

"Buck up, Sis." Edgecombe took another swig from the bottle. "She's upset, you see, because she's still in love with her brother-in-law."

"John! That is not true. This is an indignity and I cannot bear it. I will not."

He rolled his eyes. "It's obvious to a blind man."

Marguerite blinked wet eyes and sank into the corner.

"Why do you think he's dead?" Lincoln asked.

"Because where could he be if he isn't pushing up daisies? I had my man Dawkins ask in the village, after you departed, and no one there had seen him. When I arrived at Harcourt

House last night, my sister confirmed that Donald admitted to fighting with his brother at Emberly. So we know he was there, but never made it back to the village."

"He might have gone to a different village for the night."

"But we know he never made it home to London! God, man, you're supposed to be some sort of inquiry agent, yet you're not looking at the evidence. The last person to see Buchanan alive was the man he fought. Donald."

Marguerite placed her hands over her ears and screwed her eyes shut. She was close to falling apart.

"My sister doesn't like to think that her husband killed the man she loves."

Marguerite began to hum, as if she were trying to drown out her brother's words. I eyed Lincoln and lifted one shoulder in a "what-shall-we-do" gesture. He simply gave his head another half-shake.

"Harcourt doesn't strike me as the sort of fellow who would kill his own brother," Lincoln said.

"Why not?" Edgecombe sneered. "He put his own wife in Bedlam."

Marguerite's humming grew louder, and she gently rocked back and forth. I laid my hand on her knee but she jerked violently, and I recoiled.

Edgecombe laughed, a bitter, brittle sound that grated on my nerves. "He had her admitted to the asylum a few months after the baby's birth. She was still very affected by Hector's death, and she wasn't showing signs of recovery." He nodded at the humming, rocking figure of his sister, opposite. "She was much like this, as it happens."

"Her own husband," I said quietly. Poor Marguerite.

"She hasn't been the same since." Edgecombe shook his shoulders, as if shaking off the memories. "So you see why I suspect him, don't you? A man capable of such a callous action toward his wife is surely capable of killing his brother out of jealousy."

"Jealousy?" Lincoln asked.

"Of course. Jealous that his wife loved his brother more. Jealous that Andrew could father a child, while he cannot."

"My lady," I said loudly, to penetrate Marguerite's fog. "Do *you* think your husband killed Mr. Buchanan?"

Her rocking became more furious. She slammed back into the seat so hard the entire cabin vibrated. She must have heard me but she didn't answer.

"She came along to speak to you without informing him," Edgecombe drawled. "And she wouldn't be behaving like that if she thought him innocent." He leaned forward and handed her the bottle. "Take this, Margie. It'll calm your nerves."

She shook her head.

"Perhaps a cup of tea," I said.

She screwed her hands into her skirts and nodded.

"My man Dawkins will help you." Edgecombe thumped the ceiling, and his sister jumped. "Dawkins! Assist Miss Holloway." To us he added, "He's not as good as my previous fellow, but he should be able to manage a few teacups."

I was about to protest when I decided it might be a good opportunity to speak to him. Sometimes servants knew more about the goings-on in a house than their masters.

Dawkins was a stocky fellow with a thick chest and arms that would come in useful when carrying Edgecombe up and down stairs. Despite a heavy brow which shadowed small eyes, he had a rather mischievous mouth that curved up in a smile as he introduced himself to me while we walked.

"Couldn't get out of there fast enough, eh?" he asked as we climbed the front steps.

"The meeting is not quite going as expected."

"Let me guess." He held the door open for me. "Edgecombe's calling his sister names and she's shrinking into the corner so's she can get as far away from him as possible. That's how it generally goes at Emberly. I don't expect it to be much different in London."

"That sounds like an unpleasant household."

"It ain't a picnic. Between the mad toffs and the arse licking butler, it's a wonder any of the servants stay."

"Why do you?"

"I only just started and the wages are good. Very good. Prob'ly because no one else'll do what I do." He laughed an easy laugh that lifted his ponderous features. "It ain't much of a lark taking care of Edgecombe."

We headed into the kitchen where only Cook greeted us. Seth and Gus were elsewhere, running errands for Lincoln. I introduced them then we set about preparing the tea.

"What do you know about Lord Harcourt's missing brother?" I asked Dawkins.

He shrugged. "Never met him. He went missing before I started with Edgecombe."

"Have you heard any rumors?"

"Only that he's missing, maybe dead, after he visited Emberly. I hear he's got an eye for the lassies. The maids are all crying into their aprons and her ladyship's fretting."

"What about Lord Harcourt? Does he seem worried to you?"

"Don't know. I only just met him afore he left for London."

"What about Mr. Edgecombe? How does he seem to you?"

"Bloody-minded, angry and drunk. He's a task master, that one. Always yelling at me to carry him here, push him there, fetch this, do that, and calling me names too. If he weren't paying this good, I'd leave him outside in the rain."

Cook handed me the teapot. "I'd be bad tempered too, if I couldn't use me legs."

"Ain't no excuse to be a curmudgeon, in my book. Only time I get peace is when he's asleep. Thank God and Dr. Turcott for the sleeping draft. Knocks him right out, as good as dead."

We returned to the carriage and handed out cups of tea. Mr. Edgecombe refused, holding up his bottle, until I snatched it off him.

"Tea is better for the body and soul," I told him.

"Bloody hell," he muttered. "You're worse than Harcourt and Yardly combined." Nevertheless, he took the cup and eyed his sister over the rim as he sipped.

Marguerite seemed more composed, although the remnants of her hysteria were still visible in the tear stains on her cheeks. In my absence, they had been discussing the possibility of Harcourt having killed his brother and burying the body somewhere on the estate. Edgecombe was suggesting possible spots. While Marguerite didn't meet anyone's gaze, she seemed resigned to the fact that her husband was the main suspect in her past lover's disappearance. Put like that, I wasn't surprised that she felt somewhat fragile.

"So, what happens now?" Edgecombe asked Lincoln. "Will you confront Harcourt today?"

"No," Lincoln said.

"What? Why not?"

"While your own suspicion is new, you haven't presented me with new evidence. You've told me nothing I haven't already considered. I can't accuse Lord Harcourt of murder, when it's quite possible that no crime has been committed and Buchanan will turn up alive."

"You're thicker than you look." Edgecombe snatched back the bottle and pointed it at Lincoln. "Very well, go in search of more evidence, but you'll forgive me if I insist my sister remains at Harcourt House rather than return to Emberly with her husband."

Marguerite stared down into her teacup. Her shoulders drooped, her mouth was slack, and her body slumped. She looked as though she'd given up altogether. It was hard for her. She may not love her husband, but she seemed to depend upon him. Now a long, dark shadow had been cast over his honor. It must feel like the very ground trembled beneath her feet.

"I must insist that his lordship is not made aware of your suspicions," Lincoln said. "Not yet."

I touched Marguerite's knee again, rousing her. She blinked at me then handed me the teacup. "I would like to lie down now," she announced.

Lincoln and I alighted from the cabin and watched it roll away. Dawkins, standing on the footboard at the back, waved at me. I waved back.

"Did you learn anything from him?" Lincoln asked as we returned inside.

"He hasn't been there long enough to have heard much. Yardly is very loyal, though. If he helped Lord Harcourt remove Buchanan, he wouldn't tell us."

"Remove him to where? If he's not dead, he must be held prisoner somewhere. Not at Emberly, or the other servants would know; I doubt all of them are so loyal to Harcourt that they would cover up murder for him. The village is too public. He could be paying a farmer to use an isolated barn. But why? What's the point?"

"Revenge? Frustration?" I shrugged. "To lord it over his brother and prove that he has all the power and money? If he's jealous of Buchanan, it might simply be a case of one-upmanship. Perhaps being pressured to pay off Buchanan's debts was the last straw."

"True, but it brings us back to the question of where he's being held."

We returned the tea service to the kitchen, and I set to washing the dishes in the scullery, mulling over the problem of the missing Andrew Buchanan. The more I thought about it, the more I suspected Edgecombe was right, and Lord Harcourt must have a very big hand in his brother's disappearance. He'd fought with Buchanan and had the power to keep the servants quiet if they saw anything.

Buchanan wasn't dead. We'd proved that. So where was he? Where could Harcourt hide a person *and* keep him alive without raising an alarm? Somewhere that Buchanan's shouts for help couldn't be heard.

Or wouldn't be believed.

I dropped the teacup into the water and ran out of the scullery. I dried my hands in my apron as I sprinted through the kitchen.

"Charlie?" Cook called. "Where you off to in a hurry?"

I didn't stop to answer. I took the stairs two at a time and burst into Lincoln's sitting room without knocking. He was near the door, as if he'd been expecting me, which, I supposed, he probably was.

"What is it?" He searched my face, his own handsome one marred by signs of worry. "What's wrong?"

"Tell me about Bedlam."

CHAPTER 14

Bethlehem Hospital for the insane—Bedlam to most of us—looked more like a museum or courthouse with its imperial dome and columned entrance. Located in St. George's Fields, behind a tall iron fence, it took us some time to get there in the midday traffic, allowing me to quiz Lincoln about the place. What he told me chilled me to the bone. Apparently near relations could have someone committed for madness simply by filling out a few forms. After a medical assessment, which could be bought for an undisclosed sum, the madman or woman was then admitted and treated. Treatments varied according to the severity of the madness, from undertaking simple tasks like embroidery or laundry, to cold baths, shackles and isolation. It seemed so medieval.

"This is where Lord Harcourt sent poor Marguerite," I said as we entered the vast, empty entrance hall. "And all because she was sad over her baby's death."

"Also where he may have committed his brother."

We'd briefly discussed the likelihood of Buchanan being sent here and decided it was very much a possibility. Harcourt knew about this place after having his wife committed a few years ago. It would be easy enough to take

Buchanan there after a fight if he was dazed from a head wound, and administering certain drugs would insure his continued compliance. Any complaints would be dismissed as the ramblings of a madman. Buchanan could disappear in this vast hospital, and Harcourt knew it. If he wanted to be rid of his brother without killing him, this was the place to send him.

Our footsteps echoed around the clean, too-bright entrance hall. A nurse dressed in crisp white looked up from the desk. Her lackluster hazel eyes flared briefly as she took in Lincoln's face, his dark hair tied back, and his gentleman's clothing.

"We're looking for a patient by the name of Andrew Buchanan," he said. We'd decided not to *ask* if he was in here, but assume.

She folded her hands on top of the open leather-bound ledger in front of her. "And you are?"

"Mr. Henry Buchanan, Andrew's cousin, and this is my wife."

Wife? We hadn't discussed playing roles, but I supposed relatives might be allowed entry whereas strangers would not. I took his arm in a picture of wifely affection. His muscles tensed.

"I'm sorry, Mr. Buchanan, but visiting days are the first and third Monday of the month, unless the governor is escorting you on a tour."

"The third Monday is more than a week away."

She gave him a tight smile. "Yes."

I was worried that Lincoln might bully his way in when a door to our right opened and two gentlemen emerged. They shook hands and one thanked the other for the tour, promising to fill in the requisite paperwork and return it forthwith.

"Is that the governor?" Lincoln asked the nurse.

"Yes."

Lincoln peeled away as the visitor departed. "Sir! A word, please."

The governor waited with a strained smile and an impatient glance at the door. "Yes?"

"My name is Henry Buchanan, cousin to Andrew Buchanan, one of your patients."

"Visiting days are the first and third Mondays of the month," the governor said as he walked off.

"I don't want to visit, I want to have a tour."

The governor stopped again, his feathery eyebrows raised in an expectant air. "Go on."

"I have a family member I'd like to have admitted. My cousin, Harcourt, told me all about the new techniques used here and I thought I'd give it a try."

"Excellent!" The waxed pointy ends of the governor's moustache twitched. "Your cousin is a wise man. His brother is progressing admirably under our care. Ordinarily I require an appointment, but since you're here, I'll give you a brief tour. My name is Fourner."

"Thank you, Mr. Fourner, my wife and I appreciate your time."

I could hardly contain my excitement. Fourner had admitted that Buchanan was a patient. We'd found him.

"If your wife wouldn't mind staying here," Fourner said. "We wouldn't want to upset her delicate sensibilities."

Oh, good lord. Every time a man spoke about my "delicate sensibilities," I wanted to prove to him that I had none. It also made me appreciate Lincoln even more. He might be overly protective, but he never expected me to faint if I heard a crude word or saw something improper.

Well, if Fourner wanted delicate sensibilities, he was about to get them in abundance. And I was going to get myself admitted to Bedlam as a patient.

I withdrew my hand from Lincoln's arm and covered my face. I was about to pretend to burst into tears and then faint, when Lincoln's fingers gripped my arm so tightly that he cut off the blood flow.

I lowered my hands and met his severe glare. His jaw was set as hard as granite. Fourner had already walked off toward the door, his steps quick and short. If he'd noticed my aborted act, he gave no indication.

Lincoln forced out a chilly "Don't," between clenched teeth.

"I had a plan to find Buchanan," I whispered. "I would get myself admitted as a patient today then go in search of him tonight when everyone is in bed."

"I know." He clasped my arm and pulled me into his side then marched me to the door where Fourner waited with a strained smile.

"And who is it you wish to have admitted?" he asked Lincoln.

"My ward. He's mad. Does and says the most foolish things, doesn't he, dear?" His eyes gleamed with what I suspected was mischief.

"Alas, yes," I said. "Yet he's excessively clever and lively and one can't help but admire his quality."

"It's often the clever, lively ones who need to come here," Fourner assured me. "I see quite a lot of that type, sadly. Your ward will be very welcome at Bethlehem Hospital, and I'm sure he'll be cured within the year with our treatments. Did Lord Harcourt inform you of our fees?"

"He did," Lincoln said. "The cost is not a problem. Indeed, I plan to give extra to insure my ward's comfort."

Fourner's eyes lit up. "Capital! Now, Mrs. Buchanan, if you wouldn't mind waiting here while I escort your husband through the facility. Nurse Elliot will see to your needs."

"I'm coming," I told him with gritty determination. "My nerves will be quite safe with my husband here to protect me. He's so very capable, you see, and he understands me perfectly. It's almost as if he knows what I'm thinking before I do."

Fourner gave a confused little laugh. "Charming. Very well then, come with me. But do not engage with the patients, no matter what they say to you. And stay close. I'll show you the men's wing, since your ward is male."

With his warning ringing in my ears, we walked through the door into a long gallery. It looked like an extended drawing room, with comfortable armchairs spaced along the wall, and occasional tables topped with potted plants and vases of flowers. The blue and gold carpet deadened our footsteps until we paused at one of the many doors leading off the gallery.

"The ground floor apartments are for the use of our least troublesome patients," Fourner said as he entered the parlor.

Men dressed in plain trousers, shirts and waistcoats sat in armchairs, reading newspapers or journals. Some looked up and, seeing nothing of interest, returned to their reading. One man rose and bowed, as if we were royalty, and another sang quietly to himself in the corner. Yet another crouched on the floor, his gaze on the fire burning in the grate. A system of iron rails barred it, the gaps too narrow to reach through. There must be a key to open it, to allow the orderlies access to the fireplace but not patients.

Fourner droned on about the latest techniques in treating troubled patients such as these by keeping them active and stimulating their mind. Restraint and medication weren't necessary. He took us back out to the gallery, then into each room leading off it. He nodded at nurses and men dressed in blue, whom I suspected were orderlies, and occasionally spoke to a patient in the condescending manner that some adults used when speaking to children.

By the time we reached the stairs at the end of the gallery, we'd still not seen any sign of Andrew Buchanan. On the next level we found cells with up to six beds in each. There were no screens or curtains separating them, and no fires burned in any of the fireplaces. The rooms were freezing. Some beds were occupied by sleeping patients, while others were made without a single wrinkle in the covers.

"Does my cousin reside in any of these rooms?" Lincoln asked, as we headed up yet another set of stairs.

"He does."

"Is he a difficult patient?"

"Not anymore."

"Meaning?"

"Meaning his treatment has calmed him."

"What sort of treatment?"

"A combination of the latest medicines and certain incentives have seen his behavior improve considerably."

"What sort of incentives?"

Fourner stopped and opened a door. The whitewashed walls reflected the light streaming in from the single high window and it took a moment for my eyes to adjust. The room contained two copper tubs that reached to chest height with a tap sprouting from the wall into each. The room must be plumbed, as was the bathroom at Lichfield Towers, yet it contained no flushing toilet or basin.

"What is this room used for?" I asked.

"This is one of our incentives," Fourner explained with a smug smile. "Or, rather, a disincentive. Misbehaving patients are submerged to their necks in cold baths."

"Cold baths!"

"Ice-cold, Mrs. Buchanan. A few minutes in one of those tubs sees them desperate to get out again. They quickly learn that only calmness will see them freed."

I folded my arms and hugged my chest, but it didn't suppress my shiver. "Did Andrew find himself in one of these?"

Fourner nodded and ushered us outside again. "When he woke up, that first morning after his arrival, he was a ranting lunatic, shouting obscenities at my staff and making a nuisance of himself. But after the cold baths and two days alone in one of our India-rubber cells, he learned that submission is the best way to get along here at Bethlehem."

Lincoln put up a hand, halting our progress along the corridor. "India-rubber cells?"

"Lined with cork and India-rubber, actually. The lack of bedding and other amenities means they cannot harm themselves. We find the isolation gives them time to reflect in peace. It's very soothing for the mind. Medication helps too, of course."

"Of course," Lincoln said drily.

"The cells are just along here, if you'd like to take a look. One is currently occupied—" He was cut off by a high-pitched shriek that raised the hairs on the back of my neck. "Ah, yes, that would be the patient now. It must be time for his medication."

Two orderlies and a nurse rushed past us. One of the orderlies unlocked the door, but was shoved backward as soon as he opened it. A man dressed in a white gown flew out, pushing the other orderly into the nurse. She screamed, fell back, and curled herself into a ball. The syringe she'd been holding rolled away, and the patient snatched it up.

"Get him!" Fourner shouted.

But the two orderlies, while big men, were too slow. They lumbered after the patient, but he had a head start and long legs. He streaked toward us, his tangled blonde hair streaming behind him. His wide, wild eyes were fixed on Fourner, who stood in his way, blocking the stairs.

The patient bared his teeth and raised the syringe like a dagger. Fourner threw his arms across his face and spun away. The patient plunged the syringe, aiming for Fourner's exposed neck.

Lincoln leapt and tackled him to the ground. The syringe fell out of his hand and rolled into the corner, out of reach. The patient thrashed, his screech splitting the air. He pounded his fists against Lincoln's back, at the same time bucking and twisting in an attempt to get free.

"Be still!" Lincoln growled.

But the patient either couldn't hear him over his own caterwauling or didn't want to obey. He continued to thrash and punch. Lincoln sat on him but had a devil of a time trying to grasp both the man's hands to subdue him. The orderlies hung back, shouting for reinforcements, while the nurse and Fourner were both cowering messes.

I picked up the syringe and, in the same moment that Lincoln finally pinned the man's hands to the floor, I stabbed it into the man's neck. His eyes dulled, the ridges of muscles in his shoulders subsided and he became nothing more than an empty vessel, much like a body in the moment of death when the spirit exits. Except this man wasn't dead.

I looked down at the syringe in my hand. Whatever had been in it was powerful.

"Remove him at once," Fourner snapped at the orderlies. More had joined us upon hearing the shouts and screams, and two picked up the patient like a bolt of cloth and carried him to the cell. "This is outrageous! I do apologize, sir, madam. This sort of thing does not happen very often."

"Is that the medicine you spoke of?" I asked, nodding at the nurse now bustling past us with the syringe.

"It is. Good stuff. Don't know where we'd be without it."

"Is that what you used on my cousin to subdue him?" Lincoln asked.

"In the first two days, yes. After that, he showed signs of compliance so we decreased the dose. He now has some consciousness and is very content during the day. At night, the doctors administer more to help him sleep peacefully." Fourner tugged on his cuffs and eyed the door to the cell warily as the orderly locked it. "Thank you for your assistance, Mr. Buchanan. I do hope you are unharmed."

Only Lincoln's tie seemed to have suffered from the ordeal. I straightened it for him, locking my gaze onto his. It wasn't until he closed his hand over mine at his chest that I realized I was shaking.

"Perhaps Mrs. Buchanan would like to settle her nerves with a cup of tea." Fourner directed us toward the staircase.

Lincoln settled my hand on his arm once again, and we descended the stairs like a companionable married couple. I hardly heard Fourner's next words. He continued with the tour, making particular note of the safety measures in place to stop the more volatile patients from hurting themselves and others.

When we reached the second floor once more, I realized we still hadn't seen Buchanan. Either he was outside in the garden or asleep on one of the beds.

"May we have another look into the cells where the patients sleep?" I asked.

Fourner stopped mid-sentence and looked to Lincoln, as if asking why he was allowing me to speak. "Sir?"

"My wife has requested another tour of this floor, and I would appreciate your compliance."

"Yes, of course. Come this way." Fourner stepped lightly along the carpeted gallery to the first door. Lincoln entered and I followed. He must have had the same idea as me, because he strolled down the aisle between the beds and glanced at the faces of the men lying on them. Only half of the beds were occupied, none by Buchanan.

We looked in the next room and the next, and finally found him in the fourth. I sucked in a breath at the change in him. He lay on his side, staring at the unlit fireplace with the same vacant eyes as the mad patient after his injection. Lips that I'd only ever seen curled into a sneer, moved silently, uttering something I couldn't hear. A trickle of drool dampened the pillow and his fingers clutched the blanket as if it were an anchor. His fair hair was a greasy, knotty mess and every now and again a tremble wracked him.

I didn't like Buchanan. I'd found him to be cynical to the point of rudeness, as well as lazy. But seeing the handsome, strong man reduced to a pathetic, drooling idiot sickened me.

"Your cousin, I believe." Fourner regarded Buchanan with detached professionalism.

"Is that what you refer to as *calmer*?" I asked.

"As you can see, he's very amenable now. Our doctors work wonders with their new drugs. Would you like to meet one?"

"We've seen enough," Lincoln said.

Fourner's bristly brows lifted. "I do hope the incident upstairs didn't alarm you." He chuckled and rocked back on his heels. "But I did warn you that a lady's sensibilities are too delicate for such things, didn't I, Mrs. Buchanan?"

The pupils in Andrew's eyes contracted. His gaze drifted toward Fourner then to Lincoln and onto me. He stopped the silent muttering and instead grunted. He seemed to be attempting to speak, but was having trouble forming the words.

It was time to get away before the patient managed to say something that would throw doubt on our disguises. Lincoln must have had the same idea, because he took my hand and led me toward the door. Fourner trotted behind us.

At the second to last bed, I paused, halting Lincoln too. The man lying on his back beneath the covers was so thin that his cheeks and nose jutted prominently, while his eyes had all but disappeared into the sunken sockets. The ashen color of his skin and the rattle of each labored breath in his chest were sure signs that he was close to death.

"Why is no one tending to this man?" I asked. "Where are the nurses and doctors?"

"Mrs. Buchanan, this man is beyond Earthly remedies. He will die in the next twenty-four hours. We can't spare the staff to watch over a dying man. It's an inefficient allocation of their time."

"But someone should be with him at the last. To die alone…it's so sad."

"He's not alone. He has your husband's cousin, just a few beds away. And tonight, the other beds will be occupied. There, you see, not alone at all, if he happens to pass away in the next few hours."

He would, I felt certain. Death clung to the man like a shroud.

"Come now, Mrs. Buchanan. I see you are becoming overwrought. It happens quite often with the ladies, I'm afraid."

I closed my fist at my side. There was no one about. I could punch him in the jaw without any witnesses. Lincoln grabbed my fist and wrapped his hand around it. As he led me away, I quickly glanced at the medical chart hanging at the end of the bed.

Out in the entrance hall, the nurse at the desk handed Lincoln some papers that he perused.

"Just to be clear," he said, "I fill in these forms and sign them, then you perform your own tests to assess my ward's level of madness."

Fourner stroked his moustache. "That's it, yes."

"The signature must be mine alone, correct?"

"Only his closest relative or guardian has the authority to admit him."

"No one else?"

"No. Why?"

Lincoln didn't answer, so I said, "Just curious."

"If you get those back to me within forty-eight hours, I can hold that bed for you." At Lincoln's and my raised brows, he added, "The one in your cousin's room that will shortly become available. No longer than forty-eight hours, however. I can't hold it any longer. Our beds are in high demand, you know."

Feeling quite dazed by the entire experience, I dutifully followed my "husband" outside.

"Everything all right?" Seth asked from the coachman's seat of our carriage.

I blew out a breath. "Take us far away from this place, Seth, and quickly."

Lincoln held the door open for me then followed me inside and sat opposite. He folded the forms and tucked them into his inside jacket pocket. "You thought it a good idea to get yourself admitted to Bedlam?" he snapped.

"You're bringing *that* up? After everything we learned in there?"

"Are you mad?"

I sighed. "That was the idea, yes. Once inside, I could have gone in search of Buchanan and helped him escape. Only I didn't know he'd be in that state. He probably can't even walk." I bit my lip. While my idea had merit, I'd grossly underestimated Buchanan's level of "calmness." There was no way I could have carried him out.

"You think I care what happens to Buchanan?" His waspish tone hadn't diminished in the least. "I don't care if he rots in there. His freedom is not worth risking your safety."

I swallowed my retorts. They made me sound ungrateful, in light of his concern. "It wasn't the most sensible idea, now that I know how that place works. Anyway, I have another plan for getting him out. You probably won't like it either."

"You are correct, I don't. You're not summoning that spirit when he passes on."

"Why not? I can manage the whole thing from outside. Neither of us will have to enter Bedlam at all."

He considered this for a moment then shook his head again. "He might not die for some time."

"He'll be gone in a few hours." I checked off points on my fingers. "I saw his name on his medical chart, so I can summon him. He'll know who Buchanan is, since he shares a room with him."

"We don't know that for sure."

"Once he's back in his body, he'll be strong enough to carry a man out to us, where we will be waiting in the carriage."

"He'll need to get through locked doors. Without keys, that will become noisy unless he was an expert lock picker before he entered Bedlam."

"If he hurries, the noise won't matter. He'll be gone before he's seen."

"No, Charlie."

"Why not?" I said crossly. "It's better than the alternative."

He arched a brow. "Which is?"

"That you enter and put yourself in danger." I crossed my arms and turned to look out the window. The color rose in my cheeks, but I didn't dip my head. Let him see. He already knew I cared for him anyway.

"You're worried," he said flatly.

"Of course I am! You saw that madman fly at us."

"Those tend to be locked away, it seems."

"And what about the orderlies? What if you're caught and they inject you with whatever was in that syringe? You'll fall asleep in seconds."

"Then you have my permission to do whatever it takes to rescue me."

I slumped back in the seat. "In that case, I will have to return with you tonight. Do not argue," I said when he opened his mouth. "I've decided. You need a…partner. One who's capable of raising that spirit if necessary."

He sighed. "I left myself open for that, didn't I? Charlie, I can manage alone. I always have."

"You don't need to anymore, Lincoln. You have Seth, Gus and me. We're all employed to work for you in the ministry, and it's about time you allowed us to help with more than just driving the coach or polishing the silver."

"So, you're not worried about me, you simply wish to be involved. Correct?"

I sighed. "Lincoln, you are the most capable man I know. While I've never seen you descend three flights down a drainpipe while carrying a fully grown man, I have no doubt you can manage it. However, if there is a chance that something can go wrong and a chance that I may be able to help, I'd rather be safe. So, yes, I am worried. I would hate myself for doing nothing when I could have helped, just as you would hate yourself for doing nothing if the roles were reversed. Does that answer your question?"

He stared at me for so long and with such a curious expression on his face that I wished I knew what he was thinking. But I couldn't read his thoughts the way he could read mine, so I simply came out and asked him.

"What is it? Why are you looking at me as if you're trying to see into my head?"

He quickly turned to look out the window. "Your answer was…adequate. Thank you for explaining your thoughts to me."

"I thought you could read them without an explanation."

"Not to that extent. Your emotions are as clear as crystal, but your actual thoughts are shrouded in shadows. I can't see them."

Thank God for that. At least I could retain some privacy.

* * *

When we laid out our plan, Seth and Gus insisted on both returning to Bedlam with us that night. They presented an excellent argument, involving the coach and number of horses, and after an initial refusal, Lincoln gave in. The fact that he gave in was quite an achievement. Seth and Gus congratulated themselves with pats on the back when Lincoln wasn't looking.

"Why not just speak to Harcourt?" Cook asked, over dinner in the kitchen as we discussed the plan in more detail. "Tell him you know what he done, then make him get his brother out."

"Tomorrow," Lincoln said. "Once we have Buchanan and we have had a chance to question him."

We waited until midnight before driving back across the city to St. George's Fields. It was a much faster journey, not only because there was less traffic, but also because we had four horses instead of two. Seth rode postilion on the front left horse while Gus sat in the coachman's seat. Apparently the arrangement allowed for greater control, and that, in turn, allowed for faster speeds. A smaller carriage was out of the question if we needed to smuggle an immobile Buchanan out.

We closed the shutters on the coach lamps once we reached Bedlam's fence. The glow from two streetlights near the gate struggled to penetrate the darkness, and another two lamps near the hospital entrance were mere pinpricks in a black canvas. The hulking expanse of the hospital itself swallowed the horizon.

Lincoln slipped out of the carriage and into the shadows hugging the fence. There was no need for discussion. We'd already gone over the scenarios together, along with Seth and Gus. I watched as he scrambled up and over the fence, easily avoiding the spear finials, and dropped silently on the other side. The coach hid him from the street, but there was nobody about at this late hour anyway.

I soon lost him in the darkness. Seth appeared at the window, and I lowered it to speak to him.

"How long should we give him?" he whispered.

"He only just left!"

"I know, but we didn't discuss a time."

"Do you have a time piece?"

"No."

"Nor do I, and if we did, we wouldn't be able to see it in the dark. That's why we didn't discuss times."

He sighed and leaned against the door. "We'll give him thirty minutes."

We waited. Seth tried to make frosty breath rings in the cold air, while I peered into the darkness, seeking out any movement. There was none. Gus hummed a quiet tune until Seth told him to shut up.

"How long do you think it's been?" I asked, after what felt like an age.

"Hours," Seth grumbled. "I should have gone with him."

Gus snorted. "You'd have stabbed yourself on the fence spikes before you even got in."

"Hardly. My arse isn't as lardy as yours."

"Go on then. Try it."

"Stop it, both of you," I hissed.

We waited until I was sure thirty minutes had passed. "Something must have gone wrong. I'm going to summon the spirit and ask him to take a look."

"That wise, Charlie?" came Gus's voice from the driver's seat.

"It'll just be a peek, and he'll be in spirit form. No one will see him."

"Capital idea," Seth said. "Do it."

Gus grumbled something that I took as agreement, despite the tone. "I summon the spirit of Gerald Mason McIlroy," I said, calling up the name written on the dying patient's medical chart. Come to me, Gerald Mason McIlroy. I need your help."

The final words were hardly out of my mouth when the ghostly mist whooshed past Seth and came in through the open window. It stopped in the corner of the cabin and coalesced into the shape of the man I'd seen lying in the bed earlier, only without the gauntness of death.

"Blimey!" He laughed. "That was a lark." He glanced down at his misty form, then swirled around and around, like a dog chasing its tail, as if trying to see himself from different angles. He laughed again, but it was more of a wild cackle.

I braced myself as his gaze settled on me. While Andrew Buchanan wasn't mad, most other patients in Bedlam probably were. This could be an interesting discussion.

"Good evening." My voice startled Seth more than the spirit. "My name is Charlotte Holloway, and I summoned you here."

"Is that so?" McIlroy scooted along the seat, until he was directly opposite me, and leaned forward. He reached out to touch my face but his misty fingers sank into my skin. "Blimey!"

"I'm alive and you're dead," I said matter-of-factly. "Do you understand, Mr. McIlroy?"

"Perfectly. It's rather a shock, you know, being dead. I've been sent to a place known as the Waiting Area. Do you know what we do there, Miss Holloway? We wait." He leaned his chin on his hand and grinned. "Where do you think they send the mad ones? Heaven, Hell, or somewhere else?"

"Mr. McIlroy, I have an important task for you. A friend of mine has entered Bedlam—"

"Tell him to get out of there!" he gasped. "If there is a hell, it will look like the cold bath room, I'm sure of it." His mist shimmered and he pulled a face.

"He's not a patient, but has gone inside to get one out."

"An escape! Capital idea. Wish my friends had thought of that. Wish I'd had friends. Or family. Oh, I had a brother, of course, but he never liked me. Said I was soft in the head." He tapped his temple. "He said I was a few cards short of a full deck." He chuckled into his hand. "I don't know what that means, but all his friends thought it a good joke. Do you think it's amusing, Miss Holloway?"

Good lord, I was going to trust this spirit to report back on Lincoln's progress? Perhaps I was the mad one. "Listen very carefully, Mr. McIlroy. I'd like you to enter the hospital—"

"No!" he screeched. "I'm not going back in there again, not now that I'm out."

"Just for a few minutes. Besides, nothing can harm you now. You're already dead."

"But…there are ghosts in that place."

"Mr. McIlroy, *you* are a ghost."

He looked down at himself again and straightened. "Oh. So I see. But…the doctors are more frightening than the ghosts." He rubbed his wrists, pushing back the sleeves to reveal what looked like scratches or cuts. "They shackle you to the bed at night," he whispered, once more leaning forward. "Those of us who wander at night are chained up. The dangerous ones are given medicine to make them sleep. It's horrible, Miss Holloway. I called for my nurse, but she didn't hear me. She left, you see, when I was twelve. They said I was too old for a nurse, but I didn't think so. What was her name again?"

"Mr. McIlroy, please try to focus your attention on me and the task at hand."

He blinked and nodded firmly. "Yes. I will. What is it you want me to do?"

"I want you to go inside the building and look for a man dressed all in black with longish black hair. He's neither a patient nor a staff member. He is attempting to rescue Mr. Buchanan, your old roommate. Can you do that?"

"I am almost certain that I can."

"I'm afraid I have the power to order you to do it, but I prefer your acquiescence."

"Then you have it. Do you have a pistol?"

"Why do you need a pistol?"

"So I can shoot anyone who gets in my way. Particularly Dr. Freeman and a certain orderly by the name of Daniels." He snickered as if it were a great joke.

"Dr. Freeman and Mr. Daniels are most likely at home in their own beds, not in the hospital. There is no need for weapons, and you cannot hold them anyway. Just go inside, look for my friend, then come back and report to me. Do you understand?"

He nodded. "Shall I go now?"

"Yes!"

"Right-o." He flew out the window and into the night.

I tipped my head back against the wall. "That was exhausting."

"Has he gone?" Seth asked.

"He has. And now we wait again."

We didn't have to wait long. Almost immediately, the ghost flew back, tumbling through the open window and landing on my lap.

"I found him!" he gasped out with a triumphant smile.

"And?"

"And he's in my old bed."

"What do you mean?"

Seth leaned through the window. "Charlie? What's happened?"

McIlroy eyed Seth and lifted one shoulder. "I mean he's lying in my bed. Black haired fellow, longish *et cetera*. He's real still and there's blood everywhere."

"Blood!" I shoved open the door, pushing Seth aside. "Lincoln has been captured," I told him.

"Are you sure?"

I grabbed his jacket at his chest and scrunched it in my fist. "I have to go in and get him out. Come Mr. McIlroy. I'll need your help."

"I'm going too," Seth said.

"Don't get caught," Gus said from the driver's seat. "I can't carry all of you out *and* keep the horses quiet."

I wasn't as deft as Lincoln in getting over the fence, but I managed it without tearing my clothing. Thank goodness I'd worn boys' clothes instead of skirts. That was my last clear thought that wasn't about Lincoln as I raced across the lawn with Seth on my left and McIlroy's spirit on my right.

CHAPTER 15

I didn't know how Lincoln had got inside. Broken a window? Picked a lock? He hadn't deemed it necessary to divulge such particulars to us before we set out. It meant that Seth and I now stood outside the front door, wondering what to do next.

"Perhaps one of the upper floor windows is open," he said, tilting his head back.

"How do you propose to get up there? Fly?"

Seth swore. I sighed.

"I can fly." To prove his point, McIlroy's spirit did a flip in the air then he cackled with glee.

He gave me an idea. "How did you get in before?"

"Through the keyhole."

"Listen to me carefully, Mr. McIlroy. Do you know where your physical body is now?"

"The basement, most likely. That's where they take the bodies until someone from the mortuary comes. Do you know when I died? I can't seem to recall much about my final days."

"We were here around midday, so some time after that."

"What's he saying?" Seth asked, warily.

"That his body is in the basement. Mr. McIlroy, I need you to go back inside, find your way to the basement, and re-enter your body."

"Re-enter?" McIlroy screwed up his face like a child served a dish full of beans.

"Just lie on it and allow your spirit to sink through. Then…get up and walk." It was the best explanation I could give. None of the other spirits I'd raised had any trouble working it out, so hopefully McIlroy wouldn't either. "Come and unlock this door for us. Be as quiet as you can."

"Is he gone?" Seth asked, glancing around.

McIlroy saluted Seth then his mist slipped through the keyhole.

I blew out a measured breath. "Yes."

We waited for an interminably long time, or so it seemed. Despite the darkness, the night wasn't quiet. The distant rattle of wheels and clip-clop of hooves provided a familiar and comforting backdrop to the unfamiliar and eerie wails coming from inside the asylum. My skin prickled and a shiver rippled down my spine. I sidled closer to Seth.

He put his arm around me. "This place gives me the jitters too."

The sound of thumping had us both bristling. I shushed Seth when he began to speak and listened. There it was again, followed by a low, male voice. Finally the lock clicked and the door opened a crack. The cadaverous face of McIlroy emerged through the dimness.

"This is a jolly lark," he said, chuckling. "Come in, come in."

"Was that you thumping?" I asked as he closed the door behind us and we were swallowed up by the darkness.

"Walked into some furniture. Damned hard to see in here."

As if he just remembered he'd been holding it, Seth opened the shutter on the lantern he'd removed from the coach. Its circle of light didn't reach far but it was enough to help see the furniture before we walked into it.

"Which way?" he asked.

"Follow me."

I hurried along the gallery in the men's ward and tiptoed up the stairs at the end. Light came from one of the rooms ahead. A quick count of the doors told me it was Buchanan's dormitory. Murmurs drifted along the gallery, one male, the other female, but the words were drowned out by a high-pitched cry from the depths of the building.

I froze. Seth crowded close at my back, his presence a comfort until I felt him shiver. "What was that?" he whispered.

"Garvey," McIlroy said. "He's always making a fuss at night. I think he does it on purpose to get the orderly on duty out of bed. Don't know why he hasn't been subdued yet."

"Perhaps because the orderly's in there." I pointed to the door up ahead.

"Mystery solved. You're very clever, Miss Holloway." He chuckled, and I had to place a hand on his shoulder to shush him.

"Wait here." I crept closer to the door until my booted toes touched the light streaming out of the room. I peered around and saw the nurse and two orderlies standing over the bed where I'd seen McIlroy earlier in the day. A man with broad shoulders lay on his side, his black, curly hair splayed over the pillow. It was too long to be fashionable, too dark to be properly English.

I covered my mouth to smother my gasp. Oh, Lincoln.

I signaled for Seth to come closer. "We have to get him out," I whispered as he peered past me.

"Has he been injected with anything?"

I shrugged and looked into the room again.

"What a bloody mess," said one of the orderlies, a bulky man with a narrow face and receding hairline. "Why didn't you do something, Mathews?"

"I tried, but he had the knife," said the younger orderly.

"It's done now," the nurse said. "No use crying over spilled milk."

The narrow faced orderly snorted. "Spilled something, all right, but it ain't milk. How're we going to clean this mess up?"

"Linen'll have to be thrown out," the young orderly said. "Mattress scrubbed, blankets washed. Bloody lot of work."

"Aye." Narrow-face grabbed Lincoln by the arms and hauled him into a sitting position.

That's when I saw all the blood. It was everywhere. It coated the length of his arms, his hands and chest. It covered the blankets and matted his hair.

"No!" I muttered. "Oh, God." Hot tears welled. I felt myself tipping forward, falling onto my knees.

Someone caught me—Seth perhaps. I clutched at his arm and stared at the lifeless body being hefted from the bed. So much blood…

I pulled away from Seth and lurched into the room, stumbling forward on weak, wobbling legs. The orderly dropped the body in surprise and leapt back with a shout. But I only had eyes for—

It wasn't Lincoln. The lifeless man lying on the bed had darker skin and a softer, younger face. I fell to my knees anyway, in relief, and sobbed.

The nurse let out a high scream that was louder and more terrifying than anything I'd heard in this place. She shrank back against the wall, her wide eyes on something behind me. McIlroy, I assumed.

"Seth, it's not him!" I shouted above the noise.

"I can see that." He planted his feet and prepared to fight as Narrow-face ran at us.

"Give us what we want and we'll leave," I said, regaining my courage and my strength. "No one will be hurt if you give us Mr. Buchanan."

Narrow-face didn't seem to hear me. He lunged at Seth. Seth dodged the fist and rolled on top of the body on the bed, then fell off the other side with a thud.

Narrow-face, thinking his work done, turned to McIlroy. "You look familiar."

McIlroy giggled, an innocent, childish sound that made me want to pat his back.

I edged toward the bed where Buchanan lay sleeping. He and the other patients in the room must have been medicated because our ruckus didn't wake them. I took stock of his size, and the fact that he was shackled by his wrists to the bedposts, and swore under my breath.

I was about to call for McIlroy when a shadow emerged from the deeper shadows in the corner near the fireplace. "This is not going the way I planned."

"Lincoln! Oh, thank God." I raced around the foot of Buchanan's bed and threw myself at him. He caught me and breathed deeply before setting me aside. "I thought you were dead."

"I'm not," he said, as Seth's grunt had us turning to see that he was all right. He was, but he was fighting both orderlies on his own. McIlroy stood aside and watched, echoing the movements with his own fists punching thin air.

"There appears to have been a mix up," I said. "That'll teach me to ask dead madmen for assistance."

Narrow-face drew a knife from his sleeve, and the young orderly followed suit. Seth backed away before he too removed the knife he'd tucked into the waistband of his trousers.

"Explain later." Lincoln rushed low at Narrow-face. With his back to us, the orderly didn't see Lincoln coming. He toppled to the ground, taking his colleague with him in a loud crash and tangle of limbs.

Seth laughed as he stepped into the fray and grasped the young orderly's wrists. "You make that look so easy." He removed the knife as Lincoln jabbed his fingers into Narrow-face's throat. With a gurgling choke, he too relinquished his blade.

The nurse screamed again, so I went to her and covered her mouth. "You will not be harmed, but you must be quiet." She settled down to a whimper and nodded.

"Now, give me the keys to that man's bonds." I pointed at Buchanan.

She shook her head and I removed my hand. "I don't have the keys. The orderlies do."

By the time I turned, Seth and Lincoln were already searching their pockets.

"You want to free him?" Narrow-face said. "You're as mad as him. Maybe madder. You don't want to free any of 'em, especially those that got to be locked up at night. They're bloody dangerous."

Lincoln smashed his fist across the orderly's cheek. The nurse screamed, and I winced, both at the sound and Lincoln's lack of mercy. Sometimes, my ability to forget what he was like amazed even me.

An answering scream came from somewhere distant in the asylum. I heard pounding footsteps at the same time the others did. More orderlies, perhaps.

"Where's the damned keys?" Seth growled.

"We don't need a key," I said, stepping away from the nurse. "McIlroy, you're very strong now. Break open the shackles."

McIlroy loped over to Buchanan's bed. He lifted one of Buchanan's lifeless arms and shook it. The chain connecting the iron wrist band to the bed rattled.

"Break it apart," I urged him, placing a reassuring hand on his shoulder. When he continued to hesitate, I added, "Hurry or more orderlies will be here. If they catch me, I cannot release your spirit. If I can't release you, you will be stuck here."

He wrenched open the wrist band with no more effort than pulling apart a loaf of bread, then followed suit with the other. Without instruction from me, he pulled back the blankets to reveal Buchanan, dressed in a nightshirt. He hefted the sleeping man onto his shoulder and, with a look of single-minded determination, walked steadily to the door.

"Bloody hell," the young orderly muttered, his wide gaze on McIlroy. "How'd he do that?"

"That fellow…he…" The nurse pointed a shaking finger at McIlroy then at the dead man I'd thought was Lincoln. His wrists were slashed, and a barber's razor lay in a patch of blood on the bed beside him. His spirit was nowhere to be seen. "He used to occupy that bed…until this afternoon."

"Can't be," said Narrow-face. "He's dead." He squinted, but McIlroy now had his back to us.

The other orderly began breathing heavily. He licked his lips and his eyes darted between us. "It's him," he whispered. "Oh God, oh God. I hate this place. Why'd I ever come here?"

Seth searched the now shaking man and finally found a set of keys in his inside pocket. "Which one for this room?"

But the orderly was no use. He was too busy praying.

"Tell us," Lincoln growled.

The nurse crawled over and, with a shaking hand, picked out a key.

"Thank you," I said. "We are sorry about all this, but it can't be helped." I hadn't finished talking when Lincoln took my arm and steered me out of the dormitory.

Seth picked up the lantern that he'd left in the corridor, and Lincoln locked the door. McIlroy was already at the top of the staircase with Buchanan by the time we caught up to him.

We raced down the stairs to the front door, then across the wide lawn to the fence. Gus spotted us and swore under his breath when he saw McIlroy. "Another dead man?"

Lincoln climbed the fence first, but did not descend on the other side. He balanced on the cross bar, his feet placed in the narrow spaces between. "Seth, the other side."

Seth handed me the lantern and climbed over. He dropped to the pavement and waited.

Lincoln directed McIlroy to pass Buchanan up to him as gently as possible. While McIlroy wasn't a large man, he was strong in his dead form and managed it easily. Buchanan suffered only one bump to his dangling foot and his nightshirt rode up as Lincoln handed him down to Seth, revealing masculine parts no innocent girl should see. I wasn't shocked.

"Link your fingers for me, please, Mr. McIlroy," I said. He did and lifted me up so that it was easy for Lincoln to assist me over the top. "Thank you, but I managed earlier," I told him.

"I'm sure you did, but allow me this…moment."

I blinked at him in surprise. He sounded far more amused than the situation warranted, but it was too dark to see his expression to know for sure. I dropped silently to the pavement as Seth bundled Buchanan onto one of the bench seats in the coach.

"Mr. McIlroy, this is where we must part," I said through the fence bars. "Thank you for your assistance. I'm going to send you back now."

"What about my body?"

"They'll find it here in the morning and dispatch it for burial as planned."

"Won't they think it odd that I'm not in the basement?"

"Most likely."

He grinned. "That'll scare the stuffing out of them. Go ahead then, Miss Holloway." He settled his feet a little apart and thrust out his chin. "I'm ready."

"Return to your afterlife, Gerald Mason McIlroy. You are released."

A white smoky haze filtered out of the body and formed the man's shape as the body itself crumpled. The spirit looked at it, looked at me, and grinned again. He gave a childish wave then disappeared.

Lincoln and I were about to step into the cabin when a bell clanged in the distance. A square of light emerged at the hospital entrance then another, both bobbing and swinging. Whoever held the lanterns moved fast in our direction.

Lincoln leaped onto the driver's seat. "Charlie, get in! And hold on."

I had hardly closed the door when the coach lurched forward. I braced myself with one hand on the seat and the other on the wall, but had to let go to stop Buchanan from rolling off. He groaned but did not wake.

We traveled at a ferocious speed, taking corners with reckless abandon. I had a devil of a time keeping myself from sliding around, let alone Buchanan. At the first corner, I held him back with a foot against his chest, but his legs slid off the seat. At the next corner, a sharp left, I smashed into the wall and needed both my feet and arms to steady myself. Buchanan fell of the seat altogether and landed in a heap on the floor. He snored loudly.

After that, I gave up trying to keep him in place. There was nowhere for my feet on the floor, so I stretched out along the seat, bracing myself against each side of the cabin. I winced as we turned another corner and Buchanan's head smacked into the door. He would have a headache in the morning. I found I wasn't altogether displeased about that.

We reached Lichfield in half the time it took to get to Bedlam. I was contemplating where to place my feet when the door opened, and Lincoln stood there. He looked like a wild bear with his wind-blown hair sticking out at all angles.

"I hope your journey was comfortable," he said with a gleam in his eyes so bright that even the wan moonlight picked it out.

"Thank you, yes. Although I'm not sure my traveling companion would agree." We both looked to the crumpled form of Buchanan, his body twisted into the narrow space on the cabin floor.

Lincoln lowered the step and held out his hand to me. "Seth, bring Buchanan."

Seth appeared behind him, his face as pale as the moon and his hair also disheveled. I suspected he didn't enjoy riding postilion when Lincoln drove like that. Gus opened the coach lamp shutters with a shaking hand.

"Should of done that before we took off," he muttered. "Remind me next time you decide to drive at night, sir. It might help my innards stay put if I can see, instead of leaping up and down."

"Or it might make you toss your dinner if you see *how* fast we're going," Seth said.

He carried Buchanan through the back door while Gus drove the horses at a more sedate pace to the coach house. Their necks gleamed with sweat and their nostrils flared with each snorting breath.

"Put him in the tower room then help Gus," Lincoln told Seth at the base of the staircase.

Seth gave the stairs a baleful look. "All the way up there!"

"Do it."

"Want me to lock him in?"

"No!" I cried. "He's not a prisoner."

"Don't lock the door," Lincoln said, "but someone will have to keep watch. He'll be confused when he wakes."

With a sigh, Seth trudged up the stairs. Buchanan's loose arms dangled down Seth's back and the hands smacked into his knees with each step.

"Go get some sleep," Lincoln said to me.

"You expect me to relax so soon after our adventure? Hardly."

"Then help yourself to a brandy while I assist with the horses."

I eyed the stairs. "I wonder if Cook will be mad if I wake him to tell him all about it."

"You'll know if he serves you cold soup tomorrow." He strode off and I followed. I wasn't ready to put myself to bed, so I might as well assist in the coach house too.

Lincoln helped Gus unharness the horses from the coach while I insured they had enough food and water. When Seth joined us, we led them to the stables and brushed them down while they munched oats and apples.

My nerves still hadn't settled by the time we finished. I couldn't get the image of the dead man covered in blood out of my mind. When I'd thought it was Lincoln lying there… I shook my head and rubbed my temples. It didn't bear thinking about.

"They must have decided to fill McIlroy's bed after all," I said. The four of us sat in the library with glasses of brandy as the clock struck two. The liquid burned my throat as it went down, but then it warmed me from the inside out.

"It's free again," Seth said, swirling the liquid in his glass. "Poor chap. Killed himself," he told Gus. "Razor blade to the wrists. He must have smuggled it in."

"Blimey," Gus muttered. "Man's got to be desperate to do that."

"Or mad," I muttered.

"We thought it was you lying there," Seth said to Lincoln. "Charlie was beside herself."

I would have kicked Seth if Lincoln's hooded gaze hadn't slid to me.

"I saw everything," he said.

"Why were you hiding?" I asked.

"I was waiting for the nurse and orderlies to leave. The moment I walked in, the patient began shouting that he was going to kill himself."

"It's not like you to hide, sir," Seth noted. "Usually you'd knock them all out or…worse."

"I'm turning over a new leaf." Lincoln stretched out his legs and crossed the ankles. "I thought it best to wait for them to leave so as not to raise the alarm."

Gus snorted. "That didn't work."

"Clearly."

"It was bedlam in there." Seth chuckled at his lame joke, earning a groan from Gus.

"Your new leaf turning is all well and good," I told Lincoln, "but in this situation, my nerves would have preferred you to knock them out and rejoin us as soon as possible."

"If they'd taken too long, I would have." He sounded frosty, as if the entire debacle could be blamed on my nerves. But I was not a silly female suffering from hysteria, thank you very much.

"You were gone an age!"

"No more than twenty minutes."

"Really? Is that all? Are you sure?"

His gaze narrowed further.

Seth finished his brandy then stood. "Right. I'm off to bed. Gus, you've got first watch on the tower room."

"Why me?"

"Because all you did was drive. I rode postilion *and* went inside. It was exhausting. Good night." He strode out of the library despite Gus's grumble.

"Finish your brandy," Lincoln said to Gus. "You have work to do."

Gus drained his glass and set it on the table. "Right-o then. Good night, all."

"Fetch me when Buchanan wakes up."

"Yes, sir."

I toyed with my glass, suddenly feeling uncomfortable at being alone with Lincoln in the dimly lit library. It was silly. We'd been alone often before. Then again, those times usually ended badly, or awkwardly, or both.

"I'm going to bed," I said, gathering up Seth and Gus's empty glasses in one hand. "Thank you for allowing me to come along tonight. I know it went against your better judgment, but I hope I didn't disappoint you."

"Disappoint?" He sounded genuinely surprised. "I'm not disappointed. It's not your ability, or lack of it, that feeds my reluctance, Charlie. It's concern for your wellbeing."

"Oh."

He lowered his head to peer down into the glass. The dark curtain of his hair fell across his forehead and shielded his eyes. "And, occasionally, your impatience and rashness," he added quietly.

"Impatience? Rashness?" Why did he have to taint his praise by saying things like that? It would seem he wasn't going to break the cycle of our conversations ending badly just yet. "Are you referring to me coming inside to look for you?"

He held his hand up the way he did when he wanted to interrupt. But I had something to say and I was going to say it.

"For your information, McIlroy reported back that you were lying on the bed covered in blood. Perhaps I shouldn't have trusted the word of a childlike man, but I'm quite certain you would have reacted the same way if the situation was reversed and I had been inside instead of you. I think I acted appropriately and carefully at that point. Not only did I have Seth with me, but McIlroy too." I stamped my hand on my hip and arched my brows at him.

"Are you quite finished?"

I nodded.

"Good, because I want you to know that is precisely what I was about to tell you."

"Oh." I lowered my hand.

"If I'd heard you were lying in that bed, covered in blood, I would have attempted a rescue, and with considerably more force. So I have no right to be angry, just as I had no right to be mad at you for raising the spirit of Estelle Pearson."

"Oh," I repeated dully.

"And what's more…" He studied his glass again, then he drained the contents in a single gulp. "What's more…I liked that you were worried enough to attempt a rescue."

I sat heavily on the chair. I blinked at him, trying to determine what tone he'd used—*had* he used a particular tone?

"I am…unused to people worrying about me," he said to his glass. "It's…new and…feels odd."

"The general never worried about you? Or your tutors? The housekeeper?"

He shook his head. "Why would they?" Despite the angle of his head, I could just make out the grim set of his mouth, the firming of his jaw. "I believe gratitude is in order."

He wanted to show me his appreciation? That was all? I suppose, given his refusal to take our kiss to its natural next step, it was all I could hope for.

I waited for him to say something further, but he did not. He touched his finger to his lips and I had the impression he was silencing himself. But that could have been my imagination. It tended to run rampant where Lincoln was concerned.

After a drawn-out moment, which felt like it lasted five minutes but was probably only five seconds, I stood. "Goodnight, Lincoln."

He looked up and blinked in surprise. Did he want me to stay longer? Why? I knew why *I* wanted to stay, and I hoped he had the same thoughts, but I wasn't going to throw myself into his lap and kiss him all over like I wanted to. If he wanted to change the situation between us then he would have to instigate it. I was tired of his seesawing emotions. My heart still bore the bruises of his rejection. He knew how I felt, and it was now up to him to do something about it if he wished. I was no longer going to make a fool of myself where he was concerned.

"Goodnight," he muttered, reaching for the bottle on the table beside him.

* * *

Black hair splayed across white pillow. Red blood blooming over white sheets. Lincoln was dead and not even his spirit could hear my scream.

I awoke with a start and the sensation that I was not alone in the bedroom. "Lincoln," I said on impulse.

"I'm here." He stood close to the bed, his face in shadow.

He was here. But why?

CHAPTER 16

"It was only a dream," I said, as much to reassure myself as Lincoln. I passed a trembling hand across my eyes and sucked in a deep breath in an attempt to calm my rapidly beating heart. It didn't work, and I felt more unraveled than ever. I hadn't been this shaken when I'd first seen the dead man I'd thought was Lincoln.

To my utter horror, my face crumpled and my emotions gushed to the surface. I pulled up my legs and embraced them, then buried my face on my knees. I bit my lip hard in an effort to keep silent.

The mattress beside me sank, and Lincoln's arm came around my shoulders. He pressed his lips to the top of my head, and I leaned into him. He was solid and *alive*. Thank God. His warmth seeped through my nightdress, chasing away the chill that had crept into me through my dreams. How could a man so versed in the art of cool emotions be so warm?

I didn't dare think what his presence in my room meant. Perhaps it meant nothing. Perhaps it was his way of being protective. All I knew was that I liked the way he held me, and the way I could feel his heart beating, and smell the scent of spicy soap on his skin. I liked how I was now thinking of these things and not my nightmare.

I adjusted my position and tucked my head under his chin. His arm tightened, much to my surprise. I'd expected him to withdraw and mutter a conviction that it wouldn't happen again.

"Better?" His voice rumbled through his body, sending vibrations through mine.

"Yes. Thank you for waking me."

"I wasn't sure if it was the best thing to do or not."

"It was. Believe me, I'd rather be awake all night than dream…that."

I expected him to ask me what it was about, but he didn't.

"I must have been loud for you to hear me from your rooms."

"I couldn't hear you. Not in the literal sense."

"You sensed me?"

He nodded. "This time you called my name. That's why I came."

I pulled away to look at him. "This time?"

"I often sense you having nightmares, although they have lessened considerably these last few weeks. Until tonight." His face was close to mine, but it was too dark to see more than his silhouette. "I don't like that you have nightmares about me," he murmured, stroking my hair.

"You do know that you're not the villain in my nightmares, don't you?"

"I…wasn't certain."

Oh, Lincoln. "I was afraid *for* you, not *of* you. That man in the bed…the one who killed himself…" I shook my head. The memory was still too raw to discuss it.

He cupped my cheek. "Tell me what to do to stop them."

My heart ground to a halt. My chest hurt. "Being here with me helps."

"I was afraid you'd say that."

"I had fewer nightmares when I stayed in your rooms, back when you thought I was a boy."

"That's not possible anymore, Charlie," he said heavily.

I tucked my head beneath his chin again and wrapped my arms around him. I wasn't willing to let him go yet. "So is this it? Is this what we're reduced to? A few snatched moments in the dead of night, when you wake me from a nightmare, and then in the morning, everything returns to how it was before?"

"Not…quite as it was before."

I pulled away again. "What do you mean?"

"I mean…" He blew out a breath. It smelled faintly of brandy. "I have tried to distance myself from you. I've tried telling myself that what I feel is merely fleeting desire, nothing more. I've tried not to like it when you worry about me." He rubbed my shoulder and drew in another deep breath, then another. "But I've failed, and I continue to fail every day, every hour."

"Oh. This is…an interesting development."

"Interesting is not the word that sprang to my mind," he said wryly.

"So what are you going to do about it?" *Kiss me, you big fool.*

"I am yet to come to a conclusion."

My heart plunged. Some of the coolness had returned to his voice. I was losing him. The emotional man was being slowly taken over by the unemotional one again. "You're thinking through all the possible repercussions, aren't you? All the positives and negatives?"

"It's who I am; how I work."

"This is not work, Lincoln. I am not a task you have to schedule or a mystery to solve."

"You're wrong. You're the greatest mystery, Charlie. Attempting to solve why I feel for you what I do takes a lot of my energy."

"Then stop using your head and use this instead." I placed my hand against his shirt over his heart. It beat a little erratically. "Give in to what you *feel*, Lincoln. Perhaps it'll become easier to understand once you do."

He brushed the pad of his thumb across the ridge of my cheek. "I can't risk it," he said on a breath. "The potential to cause damage...it's too great. If I hurt you..."

You already are, I wanted to say but didn't. My throat was too clogged, for one thing, and I didn't want to scare him away even more.

"Or if you are hurt because of your connection to me..." he whispered. I felt a shudder ripple through him and tightened my grip around him.

In that moment, with that shudder, I knew he spoke with honesty. An honesty that took enormous effort to put into words. Despite his strength and competence, Lincoln was afraid. He'd never loved anyone before or been loved in return. The only person he'd ever come close to caring about—Timmy—had died, and he had died because of his friendship with Lincoln. No wonder he was afraid. No wonder he'd tried to convince himself not to care for me.

But how to set his mind at ease? We'd been through so many dangers together, and the risks were great. There would continue to be risks, particularly if he gave me what I wanted—an active role in the ministry. Looking at it that way, I'd brought his rejection down on myself by insisting I work alongside him.

With a heavy heart, I scooted back up the bed, away from him. What I needed to say required a clear head, and I couldn't have that if I was touching him. His hand dropped to the mattress like a stone.

"I love you, Lincoln. With all my heart, I love you. I can love you despite knowing it comes with risks—that you won't love me back, or that you will one day leave me, whether you want to or not." My eyes burned and my chest ached but I was proud of the strength in my voice, and I was a little surprised by it, too. "But you're not ready to love me in the same way. The fear is tormenting you, and it will continue to torment you until you make the decision not to let it anymore. Love and fear are intertwined, Lincoln. You cannot have one without the other, and until you understand that, I'll never have all of you. And I want every last piece of you. I'm selfish that way." I sucked in a shuddery breath and let it out slowly. I wished I could see his face but it was too dark. He didn't move. "Come to me when you're ready."

His hand moved an inch toward me then settled on the mattress again. "How will I know when I'm ready?" he asked in a raspy whisper.

"When having me for just a moment is worth any risk, including losing me forever."

I heard his swallow in the dark then he stood. "I'll think about what you've said."

I smiled, despite the weight pressing down on my chest. He wasn't someone who could separate thinking from feeling. At least not yet.

"Get some sleep, Charlie." His silhouette melted into the shadows and the outer door clicked closed.

I sank beneath the covers and sighed. Had I really just thrown away the opportunity of having him? Would he ever understand what I was trying to tell him? Or would he come to me again one day, and tell me the risks were worth it?

Dear God, I hoped so. Otherwise, I was the biggest fool in England.

* * *

Andrew Buchanan slept late. When he finally awoke, the entire household knew it from his foul-mouthed shouts. Gus's responding shouts for him to calm down went unheeded, and it wasn't until Lincoln appeared that Buchanan quieted.

"Fitzroy! What the devil is going on?" he snapped from where he was pinned against the wall by Gus's forearm. "Who is this oaf? Where am I?"

"You're at Lichfield Towers," Lincoln said, nodding at Gus to release him. "Gus is my employee, as are Seth and Miss Holloway. We rescued you last night from Bedlam."

"Bedlam? Is this some kind of a joke?"

"I don't joke."

"It's true, he doesn't," Gus chimed in, earning a glare from Seth.

Buchanan glanced between each of the men then his gaze flicked to me. A small frown settled between his brows then he quickly looked away. The color rose in his cheeks. He stretched his neck and folded his arms over his nightshirt, as if embarrassed to be seen dressed like that. Along with his disheveled hair and stubbly chin, he looked nothing like the gentleman I'd first met at Harcourt House.

"There are clothes in your room, Mr. Buchanan," I said. "Perhaps you'd like to dress then join us for breakfast. Seth will assist you."

Buchanan stretched his neck again and looked down his nose at me. "You look familiar. Have we met?"

"My name is Charlotte Holloway. We met when I called upon Lady Harcourt."

He pursed his lips and shook his head. "Can't recall."

Not surprising; he'd been three sheets to the wind at the time.

"Miss Holloway is my assistant." The sharp edge to Lincoln's tone wasn't lost on me, but no one else seemed to notice it. "Get dressed, Buchanan. I want answers."

"You're not the only one," Buchanan muttered.

"Why are you his assistant and we are only employees?" Gus whined as he and I headed into the kitchen. Lincoln had gone to his rooms. "We assist too, and we been doin' it longer."

"You should bring it up with him," I said.

We'd all eaten breakfast so we only needed to prepare enough for Buchanan. I carried plates of bacon, toast, sausages and eggs on a silver tray and deposited it on the dining room sideboard.

Lincoln joined me. "I'm glad to see you wearing it," he said, touching the chatelaine at my hip. They were the first words, aside from "good morning," that he'd spoken to me all day. Perhaps, like me, he felt the awkwardness of our overnight conversation. It was one thing to bare one's soul in the dark; it was quite another to do so in the daytime.

"It's almost too beautiful to wear, but I couldn't resist. Thank you again, Lincoln. I'll treasure it."

Buchanan took that moment to stroll into the breakfast room, Seth at his heels. His jaw was clean shaven, his hair neatly combed and oiled, and he wore Seth's spare clothing.

"Come and eat," I said when no one else spoke. "Then we'll talk."

Buchanan gave me a slight bow and swaggered over to the sideboard, his step lazy and cocksure. At first glance, he appeared to be back to himself, but on closer inspection I noticed his eyes darting about and the slight shake of his hand as he helped himself to bacon.

Gus served tea then joined us at the table.

"Now, if you'll tell me what in God's name I was doing in Bedlam, I would be grateful," Buchanan said, slicing through a sausage.

Lincoln told Buchanan how the dowager Lady Harcourt had reported him missing and how we'd tracked his movements to Emberly Park but no further. He included all the details about the journal, Estelle Pearson and the baby, but he didn't mention my necromancy and Buchanan didn't ask how we'd learned about her involvement in the birth.

"You fought with your brother at Emberly, didn't you?" Lincoln asked.

Buchanan slapped a thick layer of butter on his toast. "He punched me, the turd. I hit him back, of course. Gave him a bloody nose and a black eye."

"He don't have no black eye," Gus said.

Buchanan bit off a corner of the toast and eyed Gus. "Are you doubting the word of a gentleman?" he said around his mouthful.

"My man is correct," Lincoln said with a hint of humor that I suspected none of the others detected. "You didn't hit your brother. He knocked you out, in fact. Afterward, he drove you to Bedlam, signed the papers, and perhaps paid a large sum to the governor to insure you weren't properly assessed. You remained there in Bedlam, drugged, for over a week until we rescued you."

Buchanan's chewing slowed as Lincoln made his speech, and finally stopped at the end with a loud swallow. "*Donald* had me committed."

"All evidence points to him. You fell unconscious at Emberly after your fight, so he had opportunity to bundle you into a coach. He knew how easy it was to have a family member committed to Bedlam after sending his wife there, and his signature was on the paperwork."

"Donald! I cannot believe it." Buchanan set down his knife and fork and stared at his plate. "He was deeply troubled by the methods employed at Bedlam when he learned what they did to Marguerite there. Besides, why would he need to get rid of me? We fought, yes, but we've fought before."

"What was the fight about?" I asked.

"Money."

"Not the baby?"

"Not really. Perhaps." He rubbed his forehead. "I'm not entirely sure, Miss Holloway. Perhaps he harbors a deep resentment toward me because of my virility and appeal to the opposite sex—Marguerite in particular. She adores me, you know. Always has. She's like a puppy when I'm around, following me about with her tongue hanging out." He chuckled and picked up his knife and fork again.

Seth rolled his eyes. Gus looked like he wanted to throw something at Buchanan. His fingers tightened around his teacup.

"You cannot recall anything after the fight?" I asked.

"Nothing. I remember him hitting me, then I felt like I was falling. A pain in my head…" He rubbed the back of his head and winced. "Then nothing."

Lincoln tapped his finger on the side of his teacup and seemed to be lost in thought. After a moment, he said, "We'll confront your brother at Harcourt House after breakfast."

"Capital," Buchanan said through clenched teeth. "I cannot wait to see the look on his face when he sees me."

I insisted on going with Lincoln and Buchanan. Buchanan was very amenable to the idea, perhaps because he thought I appreciated his little smiles and the occasional wink. *Ugh.* If only he knew how he disgusted me.

I was the last to be ready, and I hurried out the front door and down the steps to the waiting coach. Buchanan was already inside and Seth sat on the driver's seat. Lincoln and Gus waited for me.

"Has he thanked you for rescuing him yet?" I whispered to Lincoln as I drew on my gloves.

"No, and I expect none," he said in a low voice. "People like him don't know how to say thank you or sorry. The words aren't in their vocabulary."

Gus leaned in. "Sure you don't want to take him back to Bedlam, sir?"

"Don't tempt me."

I smiled and climbed in, settling opposite Buchanan. Lincoln sat beside me, and Gus closed the door. He was to remain behind at Lichfield. We drove in silence most of the way. Once, Buchanan muttered his brother's name again, but he mostly appeared lost in thought.

As we neared Harcourt House, he said, "Julia was worried about me, you say? Interesting." His twisted smile almost made me feel sorry for her.

The shock on Millard's face as he opened the door to his mistress's stepson set the tone for the reunion. Marguerite squealed then threw her arms around him and wept into his shoulder, whereas Julia was a little more sedate but no less effusive in thanking God and Lincoln for returning Buchanan to their midst.

Lord Harcourt also embraced his brother, only to be shoved away. He frowned, his arms still extended. "Andrew?"

"Where ever did you find him, Lincoln?" Julia asked as she studied her stepson from head to toe. "Somewhere far away, I suspect. He looks awfully tired."

Mr. Edgecombe rolled in from the direction of the drawing room, his assistant pushing the wheelchair. "Good lord, you're back! And unscathed, too. Well it's about bloody time. The uproar around here has been rather excessive. The ladies have missed your company most keenly. So, tell us. Whose bed have you occupied this past week?"

"Bedlam's," Buchanan answered.

Marguerite crumpled in a dead faint. Fortunately, Millard caught her before she hit the floor. He and Harcourt carried her into the drawing room as Julia fetched the smelling salts. The rest of us followed the main party.

Buchanan eyed his brother with such venom that it was a surprise he didn't feel it. Harcourt was much too intent on his wife, however, as she came around. She rested a pale, shaking hand on her throat as tears welled in her eyes. Her lips began to move but no words came out.

"My dear," Harcourt said, sitting beside her. "It's all right. I am here." He took her other hand in his until she noticed and snatched it back. She turned her face toward the back of the sofa, away from him.

He swallowed and slowly stood. "How did you wind up in that place, Andrew?"

Buchanan's eyes flashed. His jaw went rigid. "You swine. You pretend innocence in my own home—"

"Julia's home. What do you mean 'pretend innocence?' What are you getting at?"

Buchanan swung his fist, but Harcourt moved at the last moment and the punch merely clipped his shoulder. Lincoln was close enough and fast enough that he could have intervened but he didn't. He merely stood by, his hands at his back, and watched.

Julia gasped. "Stop this! Stop it at once. Andrew, explain yourself."

"Why not get him to explain?" He nodded at Harcourt, now safely out of reach. "He put me there."

"In Bedlam?" Julia turned her wide eyes onto her eldest stepson as he spluttered a protest.

Marguerite sat up and blinked at her husband. "You did *what*?"

"Had him admitted to Bedlam," Edgecombe drawled. "Keep up, Sis."

"I did no such thing!" Harcourt tugged on his waistcoat hem. "I would never commit anyone to Bedlam, let alone a family member. Not anymore," he added upon Edgecombe's derisive snort. "That place is worse than a prison. It's a torture chamber. I wouldn't commit my worst enemy, let alone my own brother."

"Don't play the innocent, kind big brother," Buchanan sneered.

"Andrew, listen to yourself! Why would I send you to Bedlam? What possible motive could I have?"

"Jealousy." He arched his brow at Marguerite.

Harcourt regarded his wife coolly. "Andrew, you are a fool," he said with lofty condescension. "I admit to occasionally having bouts of jealousy still, but you and I both know that Marguerite's infatuation with you will go nowhere."

Marguerite clutched her throat and blinked back tears. She looked like a china doll, all pale glossy skin, pink heart shaped lips and vacant eyes. Julia waved the smelling salts beneath her nose again until Marguerite regained some color.

"If not jealousy then simple anger," Buchanan went on. This time he sounded less certain. I, too, began to have doubts about our theory. Harcourt wasn't acting like a guilty man. "You were angry with me for asking you for money. When we fought and I hit my head, you panicked. If I died, you would be arrested for murder."

"You wouldn't have died! You were already on your way when I left you."

"On my way?" Buchanan sat and rubbed his temples. "Yes, I was. I recall walking off down the drive, away from the house."

Harcourt hitched up his trousers and sat too. "I cannot believe you would accuse me of such a thing. I would never take you off to Bedlam. Never. As to your debts, yes, I was angry when you asked for money, but that's nothing new. You often make me angry. You have ever since you were knee-high."

So if he didn't do it, someone must have falsified his signature on the admission forms and passed themselves off as Lord Harcourt to the Bedlam governor. That meant a man was involved. While it didn't eliminate Julia or Marguerite—they could have hired someone—I didn't think it was either of them. Marguerite loved him unconditionally, and Julia had been the one to come to us in the first place.

That left one man. I watched Edgecombe from beneath my lashes. Surely it couldn't have been him. He was wheelchair bound, and he'd been friends with Buchanan before his accident.

Before, but not after, perhaps. Why not? Had Buchanan lost interest in a friend who could no longer join in with his revels? Perhaps Edgecombe had been the one to pay a man to pretend to be Lord Harcourt at Bedlam. His man, Dawkins…

No, not Dawkins. He was new. The previous assistant had died—*at around the same time Buchanan disappeared.*

"Then who…?" Julia asked, clutching the back of Andrew's chair. She appealed to Lincoln with a delicate lift of one shoulder.

He looked to me, which brought her brows crashing down. "Charlie, if you please," he said. It would seem he had the same suspicion as me.

I nodded as he moved to block the doorway. "Mr. Edgecombe, what is the name of your previous assistant?" I asked.

Edgecombe blinked at me. "Good lord, you don't think *he* did it, do you? Why would he?"

"Tell her the name," Lincoln growled.

Edgecombe bristled. "It was Cleves. Norman Cleves."

"Middle name?" I prompted.

"What in God's name for?"

"It helps."

"Helps with what?" Edgecombe looked to me, then to Lincoln and on to Julia when she smothered a small gasp. She understood what I was about to do.

"What was his middle name?" Lincoln asked in that ice-cold tone that brooked no argument.

"I think it was Charter, after his mother's side."

"Thank you." I drew in a breath and kept my eye on him. "Norman Charter Cleves, please come to me. I summon the spirit of Norman Charter Cleves."

Edgecombe's frown deepened. "What the devil is going on?"

"That's what I'd like to know," Buchanan said, although his tone held curiosity not censure.

Julia clutched the choker at her throat and scanned the ceiling, as if she could see the spirit of Norman Cleves now hovering above the fireplace. Of course, she could not.

"Are you…?" Lord Harcourt stared at me. "Is she…?" His wife held out a shaking hand and he took it and sat beside her once more. They were the picture of a united couple again, reliant on one another for comfort in times of difficulty. "My god…you are."

"Are what?" his wife asked.

"A spiritualist, I believe."

"She speaks to ghosts?" Marguerite whipped around to face me. "Has she summoned Cleves here?"

"Well, well," Buchanan said, grinning at me. "You're a medium. Did Father bring you back here to question you? Thought I recognized you."

"My name is Charlie," I told the spirit of Norman Cleves as well as answering Buchanan. "I'm a necromancer, not a medium. I work for an organization known as the Ministry of Curiosities."

Cleves would have been a large, impressively-built man in his lifetime. He had the broad shoulders of a navvy, the muscular chest of someone used to carrying heavy loads—like grown men—up and down stairs. I knew this because he was naked from the waist up.

"A necromancer, eh?" the spirit said without taking his eyes off Edgecombe. "Can you turn people into spirits too, just by calling their names?"

"No, only summon the dead. Tell me about your death."

"This is ridiculous," Edgecombe spluttered. "Dawkins, I'm leaving. Julia, I would appreciate the use of your driver and other servants to assist—"

"Stay," Lincoln said quietly. "Listen."

"Listen to whom? There's no one there. Your assistant is a crackpot!"

"Mr. Cleves?" I prompted. "I can bring you justice, if it's deserved."

"Oh, it's deserved, all right. He killed me." He nodded at Edgecombe. "He bloody killed me, after everything I did for him." With a baring of teeth, he swooped at Edgecombe. But Edgecombe sat without moving and the spirit *whooshed* through without Edgecombe feeling a thing. "We'd been out for a drive in the brougham, just me and him. We were almost back at Emberly when we came across Mr. Buchanan, wandering along the drive, all befuddled and stumbling. As soon as we offered him a ride, he passed out. I said we should call on the doctor, but Mr. Edgecombe had this look in his eyes. A real mean look, it was. Like he hated Mr. Buchanan. Really hated him and wanted to hurt him. He said he would take him to a special hospital. He told me to go to his rooms and get his medicine, the stuff that puts him to sleep at night."

I remembered Dawkins telling me about the strong medicine that made Edgecombe sleep peacefully throughout the night. I looked to Lincoln and gave a slight nod of my head. He blinked in understanding—he must have guessed that Cleves had implicated Edgecombe.

"I returned to the curricle and injected the stuff into Mr. Buchanan, then we set off for London," Cleves went on.

"That's a long way from Emberly Park."

"Aye, miss, it is. If I'd known that's where we were headed, I would have refused to go. We drove all bloody night. By the morning, I was tired and my back hurt. But I did what my master wanted, because he's always been good to me and he paid well."

"What happened when you reached London?"

"London!" several voices echoed at once.

"What's going on?" Edgecombe growled. "What's the silly chit doing?"

Cleves grunted a humorless laugh. "Tables are turned now, aren't they?" To me, he said, "Mr. Edgecombe directed me to a hospital then told me to pretend to be his brother-in-law, Lord Harcourt. We swapped jackets, waistcoats and even boots, then I carried Mr. Buchanan into the hospital."

"*You* filled in the paperwork?"

He lifted his chin. "I can read and write my letters as good as any man. Mr. Edgecombe waited in the brougham. After, we checked into a hotel and rested. The next day, we drove back to Emberly. That's when he killed me. Not sure how. Slipped some medicine into my drink to make me sleep, I expect, then injected me with some of the stronger painkillers the doctor gives him. I never woke up. I waited for a while in this form then decided to cross over when I was called. I saw by then he wasn't going to be arrested." He shook his head. "Bloody bastard. Tell him I hope he rots in hell."

"Mr. Edgecombe," I said. "Mr. Cleves would like you to know that he thinks you're a bloody bastard and that he hopes you rot in hell."

Marguerite gasped. Julia clicked her tongue. "Really, Charlie, was that necessary?"

"Very," I assured her. "Mr. Cleves was murdered by Mr. Edgecombe and—"

The rest of my speech was drowned out by Marguerite's screeching protest. "You're lying! She's lying, Donald! John would never harm anyone! Besides, look at him. He's hopeless. He can't do a thing for himself, can you, dear? He's like a child—"

"Shut up!" Edgecombe shouted, sending spittle spraying from his mouth onto his chin. "Shut up, shut up, shut up! Dawkins, push me out of here. You," he pointed at Lincoln, "step aside."

Lincoln didn't move. Nor did Dawkins. He was staring at the back of his master's head. He muttered a few colorful words then strode for the door. "I didn't sign up for this." Lincoln let him past without stopping him.

Edgecombe pushed himself forward with laborious heaves of the wheels. He grunted on every push and sweat beaded on his hairline. "Out of my way."

"You?" Buchanan grabbed one of the wheelchair handles, stopping Edgecombe in his tracks. "Stay here. You put me in Bedlam, for Christ's sake! I'm not letting you get away with it."

"Not to mention he murdered Cleves," I added.

But no one heard me. All attention was on Buchanan and Edgecombe. Fury burned bright in both men's eyes and tensed the muscles in their necks.

"Why?" Buchanan asked. "I thought we were friends."

"Friends!" Edgecombe growled. "*You* did this to me." He indicated the chair and his useless legs beneath the blanket. "You made me like this."

"You fell of your horse." Buchanan straightened his back and turned his head away. "Nothing to do with me," he muttered.

"You shot at my horse and he bolted!"

"A competent rider would have stayed in the saddle. Besides, I didn't shoot *at* him. I saw a fox nearby..." He shrugged. "You can't blame that on me."

"If you really believed in your own innocence, then why not come to visit me in all this time?"

"Emberly is too far from London, and London is where all the pretty girls are."

Edgecombe snorted. "You stayed away because you couldn't face me. You never wrote, never asked your brother to pass on your regards."

"I'm no good at letter writing."

"Coward!" Edgecombe rolled himself forward again, this time toward Buchanan. Buchanan stepped nimbly behind the sofa. Edgecombe gave up with a frustrated snarl.

"You hadn't seen Mr. Buchanan since your accident," I said, putting the final pieces together. "All your anger and resentment toward him had festered over time, so when you saw him wandering along the drive, you decided to punish him for robbing you of the life you had."

"John," Marguerite sobbed into her husband's handkerchief. "How *could* you?"

"I *could* have killed him," Edgecombe snapped. "Taking him to Bedlam was a mercy." He pushed the wheels himself, putting all his upper body strength into it.

"No further," Lincoln said when Edgecombe was almost upon him.

Edgecombe slipped his hand beneath the blanket and whipped out a pistol. "Move!"

CHAPTER 17

Marguerite screamed. Donald pulled her into his chest, perhaps as much to smother her into silence as protect her.

"Move!" Edgecombe growled, pointing the pistol at Lincoln.

Lincoln stepped calmly aside.

"Marguerite, push this bloody chair. Julia, a carriage, driver and footman, if you please. *Now*!"

"You're just going to let him go, Fitzroy?" Buchanan's high-pitched voice was almost as ear-splitting as Marguerite's.

"He's not going to get shot for him," I said hotly. "Or for you. This is a family matter, not a ministry one, and I have a mind to let you all deal with him. We're not risking our lives for any of you."

"Really, Charlie." Julia's clipped tones fell like shards of glass in the silence that followed my tirade. "There's no need for hysteria. While I'm sure Lincoln enjoys being the object of your infatuation, it's not very helpful."

I wished I could think of a retort to put her back in her place, but for once, I was speechless. That annoyed me as much as her insults.

"Julia!" Edgecombe snapped. "Retract your claws and be useful, instead of decorative, for once. Ah, the servants are here. Good."

Millard had returned upon hearing the shouting, along with two footmen. They reared back when they spotted Edgecombe with the pistol. Each of them looked to Harcourt for direction—not Julia, their mistress, or Buchanan, the other regular member of the household. That must be galling for them both.

"You!" Edgecombe barked at one of the footmen. "Tell the driver to prepare a fast vehicle. Go!" As he ran off, Edgecombe turned to the other footman. "You look strong. You'll be assisting me. Wheel this chair, since my sister refuses to get off her arse. Do it backwards so that I may keep my eye on them all. And don't try anything stupid."

Harcourt gave a slight nod, and the footman complied, taking a wide, circuitous route to the back of the wheelchair without taking his wary gaze off Edgecombe.

"You won't get far," Lincoln said as Edgecombe rolled past him and out of the drawing room. "That's a four-barrel pistol. We're more than four."

"I'd wager you're not willing to risk four lives to capture me."

"You don't know me very well if you think that."

There were several intakes of breath in the drawing room, but mine was not among them. I knew Lincoln wouldn't take such a risk. Two months ago, yes, but not anymore. Particularly when one of the lives at risk was mine. He was not the cold-hearted killer some—including himself—thought him to be.

"Perhaps I'll start with you." Edgecombe swung the pistol in Lincoln's direction to another round of gasps, this time including mine. Lincoln didn't move.

Nor did Edgecombe. The footman had stopped and stepped away, his shaking hands in the air. "Get back here, you fool!" Edgecombe shouted. The footman glanced at each of us and at Harcourt's nod, he once again took the wheelchair handles and dragged Edgecombe backwards out of the drawing room.

"If you do not shoot anyone, there is a chance you will walk free and the family will sweep this under the carpet," Lincoln told Edgecombe. "You can live as you were."

"Not bloody likely," Harcourt said in a low threat that may not have reached Edgecombe's ears. "I don't want him in my house after this. Marguerite, cease your appeals. You cannot ask that of me." His gentle pats on her back didn't placate her as she fell into a teary mess against the back of the sofa.

"Nobody has asked *me* what I wish," Buchanan said. "Where is my justice? *I* will not sweep this under the carpet." He stepped forward onto a creaking floorboard.

Edgecombe pointed the pistol at him.

"Don't shoot!" Julia shouted.

"Andrew!" Marguerite flung herself at Buchanan, her body between him and her brother. "Don't do this, John. It's madness."

"Perhaps I ought to be the one in Bedlam then." Edgecombe's harsh cackle had me thinking that he was right. The suddenly serious, cruel twist of his mouth only reinforced my opinion. "Move, Marguerite. Give me a clear shot at the prick. He deserves to have his life ended the way he ended mine."

"You're not dead, John!"

"Might as well be."

"If you kill him," Lincoln went on, in that unruffled tone of his, "you will be arrested for his murder."

"Be quiet," Edgecombe hissed. "Marguerite, *move*!"

Marguerite broke into hysterics against Buchanan's shoulder. He winced and patted her back as if he couldn't stand to have his borrowed clothes spoiled by her tears.

Harcourt looked away as his wife fell to pieces over her lover. Only Julia remained unmoved, and the spirit of Cleves too, as he stood near Lincoln, his presence forgotten by all except me. If only there was a dead body nearby that I could force him to enter, so he could overpower Edgecombe for us.

But there wasn't. We had to use Earthly means.

"Put the gun down," Lincoln said. "I won't allow you to get out of here alive if you shoot anyone."

"Faster, man!" Edgecombe's darting eyes assessed the numbers and the exits. He must have seen that it was hopeless; he had four bullets and there were more than four against him, taking the footman and Millard into account.

"Give up, Edgecombe," Lincoln said from the doorway. "You won't get away with this. Your family will never forgive you if you shoot someone. Such a crime cannot be overlooked by them or by the law. If you surrender now, there is still a chance of being free. You can live out your life peacefully, somewhere in the countryside. Somewhere quiet and far away from the city, Bedlam, and madness. You will be free."

His voice droned on, an unrelenting rhythm of calm that must have felt like a blunt instrument to Edgecombe's mad mind for he clutched his head. He thrust his fingers through his hair as if he would penetrate his skull and dig out his brain. Perhaps he was the maddest of the lot.

"I will never be free!" He pressed the gun to his temple and fired before anyone knew what was happening.

I jumped and covered my mouth but not before a cry escaped. Marguerite and Julia both fainted, while Buchanan and Harcourt turned pale faces away from the shocking sight.

The poor footman stumbled backward and fell to the floor. He scrambled away from the wheelchair, then turned onto all fours, and vomited. He was covered in blood.

The smoky spirit of Edgecombe rose out of his body and drifted aimlessly around the room, as if caught by the drafts. When he finally stilled, he stared down at his own ghostly legs. Was he unable to believe he'd just killed himself? Or was he enthralled by his transformation into a ghost?

The spirit of Cleves strolled up to him, signaled a rude hand gesture, then came back to me. "Am I done here?"

"Yes, thank you," I said numbly. "Your assistance was most beneficial. You are released now, Mr. Cleves. Return to your afterlife."

He slipped away, and Edgecombe's spirit followed soon after, thank God. I didn't want to converse with him.

Lincoln checked the pulpy mess of the body in the wheelchair. He also held a pistol. Where had it come from? Why hadn't he used it before?

My brain was busy trying to sort through questions and answers, yet my feet wouldn't move. I did not, however, collapse into a faint like Julia and Marguerite. I attributed my stoicism not to my more robust health, but my refusal to wear a corset. My lungs were not restricted like theirs. I was able to breathe as much air as my body required.

Harcourt gently picked up his wife and carried her back to the sofa, where he waved the smelling salts beneath her nose. As she began to rouse, he wordlessly passed the salts onto Buchanan, who repeated the motion beneath Julia's nose. It would have been quite a romantic, noble scene if it weren't for the dead body and the retching footman in the entrance hall.

Lincoln tucked his gun back into the waistband of his trousers, beneath his jacket. He then took charge, ordering the servants and helping where needed. He and Millard carried the body into the mews to await a coroner, and I summoned the courage to assist two of the maids in cleaning up the mess. I liked to think my lack of hysteria helped calm them, but in truth they cried throughout and raced off to the service area to wash themselves clean afterward.

"Let's go home, Charlie. You've done enough." Lincoln gently took my bloodied hand in his own and steered me toward the door and out to the waiting carriage. Someone must have apprised Seth of the events, because he seemed unsurprised to see us in such a state and did not ask questions.

Back at Lichfield, I headed straight for the bathroom and turned on the taps. While the bath filled, I stripped off and scrubbed as much of the blood off my skin as I could at the sink without removing the skin itself. Finally, feeling more like myself, I sank into the bath and let the warm water soak away any remaining blood, fear and horror.

The knock on the door roused me some time later, when the water had begun to cool. "Charlie? Are you all right?" It was Lincoln. He must be concerned, though perhaps he was waiting for the bath himself.

"Yes, thank you. I'll be out in a moment."

"I have clothes for you."

I dried off, and with the towel around my body, opened the door a crack. The corridor was empty except for the clothing placed neatly in a pile on the nearby table. I took the garments back into the bathroom and hurriedly dressed.

I found Lincoln in the parlor, stoking the fire. He must have washed outside because he was clean, his hair damp.

"I'm sorry I occupied the bathroom for so long," I told him as I settled on the chair by the fire.

"The bathroom is all yours whenever you want it. Tea?"

"God, yes." Cook had not only provided tea, but also scones with large pots of jam and cream. He knew me so well. I helped myself to one and slathered as much jam and cream on top as would stay on.

I angled my head to the fire to help dry my hair and ate an entire scone in a mere three bites.

"Better?" Lincoln asked as he watched me sip tea.

I nodded. "Much, thank you. I think I was a little in shock for a while there."

"Nobody but me would have noticed. You carried yourself admirably, Charlie. Much more capably than the other females."

I felt the heat rise in my face at his praise. "Perhaps that's because I'm used to death now."

"Death, yes; horror, no. I'm sorry you had to see that."

"Poor Marguerite, to see her brother die in such a ghastly manner."

"I would like to tell you that she'll recover, but her mind was already delicate. I'm not sure how she'll cope with this."

I sighed. Then I frowned. "I didn't know you had a gun."

"We were confronting a man who put another into Bedlam using force and trickery. I thought a weapon might be useful."

"Why didn't you use it?"

"There was no opportunity. If I had, he might have shot you. Or anyone." His eyes banked with deeper, blacker shadows as he looked at me. "I couldn't risk it."

He couldn't risk *me* being injured. Of all the people in that room, I was the only one he cared about. It was both thrilling and intoxicating, yet troubling too to think that he might sacrifice other lives if it meant saving mine.

"If only you'd pulled your gun out before he drew his," I said.

He sipped his tea and looked at the flames.

"You could have, couldn't you? Either before or after, when his attention was on one of the others. He wouldn't have noticed you until it was too late."

Still he didn't answer, and I knew I was correct. Lincoln had deliberately not shown his hand, perhaps so as not to startle Edgecombe into shooting one of us. But perhaps also so he could calmly and very deliberately talk the man into seeing the hopelessness of the situation and his future.

"You intended for him to kill himself," I said quietly. "Didn't you?"

He slowly lowered the cup to the table. "The man hated his life. He wanted it to end. Added to which, he would have gone to prison. Buchanan and Harcourt would have seen to it."

A lump made swallowing difficult. Tears pricked my eyes. Perhaps he was right and the future he so coldly mapped out for Edgecombe was the one he would most likely have had. And perhaps Edgecombe would never have been willing to make the best of the situation. But Lincoln should not have encouraged him to end his life. He should not have played any sort of hand in Edgecombe's decision.

"I have told you, do not romanticize me," he said, standing. "I'm the man known as Death by the people who know me best."

"Not by me."

He bent and touched my hair, brushing the damp locks off my cheek and tucking them behind my ear. "Perhaps you're a fool."

"Perhaps I am."

He lowered his hand, before I could catch it, and walked away.

* * *

The dowager Lady Harcourt arrived two days later when I was in the midst of packing a trunk for my journey to France. Lincoln and I weren't set to leave for another two days, but I decided to get an early start. I had to do something or go mad from waiting to experience so many firsts—first time outside of England, first time on a boat, first glimpse of the sea, first time alone with Lincoln for several days.

I wasn't sure if Julia was a welcome distraction or not. On the one hand, I didn't want to suffer through her remarks, which had become snider and snider over the past few weeks, but on the other, I wanted to know how her family was faring after the recent tragedy.

Lincoln took the decision away from me. "You'll act as mistress of Lichfield and have tea with us in the parlor," he told me. While I was recovering from my shock he opened the door to greet her.

"Lincoln," Julia said, kissing his cheek and laying her hand on his shoulder. "I'm so pleased to see you've recovered after that trying experience."

"There was nothing for me to recover from," he said, stepping away.

Julia lowered her hand and caught sight of me, standing back near the staircase. "Charlie," she said with bland indifference.

"Lady Harcourt," I said, unable to call her by her first name when she hadn't asked me to. Some things were so deeply ingrained into one's habits that they could not be expunged, even with a large dose of spite.

Lincoln turned his back on her and arched his brows at me. His eyeballs angled toward the parlor, and I understood what he wanted me to do.

"Come and join us for tea," I said with a smile.

"Not me, I'm afraid," Lincoln said. "I have work to do."

I shook my head at him. "Surely, you can spare a few minutes."

"You *must* join us." Julia slipped her arm through his and steered him toward the parlor. "After all, I came here to speak to *you*."

I rolled my eyes as she turned her head away. "Tea, please, Gus," I whispered to him when he appeared.

"With a dash of venom for the lady?" he asked with a wink.

"She has enough of her own."

I walked into the parlor with a smooth, unhurried step that I hoped oozed confidence and decorum. If it did, it unfortunately went unnoticed by Julia. Her entire attention was focused on Lincoln as he stood near the window. I sank onto the chair by the hearth where the fire would hopefully chase the chill from my bones, which Julia's arrival had put there.

"How is Lady Harcourt?" I asked her since neither of them spoke.

"Much weaker, as is expected," Julia said. "She and Donald returned to Emberly yesterday, thank goodness. She hadn't stopped crying since John's death."

"She just lost her brother under quite awful circumstances."

"Charlie, if you wish to be a part of the ministry then you must harden yourself or you will end up the same way as poor Marguerite—witless and the butt of jokes." She held her hand up as I opened my mouth to protest. "Yes, it's cruel, but I am only the messenger, not the instigator. Do not blame me for pointing out how others will react."

Ha! She seemed to be the only one saying and thinking such things. On the other hand, I did not move in the same circles as her and did not hear the gossip. I was never more grateful for that than now.

"And the body of Edgecombe?" Lincoln asked.

Julia chuckled a throaty laugh. "Always the macabre with you, my dear. Your fascination with death continues to astound me." Her gaze flicked to me then away. Was she implying that his attention to me was due to my necromancy? "The body will be sent to the Edgecombe family estate, where a cousin will oversee the funeral and burial arrangements."

"And Mr. Buchanan?" I asked. "Has he learned anything from this experience?"

"Learned? Whatever do you mean?"

"Not to gamble, for one."

"His debts are now paid."

"By you?" Lincoln asked.

She gave a slight nod.

"What's to stop him racking up further debts and coming to you to pay them off again and again?"

"I know you think I've created a rod for my own back, but there was nothing else to be done. I would rather not have his creditors send around their thugs in the middle of the night, terrifying my staff. They've experienced quite enough trauma, thank you. I made my decision and that's final."

"Did you report to the rest of the committee?"

"I have, but since it didn't turn out to be a ministry matter, it was a courtesy only. There is no need for you to write an additional report. My husband's journals and other things will be returned to the attic and filed away once more."

"What of Buchanan's curiosity?"

"I think he no longer has any. Once I assured him that seers cannot foresee the winners of races, he lost interest."

Gus brought in tea and I poured as he silently left again. Julia accepted her cup and we waited for her to announce the reason for her visit. Part of me worried that she had discovered our pending journey to France and had come to put a stop to it. But Lincoln had assured me the committee members would not be told.

"I've come to offer my services," she finally announced, setting down her cup. "I wish to redecorate this room, among others. If you are to have young ladies of good family call upon you—"

"There will be no one calling upon me," Lincoln said.

"Tosh. Of course there will be. We must find you a wife, *poste haste*. I am in earnest now, Lincoln. And not just any wife, but the *right* wife. Someone sweet of nature, who is content with her lot in life, and not at all magical." Her smile was all teeth and no humor, and I had no doubt it was directed at me, along with her comments on the type of wife Lincoln should have. The mythical woman she described was my opposite in every way.

"Someone like Miss Overton?" I asked.

"Precisely. If only you had come to know her better, Lincoln, you would have found her company very…interesting."

"I doubt that," he said.

"Granted, she was a little silly."

I pressed my lips together to suppress my smile.

"But she is lovely, in her way, and very pretty."

I watched Lincoln over the rim of my cup to see if he agreed with this last sentiment, but he had his blank expression in place and gave nothing away.

"Thank you for your offer to redecorate," he said before she could go on. "But it's not necessary. Charlie will be redecorating the entire house."

"Charlie! But…she has no experience in these things. No offence meant, child, but a house like Lichfield requires a good eye to do it justice."

That wasn't offensive *at all.*

"And deep pockets?" Lincoln intoned.

I grinned into my teacup.

"A good eye," she said again stiffly, "and an innate sense of style and sophistication that cannot be learned."

Now I was determined to present the most tastefully redecorated parlor the city had ever seen. The only problem was, I had no idea how to go about it. She was right. I was the least sophisticated woman to be left in charge of such a task for such a grand house. How did one go about finding things to buy? Were there periodicals? Who should I place orders with? And for what?

"Charlie will do the room justice, I'm sure," he said. "Before you go, Julia, I should inform you that I will be absent for up to a week."

She lowered her cup as if it were suddenly too heavy. "Where are you going?"

"It's a private matter."

"Private?" she echoed, as if such a thing was absurd. "But…you have no…" She picked up her cup again and sipped.

"Privacy?" he finished for her. "I do understand that my life and the ministry's are tied together in the tightest of ways, but I think even you would allow me some time to myself."

"Are you going on a holiday?"

"Of sorts."

She blinked at him, perhaps trying to picture Lincoln with his trouser legs rolled up, strolling along a beach. The image was so absurd that I giggled. He arched his brows at me, and I could swear his lips lifted a little at the edges.

"I'll write to the rest of the committee to inform them," he told her.

She continued to stare at him, her tea forgotten. "But…how are we to get in touch with you if there is urgent ministry business?"

"Leave it with my staff. I'll tend to everything when I return. Excuse me, ladies, I have work to do." He set his cup down and left us.

I wasn't surprised when Julia announced that she had to leave too. I walked her to the door and assisted her with her hat. She paused in the middle of her goodbye, her gaze intent on the chatelaine at my hip. She traced the outline of the goddess figure with her fingernail.

"It's pretty, isn't it?" I said.

Her hand whipped back as if the silver stung. With a nod at me, she let herself out. I wasn't sorry to see her go.

"Lincoln," I said, when I found him with Seth in the stables, preparing the horses for a ride, including the small gray mare that he'd bought for my use alone. "Why did you tell her that I was going to redecorate?"

"Because you are. Ride with me."

"I, er, very well, but I need to change. The redecorating… She's right, and I don't really have an eye for it. I wouldn't know where to begin or even where to shop. My mother had pieces of furniture handed down from her mother, and I think the rest were items my father bought when they married." I shrugged. "She never instructed me in decorating rooms, and even if she had, it wouldn't have been on Lichfield's scale."

"You'll manage," he tossed over his shoulder as he tightened a saddle strap.

I sighed. "I don't want to manage, I want to excel. I want to out-decorate the dowager Lady Harcourt." There. I said it. Now I sounded spiteful.

Seth hauled the side saddle down from the beam and carried it past us. "There's quite a simple solution, you know."

"Don't tell me," I said, "you consider yourself a master decorator."

He laughed. "No, but I know who has the best, most sophisticated taste in all the world."

"Really? Can you introduce me?"

He pouted at Lincoln. "No, because you're not allowing me to come to France with you."

"Your friend is in Paris?"

"He is. He lived here for a while then returned home when he grew bored. His name is Monsieur Fernesse, and he produces some of the finest pieces in all of Europe. His furniture and fittings are highly sought after. I'm sure he'll guide you in all things tasteful and sophisticated."

"Write Charlie a letter of introduction before we go," Lincoln said, taking the saddle from Seth.

"Certainly." His cheeks grew rosy. "A word of warning—do not believe everything Fernesse tells you about me."

I grinned. "Oh? Is he prone to exaggeration?"

Seth's cheeks glowed. "That's one way of putting it."

I returned inside and changed into my riding habit. When I emerged from my room, Lincoln was waiting for me in the corridor. Something was wrong. He looked troubled.

"What's is it?" I asked, searching his face for clues.

"We won't be riding today."

"Is Rosie ill?" I hoped there was nothing wrong with my sweet little mare.

He shook his head then he leaned against the wall and scraped his hand through his hair. Was I mistaken, or did his hand shake?

I grasped his forearms. "What is it?"

"One of the straps on your saddle was cut. Not all the way through, but enough that it would have come apart during a ride. If you'd been riding fast, it would have slipped off and…"

"My god. When you say cut, do you mean deliberately?"

He nodded. "It was straight, not frayed, and clearly done by a blade."

I slumped against the wall too. Someone had wanted me to have an accident, perhaps even kill me. I was the only one who used the side saddle. If Lincoln hadn't spotted it… I shuddered.

It was his turn to grasp my forearms. His gaze searched mine. "It was a clumsy attempt, easily spotted. Its success depended upon a number of factors going against us. Whoever did it was either too foolish to have thought it through, too desperate, or in a hurry. It leads me to think it was merely opportunistic." He let me go to drag both hands through his hair and down his face.

"If it was clumsy, then you ought to be calmer."

"I *am* calm!" he growled.

"You don't sound it."

My lip wobbled and he took my face in his hands. "This might be the first of many attempts, Charlie. We must be vigilant."

"You think they'll try again?"

"They will and with more sophisticated methods next time. So I've decided. We're not going to France."

"What! Why?"

"All manner of dangerous things can happen between here and there."

I held onto his wrists near my cheeks and drew his hands away. "All manner of dangerous things can happen here, too! The tampered saddle proves that. Lincoln, nobody knows that I'm going to France with you except Gus, Seth and Cook. I'll be quite safe there. When we return, we can investigate."

He slumped back against the wall. "It's not as simple as that. I may not be able to keep my eye on you like I'd hope. Not on the journey over and back."

"Why not?"

"I…don't travel well by sea."

"You get seasick?" I began to laugh but bit my tongue when he glared at me. "It seems I will have to nurse you on the crossing."

"You won't be anywhere near me. You'll be locked in a cabin, alone, until we dock."

I sighed. "You're going to be a fun traveling companion."

He pushed off from the wall and strode down to his own rooms. Oh dear. I'd offended him. I ran after him and reached his door just as he began to close it. I wedged my body into the gap, stopping him from slamming the door.

"I'm sorry," I said. "I wasn't mocking you. I'm just used to you being so capable all the time. Even when you're asleep you're alert."

He grunted and moved deeper into the room. I followed.

"Seasickness is not a weakness, Lincoln."

"It makes me weak, therefore it's a weakness." He strode to the desk and gathered up some papers.

I sighed. "So it's one single weakness. If you have any others, I'm yet to discover them."

He shuffled the papers then shuffled them again. I almost interrupted, but his shuffling became more and more furious until he finally threw the pages on the desk, sending them skittering across the surface, crashing into the inkstand, and onto the floor.

He spun round. "You are my weakness, Charlie."

I balked; blinked.

"That's not what I meant." He looked to the ceiling. "I'm not very good at…this. I always seem to say the wrong thing."

"Would you like me to return later, when you've calmed down?" I said testily. I did not like him to think of me as his weakness, as something to be coddled and protected lest I bring him down too as I fell.

"No! Christ." He blew out a breath then lifted his gaze to mine. I closed my fists and bit my tongue to stop myself throwing my arms around him and telling him it didn't matter, that he didn't have to say anything. I was not going to make this easy for him. "I wanted to tell you this on the ride, but now will have to do." He blew out another breath.

"I've been thinking about what you said, that I must be prepared to risk losing you. I've thought of little else."

My tongue began to hurt so I bit my cheek instead and nodded at him to go on.

"I think you're wrong."

"Pardon?" I blurted out.

He gripped the chair back behind him. "There is risk to your safety no matter if you are with me or not, and with the ministry or not. Edgecombe proved that. He could have shot you or anyone in that room, accidentally or on purpose. And now the saddle…" He cleared his throat. "You and I are not…together…and yet there continues to be risks. So you see, we might as well be together as apart."

It wasn't very eloquent, but he wasn't a man who was comfortable with expressing his emotions. "I like how you thought it through," I said with a small smile.

His brows lifted. "And?"

I stepped closer to him. "And I like that you are not going to shut me away in this house to keep me safe, despite the incident with the saddle."

"I didn't say that."

"I want to expose the person trying to hurt me, Lincoln, not hide from them."

A shadow flickered across his eyes. It was filled with pain. I drew him into a hug and he let go of the chair behind him and wrapped his arms around me. He sighed, his breath ruffling the hair at my neck.

"You worry me, Charlie," he murmured.

"You worry me too, Lincoln. But it will be all right. We'll go to France then come back and find out who cut the saddle." I stroked his hair and relished the feel of his strong arms, his hard chest, and the way he held me tightly as if he were scared to let me go.

We stood like that for a long moment. For my part, I enjoyed the embrace, but I also wasn't sure what to do next. Kiss him? Talk further? And why wasn't he kissing me?

The knock made us jump apart. Seth stood in the doorway, a silly grin on his face. "Finally!"

"What do you want?" Lincoln growled.

"Don't get snappy with me because you were caught with your trousers down, so to speak." His grin widened.

"I would answer him, if I were you, Seth," I warned. Lincoln had gone rigid with fury. I suspected that meant he didn't want others knowing about us. His reticence seemed somewhat unnecessary considering Seth had caught us red-handed, and most of the committee members already suspected we were more than employer and employee.

"You're needed in the stables."

"Are there any more problems?"

"No, but we need another set of muscles. Cook says he's too busy to help."

"I'll be there in a moment."

"Very good." Seth whistled all the way down the hallway.

"Lincoln," I said as he folded his arms across his chest. "This…the thing that just happened between us…you are not going to pretend it didn't happen, are you?"

He smiled. Yes. *Smiled.* So he *was* capable of it. I felt quite giddy with wonder as I drank in the sight of the tiny lines at the corners of his eyes and mouth. "No." He took me in his arms again and kissed me tenderly, teasingly, pecking and retreating, exploring.

Then the kiss deepened, sending my heart racing and my mind blank. I couldn't get enough of him. Couldn't get close enough, even though our bodies were pressed together. I clutched his shoulders, holding on because he was solid and I felt in danger of floating away. His hand splayed at my back, the other at my waist. It moved to my hip and touched the chatelaine there. I groaned.

As if my voice had slapped him, he broke off the kiss and stepped away. His chest rose and fell with his heavy breathing, his eyes turned stormy. "I…we…must stop."

I nodded stupidly, unable to speak. With a steadying intake of breath, I too stepped back.

"I'll tell Seth that the committee members are not to be informed," he said.

"Oh?" It took me a moment to comprehend that he was speaking, let alone register what he was saying.

"They're too reactionary to a change of this magnitude."

Magnitude? Reactionary? I suppose he meant they might try to send me away. But surely Lincoln could just overrule them and do his own thing as he usually did.

"Eastbrooke and Gillingham already suspect," he went on, "but I can fool them a little longer. You'll still be in charge of redecorating. After the parlor, the entire house is yours to do with as you wish. I'll employ a housekeeper and maids to take over your duties. Anyone you need. You're now mistress of Lichfield, not a servant. Is that clear?"

I nodded numbly then watched him leave, his back ramrod straight, his hair disheveled from my exploring fingers.

What had just happened? The kiss. Yes. But beyond that…he didn't want the committee to know about us, yet he was talking about me becoming mistress of Lichfield. Did he mean to make me his wife after he'd worked out how to broach the subject with the committee? But that was madness.

Wasn't it?

I was a street waif, disowned by her adopted father, bastard daughter of a murderer and poverty-stricken French woman. And Lincoln was the son of someone important, of that I was certain. His mother may have been little better off than mine, but I suspected his father was a lord, perhaps even one of the men on the committee. Lincoln may not care for social distinctions but the world did. A public admission of our relationship might see him expelled from the ministry by four people who cared about such things very much.

Anyway, it was foolish to think about us being more than lovers when he'd not promised me anything. He'd even declared that he didn't want to marry, that he was unfit to be a husband. While I disagreed, I doubted he'd changed his mind so soon. So he *must* be referring to making me his lover. I didn't care. It didn't matter to me if we never formalized our union, as long as his heart belonged to me.

I plopped down in an armchair and stared at the bookshelf. I was trying to sort through my thoughts when one of the books caught my attention. It was a reference about Greek myths.

I plucked it off the shelf and flipped to the page on Aphrodite. "The Goddess of Love," was written in bold type beneath her name. My breath hitched. I read the paragraph about her then re-read it. Goddess of love!

Good lord. Lincoln may not be very good at voicing his feelings, but he certainly knew how to show them in other ways. I sat back and smiled down at the picture of the woman who looked so similar to the one engraved on my chatelaine. He'd given it to me even while he'd been pushing me away, even as he told me he was not capable of love. This was proof that he was.

I just hoped his heart would remain true when the committee learned of our relationship, such as it was, and they tried to send me away. Because I had no doubt some of them, if not all, would do everything in their power to separate us.

THE END

LOOK OUT FOR

Grave Expectations

The fourth MINISTRY OF CURIOSITIES novel.

Charlie's life is perfect. She has everything her heart desires. Until it all goes horribly wrong. With an angry dead supernatural on the loose and the committee determined to get rid of her, Charlie's time with the Ministry of Curiosities, and Lincoln, is in danger of ending.

To be notified when C.J. has a new release, sign up to her newsletter via her website: www.cjarcher.com

ABOUT THE AUTHOR

C.J. Archer has loved history and books for as long as she can remember. She worked as a librarian and technical writer until she was able to channel her twin loves by writing historical fiction. She has won and placed in numerous romance writing contests, including taking home RWAustralia's Emerald Award in 2008 for the manuscript that would become her novel *Honor Bound.* Under the name Carolyn Scott, she has published contemporary romantic mysteries, including *Finders Keepers Losers Die*, and *The Diamond Affair.* After spending her childhood surrounded by the dramatic beauty of outback Queensland, she lives today in suburban Melbourne, Australia, with her husband and their two children.

She loves to hear from readers. You can contact her in one of these ways:

Website: www.cjarcher.com
Email: cjarcher.writes@gmail.com
Facebook: www.facebook.com/CJArcherAuthorPage

16083782R00164

Printed in Great Britain
by Amazon